Poe, "The House of Usher," and the American Gothic

Poe, "The House of Usher," and the American Gothic

Dennis R. Perry
and
Carl H. Sederholm

palgrave
macmillan

First published in 2009 by PALGRAVE MACMILLAN® in the
United States – a division of St. Martin's Press LLC, 175 Fifth
Avenue, New York, NY 10010.

Where this book is distributed in the UK, Europe and the rest of
the world, this is by Palgrave Macmillan, a division of Macmillan
Publishers Limited, registered in England, company number 785998,
of Houndmills, Basingstoke, Hampshire RG21 6XS.

Palgrave Macmillan is the global academic imprint of the above
companies and has companies and representatives throughout the
world.

Palgrave® and Macmillan® are registered trademarks in the United
States, the United Kingdom, Europe and other countries.

ISBN 978-1-349-37901-9   ISBN 978-0-230-62082-7 (eBook)
DOI 10.1057/9780230620827

Library of Congress Cataloging-in-Publication Data is available from
the Library of Congress.

A catalogue record of the book is available from the British Library.

Design by Macmillan Publishing Solutions

First edition: May 2009

10 9 8 7 6 5 4 3 2 1

CONTENTS

PREFACE

This book grows out of two problems in Edgar Allan Poe studies, especially those concerned with his relationship to other writers, both writers of nongenre fiction and those in Gothic and supernatural horror writing. First, in terms of his influence on other writers, such influence studies as those by Lois Vines and Burton Pollin are important as far as they go, but they mostly overlook his influence on Gothic and horror writers (though Pollin does discuss Poe's influence on Stephen King). Whether this is because they wish to associate Poe with mainstream writers, or aren't familiar with those genres is not clear. Second, on the other side of the literary spectrum, the problem is that Poe so ranges across stylistic boundaries that he can be easily marginalized in studies of genres in which he should be acknowledged as a key player. For example, because Noël Carroll classifies Poe as a Gothic, rather than horror, writer, he leaves him out of his *Philosophy of Horror.*

Poe's influence is so enormous that one is hard-pressed to know just where to begin to account for it. In its broadest aspect, this study is meant to demonstrate Poe's impact on a number of genres that, in part, still exist in the form they do because of his enormous influence. These genres include psychological horror ("The Yellow Wallpaper"), ghost stories (*Turn of the Screw*), weird tales ("Shadow over Innsmouth"), haunted house stories (*Haunting of Hill House* and *The Shining*), graphic slasher stories (*Psycho*), and urban horror stories (*Rosemary's Baby*). We attempt to solve these problems by (1) addressing his relationship to other writers of Gothic and supernatural horror and defining Poe broadly enough so as to include him in more of the literary conversation; and (2) limiting our scope to the influence of one story, his masterpiece, "The Fall of the House of Usher."

We explore "Usher's" influence by viewing its relationship to other texts as a kind of conversation. That is, Poe's descendents, looking back at "Usher" as a model of certain effective characteristics of storytelling, enter into a dialogue with Poe's tale. While retaining certain touchstones of "Usher," writers explore new ways of developing these elements. These elements include the presence of an outsider who has a mysterious affinity with a house, often a repressed woman, and the unfolding of a process of psychological decay toward an apocalyptic conclusion. The result is that Poe speaks back. He does so by opening up in the presence of new ideas, yielding new perspectives on his tale in the light of what ideas in "Usher" were modified. Depending on the subject matter of the story being analyzed, we facilitate these literary conversations between texts with a pluralistic methodology that includes feminism, psychoanalytic and myth criticisms, and other theoretical approaches.

Acknowledgments

This project has benefited from the support of many institutions, colleagues, and friends. First, we would like to express thanks for the continued encouragement and support of the English Department and the Department of Humanities, Classics, and Comparative Literature at Brigham Young University. The College of Humanities at Brigham Young University has generously offered financial and collegial support throughout this process. We also thank the American Heritage Center at the University of Wyoming for opening up the Robert Bloch archive to us. Some portions of Chapter 5 originally appeared in "What Screams are Made of: Representing Cosmic Fear in H. P. Lovecraft's 'Pickman's Model,'" *Journal of the Fantastic in the Arts* 16.4 (2006): 335–49. We thank the editors for their kindness. Debbie Harrison read the entire manuscript through and provided invaluable and expert editorial comments.

Dennis: I am ever grateful for the loving support of Mary Lyn, Rich, Lindsey, Emily, Chris, Michael, Katie, Becky, Kirk, and Eric, whose patience with me whether I'm writing a book or not is always appreciated.

Carl: I would like to thank my wife and son for their love and kindness. I also thank my extended families for their love and support. I gratefully acknowledge my several colleagues and friends in the Gothic, Horror, and Stephen King sections of the Popular Culture Association conference, especially Tony, Mary, and Phil.

CHAPTER 1

INTRODUCTION:
THE "USHER" FORMULA

There isn't anywhere you can go in this overcast, weedgrown, blood-fertilized field of ours that [Poe] hasn't been first: the chilly blue-lit corners, the arena of onstage violence, Poet's Corner, the comedy sideshow, the Vale of Things Man Was Not Meant to Know. In the perfumed mouldy halls of horror, he is the doorkeeper, the cartographer, and the resident ghost.

—*John M. Ford*

Real art is news that stays news.

—*Ezra Pound*

Edgar Allan Poe's "The Fall of the House of Usher" is widely recognized as a literary masterwork and has been regularly included in short story, Gothic, horror, and American literature anthologies. Why Poe's dark story of madness, premature burial, and a sentient house is so important may be partially answered in the aggregate of the hundreds of critical articles and chapters that seek to explore its seemingly endless ambiguities. As Clive Bloom summarizes the problem, Poe's tale "is probably the most interpreted short story ever written, its ambiguities endlessly fascinating" (3). To summarize the body of such criticism would be an impossible task, even for an introduction to a book about its significance. Even to account with any comprehensiveness for the various theoretical and interpretive "camps" that have grown around the tale is beyond our scope and purpose. However, we hope to provide briefly something of the flavor of various key approaches to "Usher" in order to contextualize what we attempt in this study.[1]

In "The House of Poe," Richard Wilbur famously represents one important critical perspective on "Usher," exploring the notion that Poe's fictional output may largely be understood as a comprehensive, "deliberate and often brilliant allegory" (255) of the "poetic soul to escape all consciousness of the world in dream" (260). As Wilbur explains, "the scenes and situations of Poe's tales are always concrete representations of states of mind" (260). Turning to "Usher," Wilbur argues that "The House of Usher is, in allegorical fact, the physical body of Roderick Usher, and its dim interior is, in fact, Roderick Usher's visionary mind" (264). Considered as a state of mind, then, Roderick Usher becomes "an allegorical figure representing the hypnagogic state" (265). Daniel Hoffman likewise examines Poe as a writer who explores large and complex metaphors of the self in his fiction. Writing about "Usher," Hoffman points out that the house itself "is no house at all, but a profound and intricate metaphor of the self" (297). As in Wilbur, we see here the desire to read Poe in terms of grand gestures, moves that help us grasp his larger psychological implications rather than his twists and turns of plot. Hoffman goes on to explain that even the narrator's place in the story involves a "journey into the darkest, most hidden regions of himself" (297). Put another way by Eric Savoy, "of all nineteenth-century American writers, Poe seems most thoroughly our contemporary in his attempt to give language and a narrative structure to what Freud came to describe as the unconscious" (181).

Whereas critics such as Wilbur and Hoffman speak of Poe's interest in allegorizing the mind and the self, other critics, including Joseph Riddel and Gregory Jay, interpret "Usher" in terms of what it may tell us about the powers and limitations of language. Riddel writes that throughout "Usher," Poe helps us understand that the story is really about a change in the natural order of things, a change that forces us to consider the "failure of language" (891). Instead of seeing allegories of the mind, Riddel's argument considers "Usher" as a tale about the constant repetition of language's failure to signify any permanent meaning.

He writes that "everything in 'The Fall of the House of Usher' is a metaphorical detour, a delay in the course of a narrative that pushes toward its own tautological conclusion" (895). Discussions of "The Fall of the House of Usher" are not easy to classify under any one particular head. Many of the widely recognized approaches strive to make sense of the story in terms of large-scale commitments to various intellectual, theoretical, and social themes ranging from aesthetics to psychology to feminism. John Grusser recently formulated his sense of these differing approaches by stating that most criticism falls under two sets of opposing perspectives—those dealing with either "rationalism versus supernaturalism" or "reliability versus unreliability" (80). Although we do not wish to rehash the different sides in debates over "Usher," we find Grusser's comment to be a helpful means of labeling the broad terms through which scholars discuss the tale generally. What these approaches share is a desire to read stories like "The Fall of the House of Usher" in terms of a grand narrative, whether found in coming to a greater aesthetic sensibility or understanding the difficult connections between our world and our minds.

Responding to this diverse body of criticism, G. R. Thompson warned against trying to read "Usher" only in terms of a singular thematic approach. He explains that "it is misleading to conceive of the meaning of the tale as devolving solely upon any single and fixed subject, such as the supernatural character of the house, or of Madeline Usher, *as opposed* to a Gothic homily on the neurasthenia of the ultimate in narcissistic artist heroes, or as opposed to the incestuous guilt and hereditary curse of the family" (88). For Thompson, the story's main significance is that it "is a concatenation of all these, and not an either/or question" (88). Although there are thousands of pages that attempt to make sense of "Usher" in terms of one or another rather large purpose, Thompson's 1973 claim strikes us as still relevant. Finding a stable meaning within "Usher" will always be futile. After all, some of the more recent sophisticated critiques of the story, including deconstructive approaches, rely on the idea that the story not only refuses to be read but also helps us see language in terms of what it can't do.

In this project, we must turn slightly away from the surveys of literature that would normally help make up a book on a tale like "Usher." While critics will continue to explore and exhaust the kinds of debates surrounding "Usher," our interest lies in making sense out of the ways other American Gothic horror writers have read Poe's greatest short story over the years and how they have transformed their readings into important works of their own. Our approach to "Usher," then, is fairly simple. We wish to explore the influence of "The Fall of the House of Usher" on prominent modern Gothic and supernatural horror texts, an influence that has gone too long overlooked. To this end, we treat these modern fictions as not only readings of but also significant critical responses to "Usher." In so doing, we take a critical cue from George Steiner's claim that "all serious art, music and literature is a *critical* act" (11). Our project therefore is concerned less with resolving the ongoing debates over "Usher's" critical meaning but more with tracking the ways stories by other writers within the Gothic horror tradition open up ways for us to understand what makes that tale so significant and powerful.

I

There have been several books addressing the titanic length and breadth of Poe's shadow over world culture, a shadow touching everyone from Dostoyevsky to Debussy, Baudelaire to Wilkie Collins, and Melville to Ray Bradbury. His contributions have been enormous, including his articulation of a still important theory of tightly structured narratives, his invention of detective fiction, his pioneering contributions to science fiction, and his anticipation of modernism's concern with the psychology of deterioration. Although Poe's influence is broadly recognized, there remains a surprising lack of detailed discussion of his influence on writers such as H. P. Lovecraft, Robert Bloch, Shirley Jackson, Stephen King, and others who recognized his centrality to the genre and his continuing relevance. An important purpose of this project is to account specifically for the overlooked significance of "The Fall of the House of Usher," one of the primary foundational texts of modern horror, haunted house, and ghost stories. Such an oversight misses a rich opportunity to explore Poe's embeddedness in much of contemporary psychological and supernatural fiction. On the one hand, Poe's presence in horrific supernatural literature and films is so pervasive that it would be nearly impossible to document; on the other, the peculiar importance of this story itself cries out for an extensive study of its potential influence and impact.

Because of its pervasive influence, "Usher" lends itself particularly well to an intertextual study. It is a well-known critical commonplace about fiction these days that "authors have always been aware of relationships between the work they were writing and other texts" (Cancalon and Spacagna 1). Indeed, as Julia Kristeva notes, "any text is the absorption and transformation of another" (qtd. in Cancalon 2). Moreover, Michel Foucault adds forcefully that "no book can exist by itself . . . it is a spot in a network" (qtd. in Cancalon 2). Although we agree that all texts work within and against each other, we prefer Anna Nardo's formulation in her comparative study of George Eliot and John Milton, that relationships between authors of related texts may be described as a kind of intellectual wrestling match or, as she calls it, a "strenuous dialogue" (1). For this study it is just such a relationship between later horror writers and Poe's "Usher" that we intend to explore.

To be more specific, however, we want to discuss the conversation about Poe's greatest work, "The Fall of the House of Usher," as the turning point in Gothic literature in which Poe includes most of the basic rules of the game of horror writing. Here he establishes the psychological relationship between character and place in a dreamlike atmosphere that builds, both in terms of the diagesis and the narrative structure, toward an explosive climax of collapse and destruction. To this framework Poe adds doublings, inexplicability, dream logic, primitive mental states, madness, and so forth. To help us frame this conversation between Poe and his "children" (Magistrale and Poger 9), we reference Kristeva's concept of texts having two intertextual dimensions: (1) the vertical, or the orientation of one text toward other texts, and (2) the horizontal, which is focused more specifically on the writing subject and its addressee (Cancalon 13). We wish to interpret Kristeva's split focus on the text in a way that accounts for the two dimensions of a writer's strenuous dialogue with Poe. Vertically speaking, "Usher" becomes the subtext of current American Gothic horror works, becoming the framework they flesh out, including the basic "Usher" situation of an outsider coming to a strange house/setting and being absorbed by it. Horizontally speaking, the writer is trying to outdo Poe, seeking new, presumably more relevant ways of applying "Usher's" kaleidoscope of horrific possibilities. For example, vertically, *The Shining* is about Jack Torrance's being absorbed by the Overlook Hotel just like

"Usher's" narrator into the House of Usher itself; horizontally, King adds complications of telepathy, a detailed history of Jack's failures, and imagery such as the creeping boiler, the clock, and the living topiary. King uses Poe as a platform from which to stage new thrills and dimensions of blue-collar Gothic horror. Thus, *The Shining* incorporates Poe's inexplicabilities, doubles, dream life, and madness into King's ongoing exploration of more modern dysfunctional families, father-son relationships, and innovative horrific effects.

While Poe's importance has been long recognized, "Usher's" influence on subsequent Gothic horror and other supernatural tales has been only sporadically developed. Indeed, many important critical statements on Poe focus on his significance as a Gothic writer within the American literary tradition. Leslie Fiedler, for example, demonstrates that Poe literally haunts American literature by symbolizing the deep conflict between the play of fear and desire that lies at the heart of the American experience. Poe's work, Fiedler suggests, provides a glimpse into the dark nightmares of the American psyche, his obsessions creating "a series of inter-reflecting mirrors which present us with a thousand versions of our own face" (27). Fiedler is therefore able to call Poe "the eternal prototype of the American writer," because he exists in our imagination as the representative of our darkest nightmares (425). More to the point, Mark Edmundson claims that American culture is deeply divided between the Gothic nightmare and the American Dream, as epitomized by the works of Emerson and Poe. As he puts it, "Ours is the culture that produced both 'Self-Reliance' and 'The Fall of the House of Usher'" (5). Some more recent studies build on Fiedler and Edmundson by showing some of the depth Poe's influence has had on American literature. Dale Bailey's *American Nightmares,* for example, connects Poe to the larger haunted house tradition. Finally, Tony Magistrale and Sidney Poger's study *Poe's Children* underscores Poe's major influence on recent detective fiction. These two studies represent the kind of focused work on Poe's influence that helps define the purpose of our own project.

If we return to "Usher's" own importance, we note that several critics have commented on its role as a pathbreaking work of fiction. In *Gothic Horror* (1998), Bloom suggests that "Usher" not only marks "a decisive break between the Gothic of *Otranto* and the later psychological horror of the late nineteenth century but it also marks the appearance of a self-conscious aestheticism allied to, but different from, the popular tale of horror" (3). Combining physical and psychological horror, Poe created in "Usher" a space for "old-style" Gothic as atmosphere wherein the "mind isolated with itself" can be explored. Dani Cavallaro, in *The Gothic Vision* (2002), builds on Bloom's assessment: "Edgar Allan Poe's 'The Fall of the House of Usher' [1839] can be said to have generated a matrix for the exploration and portrayal of haunting situations as locations inseparable from their inhabitants' mental states" (87). However, neither Bloom nor Cavallaro builds on these insights, apparently assuming that detailed exploration and analysis of "Usher's" influence is unnecessary. Terry Heller's *The Delights of Terror* (1987) points out the irresolvable tension between natural and supernatural readings of the tale, a tension that is heightened rather than resolved as the tale unfolds (127). The inability of literary critics to bring closure to "Usher" reflects its haunting indeterminacy. Narratively and textually, "Usher" continues to haunt writers of Gothic and supernatural horror.

In this introduction we will review Poe's presence in scholarly studies of horror, terror, and the Gothic and examine the literary ancestry of Poe's "Usher," which includes the Gothic tradition in general, E. T. A. Hoffmann's "Das Majorat" (1817), Samuel Warren's "Thunder-Struck" (1835), Heinrich Clauren's *The Robber's Castle* (1812), and Charles Brockden Brown's *Edgar Huntly* (1799), as well as mentioning other more minor literary and biographical sources. We next define the attributes of the "Usher formula" itself, the key elements of Poe's tale that most characterize it and most often appear in later stories: the psychologically tainted outsider who energizes the spectral residue in a mysterious house, the presence of the inexplicable, the violence, the doubling, the psychological disintegration, and the atmosphere of dread centered around the inability to locate solid cognitive ground. Finally, we tie these various aspects of the "Usher formula" together through the concepts of spectrality, the fantastic, and the uncanny, all of which highlight the indistinguishable boundaries between the psychological and the supernatural, the aliveness and deadness (presence/absence) of the formula itself, and the spectral nature of literary texts through which Poe haunts his literary descendents.

II

Poe's "Usher," first published in *Burton's Gentleman's Magazine* in September 1839, is the culmination of the Gothic literary tradition from 1764 (when Horace Walpole's *The Castle of Otronto: A Gothic Story* was published) to the sensational short fiction of Poe's own day.[2] Walpole's short novel, together with those of Ann Radcliffe and others, establishes a narrative tradition characterized by gloomy settings centered around an ancestral house or castle complete with subterranean chambers. The activities within this dreary setting create an atmosphere of mystery, decay, and terror. More often than not there is a female victim enclosed within the castle who is threatened sexually and otherwise by a mysterious antagonist and "supernatural" happenings. In addition, these narratives are extravagant in their dark melodrama, relying on a sublime imagination, the unreality of romance, and exaggerated emotions and dialogue. Often the plots are convoluted, while the endings are happy and tidy. These stories cover a wide range of iterations: those outrageous in their supernaturalism (*Otronto*), those syrupy in their sentimentality (Radcliffe's *The Italian*), or those near pornographic in their sexual obsessions (Lewis's *The Monk*). As a result, since its inception, the Gothic form has proven to be infinitely flexible and adaptable to later literary purposes, from the social, moral, and realistic Gothic novels of Victorian England (Dickens and the Brontës) and the Gothic novels of the twentieth century and beyond (Faulkner, Morrison, and Oates) to the horror stories of Lovecraft, Straub, and King. For "Usher," Poe certainly draws on the Gothic tradition, highlighting a gloomy and decaying house and setting, mysterious events, supernatural hints, an ambiguous protagonist, a suffering female, and an atmosphere of terror. But, of course, he doesn't stop there.

One important Gothic fantasy source for "Usher" Alterton notes is E. T. A. Hoffmann's "Das Majorat" (translated as "The Entail"), which features a decaying ancestral castle in a wild and remote area, uncanny scratchings, a beautiful but nervous woman, and an antisocial inhabitant of the castle named Roderick. In addition, the house arguably functions as a symbol for the ancient family who has possessed it for generations. Unlike Poe's tale, however, "Das Majorat" is narrated in a light, fairy-tale tone much of the time: the ruined house is literally falling apart, humor and

nonsense are pervasive, the house is haunted, there is a lot of dialogue, hunting parties demonstrate a continuous social life, and
there are mundane details about area politics and estate business.
The narrative concerns the decline of a wealthy old family mired in
ancient transgressions. The current patriarch, Roderick, entails the
family property, leading to conflict between his sons. In the end,
the family implodes just as the castle tower collapses. Poe seems
certainly to have been aware of "Das Majorat" as it is discussed by
Sir Walter Scott in *Foreign Quarterly Review* (1827) and was available in various translations. While Hoffmann's story contributed
little to "Usher's" tone or narrative economy, other elements seem
too similar to ignore.

Alterton, who first suggested the above Hoffmann influence,
also pointed out Warren's "Thunder-Struck" from *Passages from
the Diary of a Late Physician* (1835), a title Poe himself mentions
in "How to Write a Blackwoods Article" (1838). Warren's anec-
dote, presented as autobiographical, has for its setting a tremendous thunderstorm, which, because of a beautiful patient's fear of
an impending apocalypse, causes her to become cataleptic. The
bulk of the story concerns Warren's attempts to bring her around
with everything from hot compresses to galvanic shock therapy.
She finally revives on her own, covered in blood from her nostrils.
Though she seems to be getting better, she sends for her fiancé,
whom she warns to "prepare" for his death. She dies soon there-
after, followed by him several months later. While the storm and
the beautiful cataleptic remind one of "Usher," more interesting
are other Poe-esque suggestions in the story, about the dangers of
a too-early interment ("The Premature Burial") and the possibility of a being able to hear all that is happening, yet being unable
to respond physically ("The Facts in the Case of M. Valdemar").
Probably the most Usher-esque moment in the piece is when the
doctor first comes upon the cataleptic, described as a terrifying
woman with arms outstretched.

Another possible source for "Usher" is Clauren's *The Robber's
Castle* (1812), translated by John Hardman as *The Robber's Tower*
for the December 1828 issue of *Blackwood's Edinburgh Magazine*.
Told in first person, the tale concerns a young man who visits his
aunt in her remote castle at the death of his female cousin. She
has been placed in the cellar, just below where the narrator sleeps.
When the narrator can't sleep during a storm, he begins reading

a curious book on rituals when he hears noise of iron clanging below him. Ultimately the dead cousin appears. The tale furthers anticipates "Usher" in using story elements, which include stringed instruments, the twin of the dead cousin, and the reflections of the castle in a lake.

Other sources have been noted for the tale's atmosphere, its famous opening sentence, and the characters Roderick and Madeleine. Lodwick Hartley, for example, wonders if the life of Lawrence Sterne's eccentric friend, John Hall-Stevenson, who lived in the Usher-esque Skelton Castle, might have contributed to the atmosphere of Poe's story. Washington Irving's opening sentence in his piece "Westminster Abbey" from *The Sketch-Book* (1820) suggests a similar autumnal mood to "Usher's" opener: "On one of those sober and rather melancholy days, in the latter part of Autumn, when the shadows of morning and evening almost mingle together, and throw a gloom over the decline of the year, I passed several hours in rambling about Westminster Abbey" (894). Certainly the words "evening," "melancholy," and "Autumn" correlate with Poe's sentence, and given Irving's importance in the 1830s, it is unlikely that Poe's effective elaboration of this passage is merely coincidental. The suggested true-life source for Roderick and Madeleine Usher are James Campbell and Agnes Pye Usher, who were the orphaned children of Poe's mother's stage friends. James and Agnes were, in fact, known to have been neurotics in a kind of psychological doubling.[3]

Not mentioned as an "Usher" source elsewhere is *Edgar Huntly* (1799) by Brown, an early American Gothic writer whom Poe admired. The main lines of similarity include the first-person narration with its emphasis on recording detailed sensations of terror and disbelief; the narrator, Edgar Huntly himself, coming across a highly strung character named Clithero who is oppressed with a mysterious grief and a cursed past; the setting of Norwalk, a wild and dangerous rocky area of Pennsylvania that is both gloomy and remote and seems to have a psychological effect on the characters; an idealized female at the center of the story who at one point seems to be dead but isn't; and Clithero's death by sinking into water. While several of these details seem generally Gothic as well as peculiarly linked to "Usher," the number of them is provocative. The most convincing connections are the psychological doublings in the story. First, the link between Edgar and

Clithero is reinforced by the narrator's sympathetic obsession and reenactments of Clithero's actions: he follows him step for step to and from Norwalk, takes on Clithero's malady of sleep walking, similarly kills in self-defense, and ends up with the girl originally chosen for Clithero. Second, the doubling of Clithero and Edgar is echoed in the link between Mrs. Lorimer and her brother (á la Roderick and Madeline), in which she feels she will die if he does. Thus, the pattern of doubling may be the most significant foreshadowing of Poe's tale.

III

Our project contributes both to the ongoing recent discussion of the aesthetics and cultural significance of Gothic literature and its branches: terror, horror, romance, and the weird tale. Other recent studies have focused on either the aesthetic or cultural work of the genre, often narrowing their generic scope to horror or Gothic tales in a way that misses Poe's influence. In Noël Carroll's *The Philosophy of Horror* (1990), for example, Poe is not central because he is labeled as a writer of terror—the category in which Terry Heller's *The Delights of Terror* (1987) places him. While Heller's reader-response examination of terror prominently features Poe's "Usher" and "Ligeia," Poe is not explicitly made central to the history of the terror tale. Louis Gross's *Redefining the American Gothic* (1989) places Poe in a Gothic tradition, but not as a central figure. In fact, Gross offers the controversial argument that Brown may even be more central to American Gothicism than Poe, a claim with which our study obviously takes issue. Similarly, Teresa Goddu's *Gothic America* (1997) views Poe as a Gothicist, though her discussion locks him in a Southern American literary tradition without reference to his ongoing influence. Poe is placed more centrally in Bloom's *Gothic Horror* (1998), tracing modern horror through Poe's important innovations to the Gothic, combining physical and psychological approaches. In fact, he centers his discussion of Poe around "Usher" (3). Following his introduction, however, Bloom spends the rest of the book diverging into the various opinions of various writers on horror, not following up on his own "Usher" thesis. In a sense, this study elaborates Bloom's hint and provides the missing individual analyses of texts in light of "Usher" that demonstrates its influence.

Reading the opening pages of Cavallaro's *The Gothic Vision* (2002), in which he quotes and agrees with Bloom's assessment of "Usher's" importance, one would suspect that our study might be unnecessary. However, Cavallaro goes on to use Poe's "matrix for the exploration and portrayal of haunting situations" in "Usher" not to focus on aesthetic concerns as much as to ground his readings of Gothic texts as "cultural discourse" and "ideological speculation" (vii). In *American Nightmares* (1999), Dale Bailey locates Poe at the genesis of a distinctive genre, one that Poe developed through "Usher." However, Bailey only begins to develop how Poe's tale functions as a significant influence in the progress of American horror writing since then.

Unlike many of its predecessors, our study doesn't wish to engage in parsing genre distinctions, asserting that Poe generally, and "The Fall of the House of Usher" specifically, looms so large over all modern variants of Gothic and horror literature that labeling Poe as of one or another genre tends to minimize his vital contributions to most Gothic-born genres. Poe is arguably the one indispensable figure in American Gothic, horror, terror, and weird fiction. A central aim of this book is to recenter Poe and to explore his enduring significance to American horror, particularly through the lens of "Usher."

Poe, like many writers, is a synthesizer of what came before him, remaking his sources to fit his own literary agenda, combining his sources, together with the Gothic tradition itself, to create a tale that has become an archetype in the collective literary consciousness. The essence of Poe's achievement is that he radically alters his sources, stripping them bare of all he considered extraneous to his chosen effect, carefully molding what was left into truly new and original material. From his general Gothic sources he removes the usual plentitude of characters, simplifies the plot to build toward one climactic event, eliminates cultural, national, moral, historical, or political contexts, and virtually invents Gothic minimalism. From Hoffmann's "Das Majorat" Poe guts the rambling plot line, the light narrative tone and nonsense humor (which he saves for other kinds of stories), extra characters, ghosts, and the love story. From Warren's narrative Poe eliminates the exaggerated emotional sensibility characteristic of the age, dialogue, and fluctuations in tone. In their place Poe gives us a tale that is more tightly wrought, infusing Gothic art with a more modern sensibility that plumbs the depths of human psychology as the central concern along with an ironic self-reflexiveness. This explains in large part Poe's, and "Usher's," continuing popularity. Having eschewed outmoded forms of sentiment and morality, Poe creates a timeless tale. The formula he establishes is so simple, yet powerful, that, like a new form of the Gothic itself, it lends itself easily to endless variations and elaborations. Like the basic three-chord blues progression (I-IV-V), which has become the basis for much of country, folk, rock, blues, and jazz, "The Fall of the House of Usher," with its infinite flexibility, has become the model for and basis of endless variations to the present day. Just as Mary Shelley's *Frankenstein* (1818) has become the archetype of a horror genre in which man's misguided creations go out of control (including the mutated creature features of the 1950s), so we herald "Usher" as a major source text for many of the best-known modern American Gothic horror tales.

The Usher formula is really a misnomer since it is not reducible to a simple definition. Rather, it is a fluid set of variables that includes plot elements, characters, imagery, atmosphere, and psychological overtones. Despite these disparate elements, the formula, though complex, makes up a recognizable pattern. We begin to uncover this formula by examining three key elements that create the basic plot line underneath "Usher" and its descendents: an outsider, with psychological problems, comes into a house on brink of collapse that is full of secrets and traumas from the past and begins to merge with the house, the house becoming a reflection of the outsider's unconscious mind with its secrets, fears, and traumas. Thus begins a process of deterioration and collapse that leads to an apocalyptic ending. Adjunct to this structure is an immured or otherwise repressed female. In addition, "Usher" is set in an uncanny dreamland, a place where reality and unreality become blurred.

Underlying the narrative structures in "Usher," and many others of his tales, is *Eureka*, Poe's origin and destiny of the universe. While *Eureka* is often cited in studies of Poe's fiction as an underlying pattern, its usefulness here is for helping us articulate the underlying dynamics of character motivation and plot trajectory. In addition, *Eureka*'s point of view is congenial with that of "Usher," since, as Susan Manning writes, it's about "the deliberate confounding of the categories of mind and world" (qtd. in

Carlson 326). This critical commonplace of using *Eureka* as a template for the tales is valuable in helping delineate the movement of "Usher's" narrative structure, explaining the conditions of things in the story's setting and characters. While *Eureka* was written some years after "Usher," it perfectly describes in abstract many of the tale's principle qualities. *Eureka* can be summarized in a three-part schema. First, originally God creates the universe whole and perfect—one spiritual particle with which we are all united in beauty, harmony, and love. Second, inexplicably he causes the fragmentation of the particle in a big bang and we, the planets, stars, etc. are all made material and separate, creating what we now perceive as the dispersed matter of the universe. Each fragment is desirous of reuniting with the others, but cannot because the original diffusive force continues to separate each fragment. This stage is characterized by Poe as scientific disharmony and fragmentation. Finally, when the diffusive/repulsive force dissipates then the fragments begin to attract and collapse in a sublime, galactic vortex, the universe again eventually becoming one perfect, spiritual particle. Poe, likening this process to a literary narrative, calls it "God's Plot." In "Usher," the decaying house and the declining Roderick, and Madeline are all on the verge of this collapse back into one another. The attractive force is evident in the endless doublings in the story. Even the inexplicable, dreamlike atmosphere of the tale witnesses the imminent collapse of the rational, fragmented universe that Poe describes in *Eureka*. In the end, Madeline collapses on Roderick, and the house collapses into the tarn—all becoming one. The sickness of the family (and the human race) is ended.

To help us explain how the "Usher" formula continues to haunt modern horror fiction requires reference to three elements that characterize "Usher": the spectral, the fantastic, and the uncanny. Each of these phenomena has as its core concept an ambiguity that is at the heart of "Usher." The spectral deals with the ambiguity between life and death; the fantastic hovers around the uncertainties of real and unreal (Todorov); and the uncanny is about the slippage between self and other (Freud).

In terms of the spectral, Abraham and Torok's theory of how the mother haunts her child by passing along secrets and traumas can be seen through the image of the house in the Usher formula—passing along its secrets and horrors to the insider and

outsider alike, triggering deterioration and collapse. The house
reveals to its inhabitants their shadow self—the other—which
is often the basis of horror. The shadow can be reflected in the
actions of the character or mirrored in a double figure—or both.
Roderick's debilitating illness is a sign of something inside him,
but might also be embodied in Madeline's own illness and the
state of high decay of the house. That is, the horrors of the house
are also what we bring to it, making the encounter self-reflective
and self-destructive. Taking the spectral another step further,
though he is anticipated here by Poe, Julian Wolfreys in *Victorian
Hauntings* focuses on traces and echoes of past texts in present
texts, creating a narrative dream state of identity and nonidentity.
As we have demonstrated above, like all texts "Usher" contains the
traces of several source texts, many of which might be ultimately
unidentifiable. This makes it impossible to experience narrative
"reality" except at a distance, through the lens of other texts. Poe,
of course, plays off of these spectral reflections in "Usher's" prism-
like structure as he causes each aspect of the narrative to reflect
every other aspect, such that Roderick is seen in the condition of
the house and of his sister and Madeline's internment is shown
in the dying house's reflection in the tarn. Not only is "Usher"
a tale haunted by the echoes of its many sources but "Usher"
also haunts the stories it subsequently influences. Unpacking the
results is the project of this study.

Todorov's theory of the fantastic is about the hesitation of the
reader to accept the supernatural. Todorov explains it this way:
"There is an uncanny phenomenon which we can explain in two
fashions, by types of natural causes and supernatural causes. The
possibility of a hesitation between the two creates the fantastic
effect" (26). Poe's concern with creating a precise effect on his
readers is behind this sense of the fantastic in his work. After
168 years, we still hesitate at the narrator's initial experience of
the House of Usher, wondering with him at "what *must* have
been a dream"—or not (*Tales* 400). Contradictory hints within
the texts continually cause us to hesitate at whether characters
are real or merely embodiments of the mind of other characters.
Is Madeline real or representative of Usher's unconscious mind
he is impelled to suppress? Is the narrator a "madman" as Usher
declares, making his narrative entirely unreliable? Poe has created
such a perfect dreamland as a house of mirrors that hesitation

seems the only rational response to the story. Hesitation, in fact, seems to have been the effect, together with wonder and horror, that Poe intends for his readers. It is "Usher's" infinite causes of hesitation that has so endlessly driven the scholarly, and creative, imagination. Such fantastic hesitation is characteristic of the texts we examine here that draw on "Usher." For example, is Eleanor, in *The Haunting of Hill House,* being infected by the house, or is she somehow igniting its manifestations from her unconscious projections?

Finally, the uncanny takes us back to the spectral idea of hidden secrets. Sigmund Freud defines "uncanny" (*unheimlich*) as applying "to everything that was intended to remain secret, hidden away, and has come into the open" (132). The true experience of the uncanny requires the constant blending of the self and other, familiar and unfamiliar, known and unknown. According to Freud, "the uncanny is that species of the frightening that goes back to what was once well known and had long been familiar" (124). This sense of an external, horrific reality in "Usher," projecting doubles from the unconsciousness of the characters, perfectly captures the uncanny in "Usher." The slippage between self and other is inevitable in this process. When the narrator sees Madeline walking in a distant room his response is inexplicable, regarding her "with an utter astonishment not unmingled with 'dread'—and yet I found it impossible to account for such feelings" (*Tales* 404). The best explanation seems to be the uncanny one, that he has projected his own fears of psychological decay on her, making her at once akin and alien to himself. Freud goes on to define the relationship between literary doubles and the uncanny as

> intensified by the spontaneous transmission of mental processes from one of these persons to the other—what we would call telepathy—so that the one becomes co-owner of the other's knowledge, emotions and experience. Moreover, a person may identify himself with another and so become unsure of his true self; or he may substitute the other's self for his own (141–42).

Again, such observations fit the relationship of the narrator and Roderick and the characters in any number of more recent horror texts. Certainly the slippage between self and other dominates *Psycho,* "The Yellow Wallpaper," and *The Shining.*

With his psychological orientation, among Edgar Allan Poe's greatest contributions to Gothic horror literature is his ability to relocate the site of fear to the primitive dream mind, creating what Freud calls the "omnipotence of thought." That is, the mind creates its own world, as among primitive people's religious ceremonies in which they recreate the world annually—not symbolically, but to their minds, actually. Removing horror from the context of reality—religious or rational perspectives—is a major paradigm shift in the literature of fear, enabling Poe to erase spatial and temporal boundaries to create a dreamlike atmosphere where magic bonds, projection, and superstition reign supreme. Nowhere does he do this more effectively than in "The Fall of the House of Usher," where every detail is a mere reflection of the narrator's mind. Poe complicates primitive thought as the basis for horror through the "imp of the perverse," adding the inexplicable to the irrational, making, in Ahab's words, "madness maddened." In essence, through these innovations Poe creates an infinitely complex matrix of horror best read through the spectral, fantastic, and uncanny, the harbingers of troubling uncertainties between life and death, real and unreal, self and other.

We have chosen to focus on a number of texts that seem to be particularly beholden to Poe's "House of Usher" in their basic orientation. Nevertheless, because Poe's tale has had such a broad influence we have necessarily had to leave out several tempting writers and novels that would have made for interesting contributions to our study. We do note the absence of works such as Joyce Carol Oates's *Haunted,* Richard Matheson's *Hell House,* F. Paul Wilson's *The Keep,* Peter Straub's *Ghost Story* and *Lost Boy, Lost Girl,* Thomas Harris's *The Silence of the Lambs,* and many others. While in many cases these works include key elements from "Usher," these influences seem to play a smaller role than the ones we focus on. Straub's *Ghost Story,* for example, serves up equal parts from James's *Turn of the Screw* and King's *Carrie* among others. Likewise, Oates's own eclectic output often invokes Kafka more than Poe. Other works, such as Thomas Harris's *Silence of the Lambs,* draw more directly on Poe's stories of detection than on "Usher" itself. Although we believe that writers like Straub, Matheson, and others are deeply influenced by Poe, such influences will need to be traced in ways outside the scope of this study.

In the chapters to follow we will explore the Usher matrix of out-siders, houses, and psychic collapse in fiction that directly engages Poe's tale: Gilman's "The Yellow Wallpaper" (1892), James's *The Turn of the Screw* (1898), Lovecraft's "Pickman's Model" (1927) and other tales, Jackson's *The Haunting of Hill House* (1959), Bloch's *Psycho* (1959), Levin's *Rosemary's Baby* (1967), and King's *The Shining* (1977). In this study we argue that Poe is the dominant ghost haunting modern American horror—not merely a source or influence. Emily Dickinson once said that "nature is a haunted house; art is a house trying to be haunted" (554). Based on its enduring influence, "The Fall of the House of Usher" has succeeded in this attempt. "Usher's" haunting influence is partly in the inspired tensions between its structural simplicity and its inexplicable mingling of supernatural and psychological aspects. In this study, we examine how Poe continues to point the way for future writers to explore the deepest and most primitive corners of the human mind and heart.

CHAPTER 2

FEMINIST "USHER": DOMESTIC HORROR IN GILMAN'S "THE YELLOW WALLPAPER"

One of the recurring claims about Charlotte Perkins Gilman's "The Yellow Wallpaper" is that it bears certain unmistakable likenesses to some of the works of Edgar Allan Poe. Over the last 20 years, several critics have explored this significant literary relationship by reading "The Yellow Wallpaper" in light of tales such as "The Tell-Tale Heart," "The Black Cat," "The Murders in the Rue Morgue," and "The Pit and the Pendulum" (Golden, *Sourcebook* 28). Furthermore, many of Gilman's earliest readers believed "The Yellow Wallpaper" to be an explicit extension of Poe's interest in themes like madness, horror, and suspense. All of these approaches share the assumption that Gilman's relationship to Poe is clear and obvious. Gilman herself clearly articulates her long-term interest in Poe not only in the many passages of her diary, but also in the section on Poe in her "Studies in Style." While critics rightly point to Poe's overall influence on Gilman, they typically overlook one of the most significant literary connections between them—the relationship between "The Fall of the House of Usher" and "The Yellow Wallpaper." Although we do not wish to dismiss other readings that compare Poe and Gilman, we want to emphasize "Usher's" unique significance for reading "The Yellow Wallpaper," particularly because of its shared interest in women and madness. In fact, we argue that "The Yellow

Wallpaper" invites us to reread Poe's tale not only from a generally more feminist perspective but also from Madeline Usher's point of view. By inviting us to see "Usher" from Madeline's point of view, Gilman helps us understand Poe's own reading of his mysterious heroine. In fact, Gilman's literary conversation with Poe may serve as one of the most striking examples of the intertextually strenuous conversations in this study. In this chapter, we argue that Gilman's "The Yellow Wallpaper" ought to be approached as a reading of "The Fall of the House of Usher," particularly because of the way it forcefully inverts Poe's predominantly male perspective. Gilman's approach is particularly significant because it tells the story from the point of view of a woman who feels trapped by the males in her life who presume a logical and rational means of explaining her "illness."

We see Gilman's dialogue with Poe paralleling Anna Nardo's claim about George Eliot's own dialogue with John Milton. As Nardo writes, Eliot puts "Miltonic language in dialogue with itself, [and evaluates] Miltonic characters and episodes by Milton's own language" (25). Likewise, Gilman may also be said to employ the language of Poe's psychological Gothicism in "Usher" in order to make a powerful and horrific feminist statement. As we read "The Yellow Wallpaper" in light of "The Fall of the House of Usher," we will recognize that there are new questions that want asking, new takes on character motivation that emerge, and new interpretations of action that demand consideration.

I

The earliest reactions to Gilman's innovative tale—particularly those based on its feminism and Poe's influence—have tended to dictate the tenor of readings and debates about the story ever since. At the time of its publication, some readers recognized it as a Gothic horror tale with a twist—"'The Fall of the House of Usher' told from the point of view of the Lady Madeline" (Scharnhorst 17). In fact, others suggested that the story was even more terrifying than Poe's work. For example, Gilman's husband, Walter Stetson, claimed that the story was "more horrifying than even Poe's tales of terror" (Haney-Peritz 95). Moreover, William Dean Howells remarked that it was "too terribly good to be printed" (vii). Even worse, when Horace Scudder, the editor of

The Atlantic Monthly, rejected "The Yellow Wallpaper," he did so by complaining that the story made him feel so "miserable" that he was loathe to share such feelings with his readers. As he wrote to Gilman, "I could not forgive myself if I made others as miserable as I have made myself!" (*Living* 119). Though they don't say so directly, both Stetson and Howells imply that their horrific response to "The Yellow Wallpaper" may have had something to do with its portrayal of female madness, something that they were clearly not prepared to deal with. But even in more recent times, despite critical emphasis on the story's feminism since the 1970 Feminist Press edition that introduced Gilman into the canon, Poe is recognized as an influence on Gilman's story. Annette Kolodny notes, for example, that "the story located itself . . . as a continuation of a genre popularized by Poe" (Kolodny 153–54).

Scudder's reaction, particularly, has received a great deal of attention over the years by feminist scholars because of its implications that Gilman's story was somehow an affront to his sense of masculinity. But Scudder's reaction, as Kolodny suggests, may present a larger problem contemporary readers had with the story. In other words, readers like Scudder brought to "The Yellow Wallpaper" a sensibility conditioned by reading Poe. Thus, "The Yellow Wallpaper" was understood to draw on Poe's influence but was innovative enough to use a female narrator and to change the setting to a comfortable summer house. As Kolodny argues, Poe's presence was so strong that it seemed to trump Gilman's larger purposes in the minds of her readers: "Poe continued as a well-traveled road, while Gilman's story, lacking the possibility of further influence, became a literary dead end" (155). She continues that "those fond of Poe could not easily transfer their sense of mental derangement to the mind of a comfortable middle-class wife and mother; and those for whom the woman in the home was a familiar literary character were hard-pressed to comprehend so extreme an anatomy of the psychic price she paid" (154–55). Such readings, Kolodny argues, fail to grasp the point of the story. Kolodny's reading generally reflects widely held assumptions about "The Yellow Wallpaper's" original reception as primarily a Gothic story. Julie Bates Dock challenges this view by demonstrating that certain "'facts' need reassessment as scholars increasingly acknowledge that literary criticism is as grounded in historical biases as the literature it seeks to interpret" (52). As Dock argues,

"Reviewers demonstrate that the story's first readers did recognize its indictments of marriage and of the treatment of women" (59–60). Indeed, though Poe's influence caused many readers to overlook Gilman's feminist point entirely, others got it.

The result of some of the feminist readings of Gilman's story is to pit her feminism against Poe's alleged literary patriarchalism. Judith Fetterley, for example, tries to distance Gilman from Poe by his more aggressive violence, particularly in tales like "Murders of the Rue Morgue." She reads Poe's story as a parable of female victimhood with the ape as man's secret animal hate and aggression. In contrast she argues for Gilman's literary independence from Poe, one that stresses a less violent emphasis that distinguishes her from her forebear. Kolodny is answered in part by Beverly Hume, who finds the "potential violence" in "The Black Cat" and "The Yellow Wallpaper" comparable: "Gilman's narrator displays a chilling potential for domestic violence that not only haunts this tale, but threatens to undermine Gilman's stated feminist goal to 'reach Dr. S. Weir Mitchell, and convince him of the error of his ways'" (4). Our position is that the critical opposition between Gilman's feminist agenda in "The Yellow Wallpaper" and her reliance on Poe's psychological Gothicism misses the point. A look at her story in light of both Gilman's personal experience and Poe's "The Fall of the House of Usher" argues for a feminism that grows out of her response to what might be called Poe's own Gothic feminism.

Gilman's interest in Poe largely coincides with the period of some of her darkest and deepest psychological anxieties. During the five years following her marriage to Stetson in 1884, Gilman struggled with that decision. She almost immediately regretted what for her were the grating routines of domestic life. When her daughter Katharine was born in 1885, her depression and anxiety increased exponentially; she later wrote about this period that she felt deep monotony, characterized by a sense of hopelessness and regret. As she puts it, "Every morning the same hopeless waking . . . the same weary drag. To die mere cowardice. Retreat impossible, escape impossible" (Scharnhorst 7). She eventually escapes temporarily to California, alone, to stay with her brother, and while there she enjoys recovery in her freedom and opportunity to do her literary work. But upon returning home six months later (March 1886), she again slipped into a state of nervous despair. Finally, in the spring of 1887, she seeks S. Weir Mitchell's "rest cure," leading her after a summer's trial "so near the border line of utter mental ruin" that she crawled about the room, hid under beds, as she recounts, "to hide from the grinding pressure of that profound distress" (Scharnhorst 10). Even worse, Mitchell failed to understand Gilman's condition completely. Elaine Hedges writes that, even though Mitchell was a confirmed "nerve specialist," he did not approach Gilman with a personalized treatment. Instead, he considered her case as something that could be resolved with a return to her domestic activities with a commitment to "never touch pen, brush or pencil as long as you live" (Hedges 128).

During these years of feeling desperately entrapped in marriage and motherhood, Gilman often turned to Poe for diversion. In fact, she often recorded in her diary the names of the Poe stories she read or had been read to her. Some passages read as follows: "Read Mother S. 'The Black Cat'" (January 9, 1885); "and he (Walter) reads to me, Poe . . . " (January 12, 1885); "Sam lends me one vol. of Poe's works" (March 21, 1887); "Read 'Murders of Rue Morgue to Hattie'" (November 17, 1893) (Knight, *Diaries*). Obviously, Poe was a regular part of her reading over an extended period of time. It may well be that reading him just at this time had a significant early influence on her writings. Could it be that her interest in Poe had something to do with her own sense of mental collapse? While we can only speculate on that question, it could be that in her mental distress she saw herself as if she were a character out of Poe's imagination, a character bordering on madness. What is certain, though, is that many of Gilman's short stories draw on her long familiarity with Poe's writings. In fact, she wrote several Gothic short stories during the same creative period in which she composed "The Yellow Wallpaper." Though not as accomplished as "The Yellow Wallpaper," Gilman's tales such as "The Giant Wisteria" (1891), "The Rocking Chair" (1893), and, in "avowed imitation" of Poe, "The Unwatched Door (1894)" drew on the kinds of Gothic idioms she almost certainly learned from Poe (Knight, *Gilman* 29). This last story combines elements from several of Poe's tales in an "attempt to capture Poe's distinctive literary style" (Knight 32). While as a struggling young writer Gilman was primarily "interested, above all, in the effect or cash-value of a work" (Scharnhorst 12), it is also possible that she found Poe's portraits of the disintegrating minds of psychologically and physically trapped characters to harmonize with her personal struggles. This idea is all the more plausible given the fact that her more natural literary bent was largely didactic and reform oriented. Even though Gilman's aesthetic interests are more didactic than Poe's explicit aestheticism, she learned from Poe some powerful Gothic ways of dealing with culturally induced psychological issues.

Gilman's interest in Poe is significant because through Poe, or more specifically, "The Fall of the House of Usher," Gilman finds a voice and a narrative structure to express her frustrations and make a powerful early feminist statement. Although we strongly agree that "The Yellow Wallpaper" represents one of the most significant expressions of nineteenth-century feminism, we disagree that focusing on Poe's influence crushes such an endeavor; in fact, we argue that Poe's influence is crucial to understanding the full impact of the story—then and now. In short, Poe has never left the critical conversation about "The Yellow Wallpaper." However, as Dock notes, Poe's influence has sometimes been questioned as a way to bolster feminist readings that wish to divorce women's issues from what some have misperceived as mere Gothic ornamentation. Dock laments the fact that many critics want "The Yellow Wallpaper" to be either a Poe-inspired tale or a work of pure feminism. To illustrate her point, Dock quotes from a 1993 Macmillan anthology that buys into the idea of "The Yellow Wallpaper" being first read as a "ghost story in the tradition of Edgar Allan Poe" (59). Why were feminist readings of "Yellow Wallpaper" overlooked for so long? According to Dock, the answer is "embedded in the ideological constructs of its time" (60). That is, "feminist critics of the 1970s garnered evidence to confirm their version of literary history as a patriarchal exclusion of women writers" (60). If we realize that Gilman's story was recognized as both Gothic and feminist from the beginning, we can explore how the two function together in the narrative. As Carol Margaret Davison argues, one recent area of study that helps us see links between the feminist and Gothic sides of "Yellow Wallpaper" is the concept of the Female Gothic. She employs this approach to counter readings of Gilman's story as either a nonpolitical ghost story or a non-Gothic feminist piece (48). Davison invokes Michelle Massé to shore up the connection between the feminist and the Gothic, noting that "'The Yellow

Wallpaper' speaks back, consciously or otherwise, to various established Gothic traditions" (qtd. in Davison 69). We agree. Of course, speaking back is an essential strategy of feminism, and we further contend that rarely has it been done so powerfully than in Gilman's dark tale of female imprisonment.

There is no doubt that if we only slavishly compare the structural elements of "Usher" and "Yellow Wallpaper" we will do justice to neither Gilman nor Poe. Even worse, we risk placing Gilman in a position subordinate to Poe and thereby denying her full credit for her rich innovation and insights. To avoid this problem, we argue that "The Yellow Wallpaper" establishes a complex dialogue with Poe, one that invites us to reread "The Fall of the House of Usher" not only from Madeline's point of view but also from the oppressive patriarchal point of view that Poe implicitly exposes. In the context of the story that Gilman writes, with its predominate themes and imagery, we can define how she "speaks back" to "Usher." In short, Gilman speaks back to Poe by resituating "Usher" in terms of genre, reading it as a Female Gothic. This is not to say that she forces an unnatural reading on the text; but, in fact, she uncovers "Usher's" essential nature as a Female Gothic scenario—a wholly innovative approach for her time. More than merely an eighteenth-century Gothic narrative told by a woman about an unjustly imprisoned heroine in a medieval castle, the Female Gothic has more recently been defined as an enduring genre criticizing oppressive patriarchies, centering on the struggle between men and women and their societal roles, and championing feminist independence. In fact, the Female Gothic is really as much a mode of reading as a genre, since early Gothic novels, such as those by Radcliffe and Edgeworth, are now often read in feminist terms.

Anne Williams has brilliantly challenged such feminist approaches of the Gothic for using psychoanalysis "more as a means of social *diagnosis* than as a model of *interpretation*," skipping past the immediate narrative details in favor of reflecting on "historical conditions" (137–38). She alludes to Janice Radway's observation that Female Gothic fiction "cannot really express 'feminist protest' because they so manifestly side with the status quo" (138). While we agree that Williams and Radway make a convincing argument about early Female Gothics, we would place "Yellow Wallpaper" in a unique category. We would argue that in her tale of female oppression, Gilman functions as a pioneering feminist critic, using fiction as her medium to reimagine and rewrite the Female Gothic in just the sorts of broad historical and cultural terms feminist critics now read early Gothic novels. Contrary to her Gothic forebears, Gilman in no way justifies the cultural status quo nor allows for a happy ending. This she does, in part, because Poe first points the way. In order to trace Gilman's Gothic conversation with "Usher," we must first identify what seems to have most impressed her about the story, evidenced by what she includes from it in "Yellow Wallpaper"; next we analyze the uses she makes of these elements in adapting them for her own political purposes. While we will use current terms to define gender relations and cultural conventions from a feminist perspective that Gilman didn't use, her anticipatory and revelatory reading of age-old women's problems is, we believe, so in sync with current critical thinking that it does not seem out of place.

II

A striking aspect of "Yellow Wallpaper" that points back to "Usher" is the narrator's insistence on exploring the dark side of her life in opposition to John's pressure to be positive and not discuss her illness. As Janice Haney-Peritz observes, the "oppressive structure that is at issue is a man's prescriptive discourse about a woman" (97). But Gilman's narrator chooses a different text to read than her husband would prescribe. Barbara Hochman writes about how Gilman's story reflects anxieties in her day about reading, "the notion that one's reading could have an enduring impact on one's life, whether benign or pernicious" (89). She goes on to note that Gilman's narrator, over the course of the story, becomes "an avid, indeed an obsessive reader—of the paper on the walls that surround her" (90). Her character reflects Gilman herself who was described as an obsessive reader. Hochman links Gilman's and her narrator's experience to that of Agnes Hamilton, who writes in her diary "about her insane passion for reading," even comparing it to an "addiction" (qtd. in Hochman 102). We want to more specifically claim that in her narrator Gilman reflects her own close, even obsessive, reading of Poe's "The Fall of the House of Usher," reflecting in her narrator the powerful pull Gothic literature had for her as a mirror to explore the forbidden aspects of her inner self. From this perspective, the excesses of Gothic literature became a model for Gilman's own psychological excesses that she was trying to both understand and express.

"Yellow Wallpaper" presents a narrator who is determined to find a Gothic story in her experience. While not stated explicitly, she gives evidence of being a fan of Gothic literature, an imaginative type like Austen's Catherine Morland in *Northanger Abby*, who overlays her Gothic reading onto her own experiences while visiting a mysterious castle. Gilman's narrator admits to John's assessment of her as having an "imaginative power and habit of story-making . . . sure to lead to all manner of excited fancies" (Gilman, "Wallpaper" 46). This diagnosis is borne out upon her first encountering their summer rental. She refers to it in language that yearns for the strange and exotic, delighting in the romance of naming it "ancestral halls," even wishing to call it a "haunted house." But, recognizing that she is being fanciful, she revealingly resigns herself by stating "that would be asking too much of fate" (41). But despite such reality checks, she continues to wonder: "Still I will proudly declare that there is something queer about it" (41). Trying to transfer her experience from mundane reality to imaginative fancy, she is disappointed that the only reason the house is deserted stems from family squabbles over the estate, which "spoils my ghostliness, I am afraid" (42). Still determined, however, to have her Gothic way, she once again gives in to her imagination: "But I don't care—there is something strange about the house—I can feel it" (42). Like the narrator of "Usher," she brings into the house with her an imagination prepared for, even hungry for, the weird and uncanny. E. Suzanne Owens contends that in the tradition of haunted house stories the narrator's suspicions about the nature of the house suggest her rationality, since such suspicions usually prove the narrator's insight (68). We disagree, for reasons to be more fully established below, including the fact that Gilman is doing anything with her iconoclastic story but following predictable genre conventions.

The narrator's yen for Gothicism is, in the context of the story, forbidden knowledge, a giving "way to . . . fancies" but a yen she can't resist (44). In this sense she is a descendent of Poe's imaginative women, Ligeia and Morella, themselves specialists in weird knowledge. In her case, she is in a psychological/emotional struggle with her doctors who are baffled by her problems. Unconsciously, her obsession with the wallpaper represents several liberating things she needs. First, it is the freedom to use her imagination. At one point she states that studying the wallpaper is "as good as gymnastics" (48). Having been restricted by her rest cure from writing—that is, thinking—her active mind hungers for an imaginative challenge to spark her "habit of story-making." Second, the wallpaper is a means of escape into an alternate reality from the stifling routine imposed upon her by her unimaginative husband. "I sometimes fancy that in my condition if I had less opposition and more society and stimulus," she complains, but even this wishful thinking is cut off by her awareness of John's presence: "But John says the very worst thing I can do is to think about my condition . . . " (42). Finally, the wallpaper enables her to journey through the darkest labyrinthine paths of her own mind in an unconscious effort to understand and cure herself. All that she imagines about the house being "queer," "strange," and ghostly are projections of her own troubled psyche.

The problem of the narrator's reading the wallpaper shares with Poe's "Usher" the problem of reading reality. The spirit's frustration at facing the dead blind wall of an intolerable reality made inexplicable by a troubled, sensitive mind may be the major insight Gilman draws from Poe's masterpiece in writing "The Yellow Wallpaper." That is, the mind can become a Gothic workshop of the imagination when it is confronted by oppressive routine. In essence, she discovers the psychological foundations of the Gothic as definitively brought out in "Usher." As Richard Wilbur argues, "The House of Usher is, in allegorical fact, the physical body of Roderick Usher, and its dim interior is, in fact, Roderick Usher's visionary mind" (264). The same becomes true for Gilman's narrator, who becomes increasingly one with the strange room in which she is imprisoned. Gilbert and Gubar come to a similar conclusion about Gilman's narrator, that she has been sentenced to "imprisonment in the 'infected' house of her own body" (qtd. in Golden 148). In "Usher" this pattern of connection between person and place begins with Poe's narrator, who, after a long day's journey, finds himself before an inexplicably melancholy, gloomy, and depressing landscape presided over by a house that to look upon becomes a "hideous dropping off of the veil" (397). His feelings become a "mystery all insoluble" precisely because they spring from his unconscious. He seems to realize this on some level when he decides that his experience "*must* have been a dream" (400). Of course it is a waking dream of an imagination that, in anticipation of Gilman's narrator, has somehow conditioned itself to project dark fancies upon reality. But, unlike the perfectly clear motivation of Gilman's narrator in her oppressive lifestyle, we are not given any background on Poe's narrator other than his early friendship with Roderick Usher.

Strangely, once inside the house, we see that the narrator's distorted imagination is nearly a perfect reflection of Roderick Usher's, full of fears and odd fancies. In the perfect construction of the tale, Poe makes the descriptions of each aspect of the story a description of the rest. So, while Roderick's cadaverous and hypersensitive condition of living death mirrors the description of the ancient house whose fissure puts it on the verge of collapsing, and of his sister who is, in fact, dying, his condition also describes the narrator's. They share a "morbid" imagination, an "anomalous species of terror" (403), and radiate gloom outward on all with which they interact (405). Why are they so alike? Why does Poe double them—and everything else within the tale? That is one of the things that have kept critics busy since its publication. We would argue that consciously or unconsciously, Gilman's answer to the question becomes a founding conception of "Yellow Wallpaper." From the perspective of her story, the narrator and Usher share assumptions about social relations that are systemic, but are now in decline. Like the Usher house itself, the system is cracked and its stones are crumbling. It radiates an "air of stern, deep, and irredeemable gloom [that] . . . pervaded all" (401). Furthermore, this atmosphere is described as unnatural, with "no affinity with the air of heaven," fed by the tarn's "pestilent and mystic vapor, dull, sluggish, faintly discernible, and leaden-hued" (399–400). This "system" infects all the inhabitants of the house and anyone who comes near. It is, in fact, killing Roderick and Madeline, the representative Gothic Adam and Eve of the latter days, whose impending fall will signal the end of the old regime and the potential for a new social construction. At least, this is what Gilman seems to have seen in Poe's descriptions. The surface inexplicability of these details, the seemingly unmotivated actions and reactions of the characters in "Usher," all point to a world that has become a Gothic madhouse—impossible to read—about to collapse under the weight of its incompatibility with human habitation.

Gilman translates the confrontation with the inexplicable into her narrator's continuing and morbid fascination with reading the "pointless pattern" of the wallpaper (48). Haney-Peritz's notice of the word "pronounced" in the description of the wallpaper suggests that the issue of reading is at the heart of the wallpaper's fascination (97). Like the House of Usher, the room in which the paper hangs is in decline: "The floor is scratched and gouged and splintered, the plaster itself is dug out here and there, and this great heavy bed which is all we found in the room, looks as if it had been through the wars" (47). The wallpaper itself has also seen better days, "stripped off . . . in great patches all around the head of my bed" (43). Like the suggestion of the decline of a venerable system in the details of the House of Usher, so her room is in constant decay that reflects, as the decay of the House of Usher, the mind of its inhabitants. With these details and others, Gilman also adds to the sense of inexplicability by an "undercurrent" of meaning that readers would wonder about that the narrator herself misses. While the narrator assumes, for example, that the room had been a playroom or nursery, it may have actually been—or is— a room in an asylum. The barred windows, the gate at the end of the stairs, and John's insistence that she stay in this particular room all point in that direction. Also, the fact that the paper is torn off near the bed "about as far as I can reach" suggests the extent of her dementia, that she is unaware that she tore off the paper herself. Is this a "summer rental" or a stay at an asylum, making the people she sees outside the window real? All of which, of course, introduces the problem of the narrator's unreliability. Brilliantly, in the tradition of Poe, the narrator tells her story in as potentially confused a manner as the wallpaper design itself. We never know when the story is accurate or when it may be plunging off "at outrageous angles" and destroying itself in "unheard of contradictions" (43). Her remark about being "too wise" and knowing things "nobody knows but me" certainly reminds us of the delusional narrator of "The Tell-Tale Heart," who repeatedly congratulates himself on his acuity (50). Hence, reading the "Yellow Wallpaper" is as difficult for us as reading the wallpaper is for the narrator. From this perspective the story becomes "broken" (46), "absurd" (46), "formless" (47), grotesque (49), and confusing (48)—in other words, unreadable.

III

Given Gilman's own mental condition, including her feelings of psychological claustrophobia in her marriage (now thought to have been exacerbated by postpartum depression), she certainly must have been struck by Poe's powerful presentation of Madeline Usher, a woman who is wordless throughout the tale and, when still alive, is screwed into a coffin that is placed in a copper-sheathed "don-jon-keep" with a heavy iron door. With the character of Madeline, Poe, whether consciously or not, creates one of the most striking literary examples of repression, particularly to his time. Not only is Madeline never seen interacting with anyone until after her death, she is kept mostly invisible within the narrative itself. Her brief appearance when alive, walking in a distant room with no awareness of those watching her, feels more like seeing a ghost than a person. The narrator, in fact, "regarded her with an utter astonishment not unmingled with dread" (*Tales* 404). Madeline is thus presented as a figure that inspires awe, even fear—a strange, inexplicable other. As D. H. Lawrence stated of "Usher," Madeline represents "the mystery of the recognition of *otherness*" (82). By burying her alive Roderick seeks to control the uncanny other. But as Diane Long Hoeveler notes, and Gilman had intuited, "the return of Madeline from the 'dead,' her strange immersion into and emergence from the depths of the tomb, complete with blood, represents that moment in the text when the signifier goes out of control" (*Tales* 393). That is, she breaks free from how she has been defined and controlled—killed, as it were—by Roderick. What must have made this aspect of the tale even more disturbing for Gilman is that Madeline was entombed alive by a brother who not only knew of her catalepsy, but who claimed her as a "tenderly beloved sister" over whom, when discussing her impending death, he "buried his face in his hands," hands through which "trickled many passionate tears" (404). Did Gilman see in this dire situation the essence of the female problem—women silenced by the loving men in their lives, making their existence a living death? Gilman's own husband at the time, Stetson, was reasonably amiable and they remained on friendly terms after their divorce. It wasn't that he was cruel or demanding, except that like most men of the period, he expected her to perform a particular role, one she was not comfortable with.

Like Madeline, Gilman's narrator is imprisoned in a room with bars, is not allowed to express herself in writing, nor speak if it is to complain about her situation. As Roderick "loves" Madeline, so John "loves" Gilman's narrator.

Perhaps the most powerfully effective "Usher" image for Gilman is the presence/absence of Madeline. While she is only seen three times briefly by the narrator—walking in a distant room, in her coffin, and returned from the dead—she virtually shapes the narrative. We learn early on that Roderick's peculiar behavior is a result of Madeline's "long-continued illness," a behavior amplified immeasurably after her death. She is the absent instigator of Usher's art and song, of his reading, particularly *Vigiliae Mortuorum* (Vigils for the Dead), and of his "anomalous species of terror" (403). Like John, Usher fears his female counterpart's unusual condition, perhaps seeing his own impending downfall reflected in her. As symbolic (Madeline) and real (Gilman narrator) mothers, their health is basic to the health of the family; their lack of health, like the fissure and the smooch, is indicative of the impending psychological destruction of the family. Her "suspiciously lingering smile upon the lip which is so terrible in death" suggests her awareness of her influence on the men, and possibly her vengeful plans (410). Each appearance of Madeline is more awesome and terrifying, until she returns from the grave and falls on Roderick, bringing him to his death. The fact that they share their fate became important for Gilman's conception of the system and how it brings down both men and women. Like Roderick, of course, John falls (in a faint) in the end when he sees his wife "creeping" around the room. Importantly, Gilman would have noted that Roderick and Madeline are twins, in person and destiny. The fissure that brings down the house, and is echoed in the "smooch" Gilman's narrator makes on the wall, is the cracked relationship between the genders. Madeline is thus the powerful, though silent and mostly absent, major agent of all action, thought, fear, and art in the story. As Gilman might have said, the repressed eventually triumph, but only tragically.

Another dimension of Madeline's presence/absence is her being Roderick's identical twin. In a sense, this makes her physically present wherever Roderick is, her image invoked by him. While little specific information is given to us about Madeline's life or habits before her illness, her likeness to Roderick suggests that she may have also been an active intellectual, reading, writing, painting, and playing an instrument. In the context of "Ligeia," published the year before, in 1838, and "Morella," published three years before that, it's quite possible that Madeline was more than a mere cipher. Various textual cues point us in this direction. First, as in the other tales, in which the narrators are secluded from the world, spending all of their time deeply studying "forbidden" transcendental and mystic works of philosophical idealism under the tutelage of the gigantic intellects of their talented wives, Madeline has been his "sole companion for long years" (404). In "Morella," the title character and her husband were speculating about "wild Pantheism," a subject closely related to the sentience of inanimate things (230). Also, as in the previous tales, Roderick is torn inexplicably between loving concern and hostility toward his sister. No more than in "Ligeia" or "Morella" is the sudden turn from adoration to loathing explained. Suddenly the man turns off his loving attention and the female begins to fade away. In the case of "Morella" the narrator becomes haunted in his studies by strange, forbidden meanings he can't articulate, turning his joy in Morella "into horror" (230). In "Ligeia," the death of the wife is also seemingly brought on by the pair getting too near knowledge "too divinely precious not to be forbidden" (316). Certainly it is possible that Roderick, also an ardent reader of strange texts, may have found with Madeline forbidden truths about the sentience of inanimate things, causing in her a physical malady, and in him, madness.

Another possibility in terms of Madeline's talent is that Roderick became jealous of Madeline's superior intellect, a quality he apparently values, since he displays his talents to his friend regularly with his painting, improvisations, and readings. Thus, he may have begun, like Morella's husband, to withdraw his love, to read on his own, causing Madeline, like her literary predecessor Morella, to pine "away daily" (231). Speculating on the above, might not John be jealous of Gilman's narrator's gifts as a writer and an intellectual, only able to tolerate her presence when she is childlike, submissive, and silenced?

A striking aspect of Poe's tale is the presence of suspicious medical men about the House of Usher, who would certainly have caught the attention of Gilman. Herself the victim of Dr. S. Weir Mitchell's ill-conceived and damaging rest cure, Gilman was critical of the reckless treatment that would prevent her from putting pen to paper ever "again as long as I lived" ("Why" 348). (She later claimed that she sent him a copy of the story, and that though he never acknowledged receipt of it, she was "told that the great specialist had admitted to friends of his that he had altered his treatment of neurasthenia since reading *The Yellow Wallpaper* [*sic*])" ("Why" 349). In "Usher" the medical men are presented as suspicious, incompetent grave-robbers whose "eager inquiries" about Madeline's burial suggest the need to secure her within the family crypt (*Tales* 409). Their clueless bafflement before Madeline's disease, and the "low cunning" of their hopes to steal her body for research, embodies a Gothic type that Gilman likely found analogous to Mitchell and his own incompetence. Further, since Mitchell's rest cure treatment, and its strictures against any intellectual activity including writing, was designed to silence Gilman's identity into conformity, she would eventually perceive him as a pillar of the oppressive patriarchal establishment. Importantly, her narrator's husband, John, is also a physician whose patronizing and dismissive manipulations of his wife witness his own "low cunning" and stubborn incompetence. His imagination is too limited to imagine his wife's being cured except by submission to his infallible will. Crucial to Gilman's reading of "Usher" on this point of medical practice is the utter inexplicability the women's illness present to their doctors. In their own way, like Poe's policemen who follow the same plodding methods in trying to solve every case, these medical men employ a Procrustean bed for every illness. In fact, in her day most misunderstood female maladies lumped under such categories as "hysteria" or "nervous depression." Like the patriarchy itself, medical science is a hardened system that assumes an absolute authority to silence and dictate.

Reflecting the cultural systems of society, including the medical, is the setting of the House of Usher itself. The importance of setting in "Yellow Wallpaper" points to Gilman's reading of the Usher House itself as an important symbol of broader issues. Its very presence induces in the narrator an "insufferable gloom," an "unredeemed dreariness of thought," and an "utter depression of soul" (397). The narrator's horrified reactions to the house, for Gilman's purposes, become a model of how she wants her readers to respond to "Yellow Wallpaper." In addition to her stated goal to "save people from being driven crazy" ("Why" 349), it seems clear that she wants to shine a harsh light on the way things are. Gilman intends to awaken readers from the opiate of traditional gender relations, to give them a "bitter lapse into every-day life," so that they can experience "the hideous dropping off of the [cultural] veil" (*Tales* 397). She wished to show everyday life as so akin to a Gothic horror story that "no goading of the imagination could torture [it] into aught of the sublime" (397). The narrator's "experiment" of looking at the house's "inverted images" reflected in the tarn serves various purposes for the tale, including its symbolic reflection of how inverted the house and family are in terms of its unwholesome history. It also emphasizes a couple of points that Gilman certainly makes in "Yellow Wallpaper," that the status quo is an inversion of the natural, equal relations men and women are capable of enjoying. Thus, like the inverted image in the tarn, the world Gilman creates around John's dysfunctional little family has "an atmosphere which had no affinity with the air of heaven" (399). In addition, the reflection of the narrator in the wallpaper suggests, like the reflection of the house in the tarn, feelings of seclusion and imprisonment.

Gilman witnesses that the House of Usher's "discoloration of ages" and "specious totality" are on the verge of collapse—its day is at hand (400). The house, like Madeline and Roderick, exists in a living death. G. R. Thompson appropriately sees the house as a "death's-head looming out of a dead landscape" (89). Poe has set his tale at the moment just before the psychological apocalypse of the Ushers. Gilman, too, sets her story at the eleventh hour for the mad narrator's remaining shred of sanity. Like Usher's fissure that has split the house precariously in two, so the oppressive social system has split the genders in two in a way that signals the possibility of a new order for the new century. As the minute "fine tangled web-work" spread across the "crumbling" stones of Usher, so the ripped wallpaper is a similar "indication of extensive decay" suggesting "little token of stability" (*Tales* 400). The fact that the House of Usher seems alive, bearing a relationship to its inhabitants' "morale," is echoed by Gilman in the ever-changing pattern of the yellow wallpaper that seems to imprison a woman. As Cynthia S. Jordan observes, the reflection of the house in the tarn represents Madeline, "Roderick's physical and psychological counterpart" (7). Thus, both houses get inside the heads of their inhabitants, driving them crazy and reinforcing their function as symbolic of a demented, all-pervasive social system.

Finally, pervading all of these images and themes that would have stood out to Gilman in her state of mind at the time she wrote her masterpiece is "Usher's" terrifying atmosphere of the Gothic. Not, however, the mere setting in a dilapidated mansion, strange occurrences, weird characters, or living burial, but the psychological Gothic of the impossibly blurred lines between reality and dream, dream and madness. Poe's entire story is the model for the wallpaper itself. It is a metaphor for an arabesque text that won't permit itself to be read: *"er lasst sich nicht lessen"* (*Tales* 506). Poe's quote from "The Man of the Crowd" captures one of the hallmarks of Poe's fiction—its inexplicability. Among the "considerations beyond our depth" that Poe's narrator senses are Roderick's fear, the parallel sounds during the reading of *The Mad Trist*, the strangely condensed storm, Roderick's secret—all of which is emphasized by images like the source of the ghastly light in Roderick's painting and the intricate passageway into the great room of Usher. For Gilman, "Usher" embodies whatever cannot be read finding its way into her story as the narrator's mental problems, John's refusal to pay any heed to her, and the design of the wallpaper itself. Among the blurred lines "Usher" spawns is the uncanny reflection of the characters in their respective houses. Poe's narrator is as much an inversion of Roderick as the tarn image is of the house, and as Roderick is of Madeline, and Gilman's narrator is of the reflection of the women behind the wallpaper and those creeping about the estate.

Not surprisingly, in both "Usher" and "Yellow Wallpaper," the liberation of the repressed is linked to the finding of the self. In the case of Madeline, the faint smile on her lips at the time of her burial signals the emergence of the self, unencumbered by Roderick's shadow. In fact, her death may be considered an act of will, an escape in the same way Gilman's narrator escapes through insanity. The latter finds herself, like Madeline, resisting the wishes of her male companion. In both "Usher" and "Yellow Wallpaper," the establishment of the female self is based in resistance to male discourse, in becoming the opposite of what the male wants. Hence, in both stories this defiance is an act of communication, of rewriting the script in amazing ways. Just as Gilman's narrator wants "to astonish" John, so Madeline's horrific arrival similarly

bowls Roderick over. They both do so by writing on themselves—
the smooch on the shoulder in "Yellow Wallpaper" and the blood
on Madeline's robes in "Usher." Such shocking self-inscription,
like both genre-breaking narratives themselves, astonishes out of
all complacency. The path into such writing is the journey inward,
represented by the room and the crypt. As in the story of the
classic heroic journey, the Female Gothic hero must be buried in
the belly of the beast, or must sojourn in Hades, before emerging victorious. Gilman's heroic, and groundbreaking rereading of
"Usher" allowed her into a conversation not only with Poe and his
great tale, but with women and feminist literature that still speaks
loud and clear.

CHAPTER 3

REALISTIC "USHER": NARRATIVE IMAGINATION AND JAMES'S *THE TURN OF THE SCREW*

To write about Henry James's *The Turn of the Screw* is a risky venture. After all, there is so much criticism of the text that reading it all, let alone engaging it in meaningful debate, seems overwhelming. There are simply too many approaches, too many possible answers to the most vexing questions: Are the ghosts real? Is the governess crazy? How did Miles die? In recent years, critics have begun to comment on the problem of the sheer volume of criticism. Wayne Booth, for example, writes that "I can think of no other work of art that has stimulated as many contradictory readings" (James, *Turn* 240). Although Booth is probably right, contradictory approaches to James's novella seem to be the least of our problems. Even worse, therefore, is the problem that there is so much criticism it has become difficult to distinguish the criticism from the text. As Vincent Pecora puts it, "one can hardly see the text except through the nearly opaque screen of more than half a century of professional critical argument" (176). We suggest that a fresh approach to *Turn of the Screw* requires that we step off the critical merry-go-round so we can examine James's most troubling story in new ways. In this chapter, we will therefore analyze *Turn of the Screw* through the lens of Poe's "House of Usher." Doing so, we argue, will not only reveal the many resemblances between the two stories but also help us comment on the larger questions concerning James's use of the ghost story model and its underlying psychological themes. Indeed, we argue that James doesn't just apply his psychological realism to established Gothic conventions, but that he specifically works off of the innovations to the genre that Poe had already established. To be sure, critics have already noticed James's connection to Poe; our approach differs from theirs in that we will underscore the importance of Poe's "Usher" to our reading of *Turn of the Screw*. By doing so, we will go beyond the old assumptions that suggest Poe only holds a minimal importance to the study of James. Instead, we will show how the two stories address specific themes concerning literary realism, narration, and the haunted imagination.

Reading *Turn of the Screw* in terms of "Usher" forefronts the fascinating and complex ways psychological realism becomes the intersection of desire and imagination. This is a particular issue since James knew so well the thin line between realism and romance, the actual and the imaginary. He even admitted in the preface to *The American* that he had stepped over the line between realism and romance by presenting an impoverished family of aristocrats denying a wealthy American suitor over something so trivial as his lack of sophistication. In *Turn of the Screw* he presents a female narrator who clearly has a romantic imagination, who sees the house's tower as a castle in a fairy tale and her charges as a prince and princess. Because of the perspective of the narrator, perhaps *Turn of the Screw*, of all of his stories most interestingly skirts the line between realism and romance, accurately portraying a delicate, imaginative mind upended by possible encounters with the supernatural and placing the reader at the mercy of the limits of the reality imagined by the narrator.

It is, of course, James's concern with this thin line between the real and the romantic that brings him and Poe into a common literary field. While Poe is not considered a "realist" per se, at least in terms of settings and situations, his attention to authentic psychological states arguably qualifies him. H. P. Lovecraft noted, for example, that Poe "established a new standard of realism in the annals of literary horror" (*Supernatural* 43). In fact, some of the terms Lovecraft uses to describe Poe's realism perfectly apply to James: "analytical knowledge," "consummate craftsman-ship," "rigorous paring down of incidents," and "maintenance of a single mood" (43). Like Poe, James's view of realism goes well beyond life's mundane surfaces and ordinary states of consciousness. Summarizing F. O. Mathiessen on how "the projection of the super-conscious was what attached [James] to the ghost stories," Georges Markow-Totevy notes that "James seems readily to speculate on the forms of consciousness that extend beyond immediate reality" into an "uncertain realm of possibilities and vagueness" (120–21). Certainly, the same could be said of Poe's explorations into abnormal states of mind. As Fred See claims, James referred to the obsessed mind he loved to explore in the late 1890s and beyond as "possessed," a mind See defines as "ambivalent, contradictory, self-opposed, above all radically bifurcated and yet fundamentally unified" (120). From a more noumenal perspective, Quentin Anderson calls possession "the naturalistic analogue of the operation of providence" (231). In other words, Jamesean realism encompasses what See calls "spiritual identity"— the deep, even unconscious, nature of his characters. James, like Poe, explores the truly inexplicable reaches of the mind. In short, Jamesean possession may manifest itself in various ways—either as redemption or as terror. In stories like *Turn of the Screw*, it refers to what we might say exists ambiguously between the imagination and reality, just as obsession functions for Poe's characters. What James referred to in his "possession" stories as "hovering prowling blighted presences" (*The Turn of the Screw*), "infected air" (*What Maisie Knew*), "some imagined appeal of the lost Dead" (*The Altar of the Dead*), and a threatening "hauntedness" (*The Sense of the Past*) might well describe the dark psychological ambiance in "Usher" and much else of Poe's work (See 123).

Given the overlap of focus on psychological realism in James and Poe, such connections between the two writers seemingly unrelated by time and sensibility should not really surprise us, though what most of us know of the relationship is only James's famous suggestion that "an enthusiasm for Poe is the mark of a decidedly primitive stage of reflection" (Buranelli 128). James's comment was made during the 1870s when, as a developing realist, he was denouncing his own boyhood enthusiasm for Poe. In *A Small Boy and Others* (1913), James recounts how he read several tales, including "The Gold Bug" and "The Pit and the Pendulum," and was able to recite "The Raven," "Lenore," and "Annabel Lee" (Pollin 26). But as Burton Pollin points out, James's views on Poe evolved over time. According to Pollin, we begin to find allusions to Poe before *The Sacred Fount* (1901), and, from then on, larger "traces" of Poe appear in James's writing (28). Such traces include "The Raven," "The Fall of the House of Usher," and "The Masque of the Red Death" in *The Sacred Fount;* allusions to "Mystification" and "Lenore," and *The Narrative of Arthur Gordon Pym* in *The Golden Bowl* (the title of which comes from Poe's "Lenore," a poem "endlessly recited by [James] and his family back in the 1850s"); and the Gothic-inspired ambiance from "William Wilson" and "The Fall of the House of Usher" in "The Jolly Corner" (Pollin 28–37). James's late renaissance of interest in Poe is not really so surprising when we note the many similarities between the two, including the fastidious craftsmanship; interest in the uncanny, the ambiguous, and the inexplicable; preference of the conceptual over emotional presentation; practicing of literary criticism; and experimental focus on the short story form. Beyond these parallels, we suggest that James looks to Poe's "Usher" very explicitly in *The Turn of the Screw.*

However, in addition to drawing on Poe's specific tales and poems, James, even more importantly, seems clearly to have drawn on Poe's theory of creating a unified effect as found in "The Philosophy of Composition" and in his 1847 review of Hawthorne's *Twice-Told Tales* and *Mosses from an Old Manse.* James, in fact, comments on Poe's review in his own book-length study of Hawthorne, by referring to Poe as a "man of genius" who, for his times, held the critical "scales the highest" while his critical comments "contain a great deal of sense and discrimination as well" (*Hawthorne* 63). On the whole James values Poe's criticism as "extraordinary," his intelligence as "frequently great," and his reviews as "very curious and interesting reading, and it has one quality ['complete and exquisite *provincialism*'] which ought to keep it from ever being completely forgotten" (63). Crucial for James in what Poe wrote, and seemingly never forgotten, were his statements outlining what has become the modern theory of the short story. Poe's emphasis is on orderly craftsmanship in building a story, "commencing with the consideration of an *effect*" ("Philosophy" 14), after which the writer "invents such incidents [to match the effect] . . . then combines such events, and discusses them in such tone as may best serve him in establishing this preconceived effect" ("Review" 586). In other words, as Poe adds, "in the whole composition there should be no word written of which the tendency, direct or indirect, is not to the one pre-established design" (586). The result is that, as with Poe, the sheer craft of James's fiction calls attention to itself in a way not seen in contemporary realists like Mark Twain and William Dean Howells.

In short, James sometimes turns to Poe as a model of precise craftsmanship and of exploring psychological ambiguity. Indeed, James actually echoes Poe's philosophy a number of times in the preface to the 1908 edition of *Turn of the Screw*. In comparing his tale's tight construction of "agreeable unity," he notes that in shorter pieces "we founder . . . when we go in, as they say, for great lengths and breadths" ("Preface" 181). As he further suggests, "the thing was to aim at absolute singleness, clearness, and roundness" through "ingenuity pure and simple, of cold artistic calculation" (182). This last statement affirms Poe's views of the almost scientific precision by which a work of literary art is designed: "no point in its composition is referrible [*sic*] either to accident or intuition," but the work proceeds "with the precision and rigid consequence of a mathematical problem" ("Philosophy" 14–15). Praising James's economy of style, André Gide notes, "James allows only that amount of steam to escape, which is needed to take his machine forward from one point to another" (qtd. in Markow-Totevy 125). But this isn't the extent of how James echoes Poe's views on fiction. While Poe, referring to the process of creating literary art, notes that "a picture is at length painted" ("Review" 586), James declares that "the analogy between the art of the painter and the art of the novelist is, so far as I am able to see, complete" ("Art of Fiction" 393). For both, the painting, with its tight, economic composition that doesn't allow digressions or tangents, ideally embodies the proper aspiration of fiction.

In *Turn of the Screw* James uses "Fall of the House of Usher" to complicate his obvious foray into the Female Gothic mode as inspired by works like *Jane Eyre* and *Northanger Abby*. James may have begun with *Jane Eyre* in mind, drawing on its setup of a young woman coming to a large country estate to care for children as a governess. She is surrounded by mysterious, and sometimes terrifying, occurrences that only become clear in the end. Like the narrator in *Turn of the Screw*, Jane Eyre is infatuated with her boss and is prone to misinterpretations, thinking Grace Poole is the crazy woman she hears and that Mr. Rochester is going to marry Blanche Ingram. With these elements of misinterpretation in place in his story, James adds complex layers of psychological ambiguity of the type found in "Usher." From Poe's model, the mysterious occurrences at Bly, seen through the governess's "bewilderment of vision," become ultimately impossible to interpret definitively (39). Her distorted vision during the course of the story, like that of "Usher's" narrator, grows out of the psychological baggage she brings to Bly—in her case, the sexual tension of her infatuation with the children's uncle, her novelized imagination (perhaps inspired by Catherine Moreland in Austin's *Northanger Abby*), her fear of failure, and her limited provincial experience. This is where *Turn of the Screw* turns away from *Jane Eyre* and moves more completely in the direction of "Usher." Unlike James's governess's interpretations of events, Jane's false interpretations don't spring from any deep psychological baggage she brings with her. Linking the Brontë and Poe stories was natural for James. Like *Jane Eyre*, "Usher" has a brooding, unhappy, Byronic figure at the center and a hidden, mysterious woman from whom strange sounds echo menacingly throughout the house. And, in the end, like Rochester's demented wife, Madeline emerges to destroy the house and the protagonist.

It is with the "Usher" part of the equation in *Turn of the Screw*, of course, that concerns this chapter. Their mutual interest in the craft of writing grounds James's conversation with the writer he loved as a boy, rejected as an emerging young realist, and with whom he made his peace as a mature writer. In this chapter we will explore how *Turn of the Screw* is framed by "Usher" from which it takes its general narrative structure of psychological collapse into the setting, blurring of the boundaries between dream and reality, and movement of the "possessed" mind toward an apocalypse.

Ambiguous issues of writing, narration, and reading are central to both "Fall of the House of Usher" and *Turn of the Screw*. "Usher," for example, begins with the narrator trying to interpret his own responses to the House of Usher: "I know not how it was—but, with the first glimpse of the building, a sense of insufferable gloom pervaded my spirit" (397). He goes on to describe in great detail the inexplicable "utter depression of soul" he feels, finding it "a mystery all insoluble" (397). He even tries to modify his first impressions by examining the house's reflection in the tarn, but upon the attempt finds only "a shudder even more thrilling than before" (398). He becomes so confused in his attempts to read his own feelings that he can no longer discern between reality and "what *must* have been a dream" (400). As readers find themselves in the hands of a narrator whose point of view is inconclusive, his confusion becomes their own. Issues concerning the impossibility of absolute discernment are pervasive in the tale, from Roderick's superstition that the house is sentient, to the narrator's inability to judge whether Madeline is dead or alive. The problem in the text of distinguishing reality from imagination is reinforced by Roderick and his art. His phantasmagoric paintings and music are associated with an "excited and highly distempered ideality [which] threw a sulphureous luster over all" and are so vague and abstract that the narrator "shuddered knowing not why" (405).

These descriptions of vague dreads and horrors, together with the tale's emphasis on subterranean imagery, can't be precisely located. Instead, the tarn's uncanny reflection of the house and Madeline's entombment in the cellar suggest the unconscious and irrational perceptions of the dream state—or of madness. These troubling uncertainties become the apocalyptic climax that is centered on the house coming hysterically to life with inexplicable storms and unsettling sounds. All the troubling hints of the weird and uncanny in the House of Usher, felt and discussed by the narrator and Roderick, seem to escape from their repressed unconscious minds as a terrifying external display they both experience visually and aurally. Could the storm actually be located only immediately about the house and "glowing in the unnatural light of a faintly luminous and distinctly visible gaseous exhalation which hung about and enshrouded the mansion" (412)? Could the events of Ethelred's adventure actually be simultaneously echoed by Madeline's impossible escape from the tomb as a living corpse? Could the mansion collapse into the tarn at just the moment that Madeline collapses onto Roderick? Or is all this merely psychological sound and fury signifying nothing? Correctly answering these questions is made impossible by a narrator whose tale cannot be corroborated. In the end, the point of the story seems to be the effect on readers through defying their false expectations that the narrator will, in the end, explain the various mysteries in the story. Poe's purpose is more about mystifying perceptions than it is about revealing plot points. Paving the way for James's *Turn of the Screw,* Poe's great anti-tale removed conventional Gothic horror to a realm of dizzying inexplicabilities told by a *"madman"* (416).

In *Turn of the Screw,* James, like Poe, highlights the theme of reading through his narrator's highly developed and possibly distorted imagination. Like the "Usher" narrator, the governess constantly analyzes her own unusual impressions, hearing, for example, the "recurrence of a sound or two, less natural and not without but within" (30). During Flora's conducted tour of Bly, the governess sees it all in literary terms: "I had the view of a castle of romance inhabited by a rosy sprite, such a place as would somehow, for diversion of the young idea, take all colour out of story-books and fairy tales" (32). Like the narrator in "Usher," she even invokes the idea that it may not be real: "Was n't [*sic*] it just a story-book over which I had fallen a-doze and a-dream" (33). She seems, in fact, unable to see anything free of the "trap" of her imagination (38), which causes her to see Flora as "one of Raphael's holy infants" (31). After learning of Miles's dismissal from school, the governess's imagination becomes noticeably darker. As her imagination takes her into speculations about Miles's nature, that "he's an injury to the others," she moves from narrating a fairy tale to narrating a Gothic tale of dark and inexplicable mysteries (34). The governess asks, "Was there a 'secret' at Bly—a mystery of Udolpho or an insane, an unmentionable relative kept in unsuspected confinement?" (41). Her question obviously turns on the idea that Bly itself is a kind of Gothic mansion, a place where secrets are withheld from the common observer. She, it seems, is compelled to come to grips with the events taking place there. Of course, as with "Usher's" narrator, it is actually the governess's mind that seems to be haunted.

Just as Roderick can't help speculating wildly about the House of Usher, its sentience, the meaningfulness of its arrangements and its reflection in the tarn, so the governess's experiences at Bly fuel her speculative imagination. She imagines herself as part of a fictional tale, one in which she is the heroic protagonist. She explains how nice it would be if her life were "as charming as a charming story" (39). Even better, she hopes that the plot of her story would turn on the idea of her "meet[ing] some one" (39). This charming and romantic tale she imagines must end with her happiness, or else life has little meaning at all. In fact, she lives with the hope that perhaps "some one would appear there at the turn of a path and would stand before me and smile and approve" (39). Indeed, her hope that someone (presumably the children's uncle) ought to come and "smile and approve" suggests that these specific gestures must be welcoming enough for her to find herself squarely within a Gothic romance plot, like *Jane Eyre,* wherein the desirable master of the house would notice her superior qualities and fall in love with her. But the story the governess fashions will turn into a much darker type of Gothic tale. Now completely possessed by an irrational state of mind, like the narrator of "Usher," the governess is unable to save her charges. When she explicitly announces to Miles that her purpose is to save him, the apocalyptic clock begins ticking with an Usher-esque "blast and chill, a gust of frozen air and a shake of the room as great as if, in the wild wind, the casement had crashed in" (James, *Turn* 95). Like the storm that kicks up during the ending scenes of "Usher," the setting itself seems to sentiently respond to the tensions between the governess and Miles.

Her disillusionment begins during her evening walk when she recognizes that Peter Quint is not the kind of man who would "smile and approve" (39). The governess then confesses to experiencing "a bewilderment of vision":

> It produced in me, this figure, in the clear twilight, I remember, two distinct gasps of emotion, which were, sharply, the shock of my first and that of my second surprise. My second was a violent perception of the mistake of my first: the man who met my eyes was not the person I had precipitately supposed. There came to me thus a bewilderment of vision of which, after these years, there is no living view that I can hope to give.
>
> (39–40)

Her bewilderment echoes that of "Usher's" narrator at trying to make sense of his depressed gloominess before the House of Usher, his confusion between reality and dream. In addition, just as "no goading of the imagination could torture [the landscape] into aught of the sublime" for the narrator, so too the governess can't maintain the happy charm she felt before seeing (or imagining) Quint (Poe, *Tales* 397). Instead of feeling like the heroine in a Gothic romance, she becomes the victim of her own haunted imagination as she ponders the perverted possibilities of Quint's (and later Miles's) behavior. Both "Usher" and *Turn of the Screw* ultimately revolve around narrating the impossible, about making sense of the inexplicable. And, in both cases, the inexplicable is located most disturbingly in the imaginations of the tales' narrators. That is, these tales ultimately share the inexplicability of how people think, perceive, and interpret.

In the case of the governess, her imagination is that of a young and naïve provincial daughter of a rural minister. Such a background, so limited in scope, has conditioned her to think in stark absolutes. Her mind is further conditioned by her childhood reading of fairy tales, romances, and Gothic novels, all of which have nurtured a tendency to imagine reality in storytelling forms. Thus the governess is "possessed," in the Jamesian sense, of a certain predisposition toward fantasy. Roderick's imagination, too, has been influenced by the outlandish texts in his own library that contribute to his horrific fantasies about the House of Usher. In *Turn of the Screw*, the governess's confident belief in her outlandish theories lies behind the unspoken central mystery of the story. In essence, she has a dual personality: the charming, seemingly rational young woman with whom Douglas later becomes infatuated, and the unstable young woman with a disturbed consciousness that processes reality through a literary imagination that vacillates between idealized dreams and horrific nightmares. The first personality and the second are, in a sense, distinct; the one lucidly and logically interprets and expresses, while the other relies on a haunted imagination. These dual propensities of the governess create a story that endlessly baffles our attempts to knit together all of its pieces.

Split down the middle like the fissured House of Usher itself, "Usher," too, proves to be a text that refuses to render a unified reading. Like *Turn of the Screw*, the story becomes impossible to read because it does not represent the straightforward observations and insights of its narrator. The narrator, like James's governess, also has a dual focus—on the one hand, maintaining distance between his own and Roderick's ideas; and on the other, slowly absorbing Roderick's dreams. As Richard Wilbur notes, "we must understand 'The Fall of the House of Usher' as a dream of the narrator's" (265). Rather, what we experience along with both

Poe's and James's narrators are the distorted, expressionist depictions of the unconscious, dream mind. That is, what "Usher's" narrator describes of the house on that dark and soundless day of his arrival is the edifice of his own unconscious imagination. Like the house itself, his psyche is split down the middle: one half of him creates a fantastic Gothic narrative about his experience with the Ushers that his other half, unaware of his unconscious side, attempts to interpret.

James complicates his conversation with "Usher" by echoing its incessant doublings. Among James's turns of the "Usher" screw are the doubling of the strange male-female figures that the governess encounters. Roderick and Madeline are thus echoed in both Quint and Miss Jessel, as well as in Miles and Flora. Like Quint and Jessel, Roderick and Madeline are death-like figures. Roderick is described as "cadaverous," with a "ghostly pallor," and the narrator has a difficult time connecting Roderick's "Arabesque expression with any idea of simple humanity" (401–402). Madeline, like Miss Jessel, is seen wandering aimlessly about, a death-in-life figure rarely seen but having a powerful influence on the others in the house. It is suggested, at least by the governess, that Miles and Flora are younger versions of Quint and Jessel in the process of beginning their corrupt careers of secret evil. These pairs of doubles are further linked by hints of sexuality. In fact, the many readings of "Usher" as an incest narrative prefigure the sexual suggestiveness of Quint and Jessel's relationship and their insidious desire for the children. Another way James doubles Poe is by complicating the narration with a frame story, introducing an additional perspective on the governess's tale. The contrast between the mundane world of the leisured class in the frame story and the governess's fantastic narrative punctuates the latter as a horror story. Thus, James's conversation with Poe veers in the direction of mystification through craftsmanship, thereby both celebrating and challenging Poe as the master of psychological terror.

Another important influence of "Usher" on *Turn of the Screw* is how they both exploit the conventional ghost story. Both writers, in fact, challenge the notion of what it means to be haunted by emphasizing the psychological, suggesting that haunted imaginations raise just as many specters as the chiming of midnight. Poe, of course, never wrote a ghost story in the most traditional or generic sense, though he figures prominently in scholarly studies of ghost stories. In *American Nightmares,* for example, Dale Bailey claims that Poe's contributions to the Gothic "would eventually provide impetus for the thriving (dare we say) cottage industry of paperback haunted house novels" (17). As Julia Briggs writes, "the narrowest definition of the ghost story would describe it as a story about the spirits of the returning dead, but many of the best-known examples of the genre do not conform to this description" (123). This is particularly true of a writer like Poe who treats the theme of haunting through his poems and tales to blur the boundary between the haunted mind and the seeming reappearance of the dead. As Briggs explains, Poe's lack of a traditional ghost story in his work does not preclude his major impact on the subsequent "vocabulary" of such tales (125). As she writes, Poe's "work remains seminal to the form," particularly through his skillful development of the uncanny (125). Poe's contribution, as he sensed himself, is that haunting requires more than rattling chains and creaking doors; what is needed is little more than a troubled imagination and a struggling soul. Indeed, many of Poe's narrators are haunted by powerful obsessions that, once combined with their equally strong imaginations, produce the very phantoms they fear the most. It is this productive quality of the imagination that makes Poe so influential to writers of haunted tales. As Briggs argues, "the ghost story reverts to a world in which imagination can produce physical effects, a world that is potentially within our power to change by the energy of our thoughts, yet practically alarming" (124).

Poe conveys a powerful sense of feeling haunted by showing how imaginative powers within the human mind may psychologically and physically create a ghostly atmosphere. According to Kenneth Silverman, Poe effectively "dramatizes how dream and memory invariably lead back to specters" in his poem "Dream-Land" (227). He demonstrates how lines like "the traveler meets aghast / Sheeted Memories of the Past" help convey the anxiety and long-ing bound up with the play of reality and unreality (*Poems* 344). In "House of Usher," as in Poe's other "ghost" tales, he further plays with boundaries by exploring the ambiguous divisions within the psyche that become the basis of the haunted mind. Roderick, for example, sees death with both fear and desire. As Poe describes him, Roderick seems to want two things equally—to depart the rational world (by dream, madness, or death), and to maintain life as it is. In other words, oblivion is a temptation, but a horrifying one. Such a dual impulse is common in Poe's tales and poems. In his poem "The Lake," the narrator, in contemplating the terrifying possibility of death in the lake, notes that "yet that terror was not fright, / But a tremulous delight—" (*Poems* 86). Usher's mind is similarly split as reflected in the fissure that divides the House of Usher. Roderick's psychological division is further doubled when he puts his twin sister Madeline alive in the tomb. In this way she becomes a symbol of Roderick's psyche, particularly the part that wishes for oblivion. At the same time, Roderick's self-destructive imp of the perverse is reflected in his knowledge that she is still alive. Though he fulfills half of his psyche's needs by entombing Madeline, his other half becomes increasingly fearful and agitated. Ultimately, when Madeline returns from the tomb and bears Roderick down to a watery grave, her "ghost" becomes the emblem of his unconscious mind becoming, finally, the more powerful half. The ineffable essence of "House of Usher" lies in Poe's doubling of character in narrative action, thereby haunting and disturbing the reader through its inexplicably dreamlike story connections.

Returning to James, we may readily see how *Turn of the Screw* serves as perhaps the major example of a Poe-inspired ghost story. When the governess sees Quint for the first time, she initially believes that he comes from the power of her imagination. As she explains it, "What arrested me on the spot—and with a shock much greater than any vision had allowed for—was the sense that my imagination had, in a flash, turned real" (39). Such comments suggest a relationship between her powers of mind and her powers of sight, a relationship that draws on Poe's idea that the ghostly lies at the threshold of the imagination and may even produce physical effects. James further enhances the sense of haunting by causing the atmosphere to change dramatically. The governess notices that the natural surroundings have somehow paused in their movement and sound. She notes that "the place moreover, in the strangest way in the world, had on the instant and by the very fact of its appearance become a solitude" (40). Moreover, she writes that it was as though "all the rest of the scene had been stricken with death" and that evening fell with an "intense hush" (40). The governess's shock suggests something of her hope that her imagination could indeed turn real. What is likewise interesting is her claim that she experienced "a bewilderment of vision" that she feels unable to explain. Could this "bewilderment" describe her feeling haunted? Here, James draws on the same play of ambiguities that Poe does in "Usher." The governess, like Roderick, is also divided and is fighting an internal war. On the one hand, she sees Quint because of the wickedness she represses within her unconscious mind (the Jungian shadow). Because she had just been dreaming of a romantic encounter with the children's uncle, her conjuring of the ghost is a projection of her guilty desires onto him. On the other hand, she will also begin projecting guilty secrets onto Miles and Flora. Simultaneously, not recognizing her suspicions as projections of her own desires, the narrow religious absolutism of her conscious mind reacts by embarking on a quest to save the children—though she is really trying to save and purify herself. That is, everything she does enacts the psychic drama within her mind.

Significantly, James never clarifies whether Quint and Jessell are real spirits of the dead returned or whether they are manifestations of the governess's troubled imagination. In his preface to *Turn of the Screw*, James suggests that he never wanted them to follow prescribed rules. He particularly hopes to distance himself from the expectations laid out by the pile of evidence gathered by the Society for Psychical Research. In James's day, hauntings were seen from a scientific approach that tried to explain ghostly existence, behavior, and language. But James does not want his ghosts to knock or rattle or moan. Instead, he draws on Poe's use of haunting, derived from anxiety and longing. Perhaps this is why James insists that "Peter Quint and Miss Jessel are not 'ghosts' at all, as we now know the ghost" (184). Like Poe before him, James plays with the idea that the imagination produces the most menacing specters. As James puts it, "good ghosts, speaking by book, make poor subjects, and it was clear that from the first my hovering prowling blighting presences, my pair of abnormal agents, would have to depart altogether from the rules" (184). Thus, as in "Usher," James's story develops a unique approach to the spectral. When the governess sees Quint for the first time, she initially believes that what she sees comes from the power of her imagination.

Such a reading of *Turn of the Screw* suggests alternative ways of approaching "House of Usher." Colin Martindale, for example, reads "Usher," like Wilbur, in psychological terms. While Wilbur reads "Usher" as an allegory of regression toward a state of pure poetic independence, Martindale adds a Jungian dimension that sees Madeline as a part of Roderick that he wishes to repress. But in Martindale's reading, the repression is ultimately unsuccessful. In light of *Turn of the Screw,* we can see more complex ways to read Roderick and Madeline as both parts of the narrator's psyche, thus aligning the Ushers' function with Quint and Jessel as projections of the governess's mind. As such, Roderick and Madeline are born at the moment the narrator looks down into the tarn and questions if his experiences were all merely a dream. One can readily see Roderick as the part of the narrator who wants to escape into a dream state, this desire evidenced by the decaying house and the symbolic unconsciousness of the tarn's inverted image of the house. Thus, the image in the tarn becomes the image of the withdrawal into dream. On the other hand, however, the narrator also has a concurrent desire to awaken, making Madeline's rising from the tomb a symbol of his awakening. In the end, Madeline's falling on Roderick, killing him on the spot, is the burst bubble of his hypnogogic state, and the sinking of the house and its inhabitants represents the remoteness of dream once the dreamer awakens. Thus, the confusing relationships, contradictions, and impossibilities that the narrator describes perfectly embody the random way we remember dreams, with their lost narrative connections and character motivations.

Roderick's superstitions and his "anomalous species of terror" grow out of his "morbid acuteness of the senses" that cause him to confuse reality with imagination, an imagination that grows out of a mind "from which darkness, as if an inherent positive quality, poured forth upon all objects of the moral and physical universe, in one unceasing radiation of gloom" (403, 405). This description fits James's governess as well. Her "species of terror" also springs from a "morbid acuteness" of a very dark imagination. Rather than positing sentience on the house itself, however, she applies her superstition to the children. Instead of recognizing the children as relatively innocent and normal, the governess sees their games and activities as sinister motives and secret evils. Like Roderick, the governess projects her own darkness onto Miles and Flora so that what is alive in her mind becomes alive in them.

From such a perspective, the governess's "trap of the imagination" should be defined as an uncanny state equivalent to that of the dreamer, a condition in which reality is indistinguishable from fantasy. Whether the governess's specters are real or imagined does not take away from the fact she has assigned them meanings that feed her psychological needs and desires. To a large extent, her experience follows Lawrence's insight that "House of Usher" is largely about "the mystery of the recognition of *otherness*" (82). In other words, by projecting her shadow self onto the "ghosts" and the children, the governess fails to recognize the children in terms of their otherness. Indeed, she hardly sees herself clearly. James, however, does offer one brief moment in his story where the governess feels that Mile's might be innocent and that she, perhaps, is completely dumbfounded. As she describes it, "It was for the instant confounding and bottomless, for if he *were* innocent what then on earth was I" (James, *Turn* 119). Despite this glimpse of self-recognition, the governess nevertheless attempts to wrench a confession from Miles. Her efforts, however, will largely fail. After all, by imaginatively projecting her shadow on the ghosts and the children, she can only battle the inner demons she can't confront directly. Her attempts to get Miles to confess can only drain him of life. As Lawrence's writes concerning "Usher," "to try to *know* any living being is to try to suck the life out of that being" (76). In the governess's case, her fiction-laced imagination traps Miles in an awful plot that will lead, ultimately, to his death. Vampire-like, she sucks the life out of his little body.

In many ways, the face-off between the governess and Miles suggests that James draws on "The Tell-Tale Heart," Poe's masterpiece of insane self-confidence, to open up the governess's mental processes leading up to the climax. As in "The Tell-Tale Heart," the governess is obsessed with justifying her rational deductions, to both Mrs. Grose and readers of her narrative. In "The Tell-Tale Heart," Poe's narrator confesses to his readers directly, making sure they appreciate his cleverness. He begins his narrative, after all, by placing it within the context of a certain truthfulness. Indeed, with his opening declaration—"True!"—he both concedes his nervousness and suggests that what he will confess is as true and as rational as any enlightened thinker would know (*Tales* 792). Moreover, his use of the term "true" sets up his notion that what he will explain will be told from the perspective of a person who understands the difference between truth and error. He turns his attention, in fact, to his audience by asking them, "Why *will* you say that I am mad?" (792). It is his listeners, he believes, who are being willful by insisting that he is the one who has lost his mind. As he tells them, "The disease had sharpened my senses—not destroyed—not dulled them" (792). Herein lies the narrator's sense of his own rationality. He believes that he is more sane than others because his ability to use his senses—especially his hearing—to advance his intellectual schemes is far superior to that of other people. In his mind, his nervousness, then, is merely a by-product of his overall intellectual gifts.

When Poe's narrator turns to his detailed confession, then, he does so by focusing on not only how rationally he approaches the murder of the old man but also how all the events involved in the murder highlight the depth—the "sagacity"—of his mind (793). He notes, "You fancy me mad. Madmen know nothing. But you should have seen *me*. You should have seen how wisely I proceeded—with what caution—with what foresight—with what dissimulation I went to work" (792). Later, as he describes his performance around the old man the week before murdering him, he notes with pride that his behavior was the model of rational and gentlemanly action. As he explains, he "was never kinder" to the old man than just prior to murdering him (792). Moreover, he claims to have actually "loved" the old man, despite his burning wish to kill him (792). To explain these contradictory feelings, the narrator recounts that the only motivation behind the crime was that the old man's eye "haunted [him] day and night" (792). But, as he confesses his actions, he comes to the point about the eye almost as if he realizes it in the moment of the telling. He explains that "I think it was his eye! yes, it was this!" (792). This exclamation points to his sense that the old man's eye is really the only thing that needed to be killed. The old man has to die only because he was connected to the eye. The narrator goes on to detail how "every night, about midnight . . . I turned the latch of his door and opened it—oh, so gently!" (792). Using his lantern to see if the old man's eye were open, he exclaims, almost giggling, how the reader "would have laughed to see how cunningly I thrust [the lantern] in" (793). All of which, from his perspective, proves conclusively that he is sane and rational: "Would a madman be as wise as this?" (793).

In *Turn of the Screw*, the governess also congratulates herself for the perspicacity she uses in dealing with the children and the ghosts, and, like Poe's mad narrator, spends her nights waiting and watching to find the means to bring the crisis she perceives to a rational solution. Early on she expresses concern about how her narration will be received: "I scarce know how to put my story into words that shall be a credible picture of my state of mind; but I was in these days literally able to find a joy in the extraordinary flight of heroism the occasion demanded of me" (James 53). Looking back at her reactions to the crisis she imagines, she confesses that "I rather applaud myself as I look back!—that I saw my response so strongly and so simply" (53). Recounting the methodology of her night watches, as she "listened" for "something undefinably astir in the house," the governess confesses proudly a moment in her investigations: "Then, with all the marks of a deliberation that must have seemed magnificent had there been any one to admire it, I laid down my book, rose to my feet and, taking a candle, went straight out of the room and, from the passage, on which my light made little impression, noiselessly closed and locked the door" (James, *Turn* 67). Like Poe's narrator, she periodically addresses the reader directly, again describing her nightly vigils, "You may imagine the general complexion, from that moment, of my nights. I repeatedly sat up till I didn't know when; I selected moments when my room-mate unmistakeably slept, and, stealing out, took noiseless turns in the passage" (70). Like Poe's narrator, these vigils take her inevitably to the door of him with whom she is obsessed—Miles. On one occasion, James departs humorously from the Poe pattern by turning the screw on "Tell-Tale Heart" by having Miles speak from within his room to the governess: "I say, you there—come in" (92). The governess continues to congratulate herself throughout the narration, noting that she is "amazed" at her own spirit and nerve (106), that "I was grand" (112), and crows over her "personal triumph" during the climactic encounter with Miles (117).

Thus, like the narrator of "The Tell-Tale Heart," the governess congratulates both her sanity and performance by describing her relation to the children and the ghosts as a game that depends on cleverness and subtlety. In explaining the state of the contest between her and Miles after he explains why he had gone outside late at night, the governess uses game imagery: "It was a sharp trap for any game hitherto successful. He could play no longer at perfect propriety, nor could he pretend to it" (73). The imagery of these lines, including "trap" and "play," suggest a game being played, while "pretend" points to the performative aspects of their game. In considering the meaning of the note to the uncle that Miles had purloined, she figures it will give him only "so scant an advantage" (109). The narration has turned into a play-by-play commentary over a chess match. Near the climax she turns the game imagery into more violent sport befitting the circumstances: "So we circled about with terrors and scruples, fighters not daring to close" (115–16).

Hence, the governess's tale is about playing a difficult, life-or-death game. But though Miles dies at the end of it, the stakes are almost equally high for the governess. Since the beginning of the narration, she has shown real concern over her ability to successfully handle her position, even losing sleep over it. In part, her infatuation with the owner of Bly makes her want to especially please him, vaguely fantasizing that she might end up mistress of the place. As a result, her narration is designed to justify her assessment of a dangerous situation, her response, and how it turns out in the end. In essence, like the confession of Poe's narrator, the governess's story is an affidavit testifying to the correctness and competence of her decisions and actions on the job. Only inadvertently does it turn out to also be a confession, since, like Poe's narrator, she reveals much more than she intends. Among these things her desperate need to elicit Miles's confession may hint at her own perverse desire to both conduct a detailed probe into evil and to confess herself.

As the governess turns her attention to Miles, she realizes that her pressure on him to confess feels violent. She comments on her sense of the "'perverse horror' at what [she] was doing" (115). Like Poe's narrator in "Tell-Tale Heart," the governess recognizes her need to admit that her actions may appear terrible but that they are really far more rational and necessary than they may initially seem. As she sees Miles squirm under her own watchful eye and notices that he is experiencing real fear, she resists her small discomfort with hurting Miles for the sake of winning his confession. She even admits that "it was as if he were suddenly afraid of me—which struck me indeed as perhaps the best thing to make him" (115). Whereas the governess tries to shield her charges from fearing the ghosts, she now recognizes that fear may be the secret to gaining all that she wants from Miles.

The governess's sense of her own terrible power brings to mind Michel Foucault's insight that, to some extent, acts of confession lie at the heart of Western society as a means of grasping certain kinds of truth. He writes, "Since the Middle Ages at least, Western societies have established the confession as one of the main rituals we rely on for the production of truth" (58). Since then, Foucault claims, "the confession became one of the West's most highly valued techniques for producing truth" (59). Indeed, Foucault goes on to trace the impact of confession and its relationship to truth on society and culture broadly. He writes that confession

> plays a part in justice, medicine, education, family relationships, and love relations, in the most ordinary affairs of everyday life, and in the most solemn rites; one confesses one's crimes, one's sins, one's thoughts and desires, one's illnesses and troubles; one goes about telling, with the greatest precision, whatever is most difficult to tell. One confesses in public and in private, to one's parents, one's educators, one's doctor, to those one loves; one admits to oneself, in pleasure and in pain, things it would be impossible to tell to anyone else, the things people write books about.
>
> (59)

Although Foucault's arguments about the powers of confession may be too broad, his insight that within confession lies the possibility of truth in several venues of human life invites us to consider whether *Turn of the Screw* is, to some extent, about the nature and power of confession itself.

Returning to the governess's hope to get Miles to confess, we notice that she sees his confession largely in terms of the truths she wants to understand about Miles. Indeed, she wants Miles to use his confession to draw out the truth of not only all that he has done, but also all that he knows—including perhaps the motives behind his actions. In this sense, she wants to hold Miles under her control, to probe so deeply into him that he will be left without any secrets. This last point is particularly crucial for the governess because she believes that Miles cannot truly be "saved" without his speaking all the truth to her (110). Were Miles really in danger, perhaps the governess could simply remove him from

Bly and thereby shield him from Quint's threatening glare. But, for the governess, the kind of safety she wants Miles to experience can only come from confessing all the truths that lie deep within him. Moreover, the governess needs all this knowledge to make sense of all that she has done with the children. In her mind, Miles's confession, then, holds the power to release both his secret actions and the governess's explicit choices.

Curiously, Miles seems to understand a little bit about the larger game behind the governess's constant wish for a confession. Finally, Miles agrees to tell the governess "everything," as if he has finally realized that the governess won't relent until he has explained himself completely. Has he come to understand that his confession holds the key to the governess's feeling saved or is there something more? After Miles promises to tell the governess "everything," he revises his promise (James, *Turn* 116). Instead of "everything," he explains, "I mean I'll tell you anything you like" (116). It seems important here to reflect on the differences between the promise of "everything" and the promise of "anything" (116). Has Miles realized in this instant that the governess somehow requires more to his confession than a mere recital of the facts of his actions? Perhaps he understands that his confession has more to do with her than with what he has actually done. Moreover, his promise to tell her "anything you like" comes as part of a larger hope that she will "stay on" and that "we shall both be all right" (116). In other words, Miles recognizes that what he says will contain significant power that will impact both him and the governess.

To help make the suspense complete, James not only delays Miles's confession, but also introduces Quint back into the narrative. With his "white face of damnation" looking on, Quint's presence is meant to suggest that Miles stands at a crossroads, one that offers either salvation or damnation. For the governess, Quint's presence operates much like the tell-tale heart itself, an insistent source of intensive beating that prods her to act in a hysterical fashion. She is the one, after all, who sees in Quint's presence nothing less than "the hideous author of our woe" (119). For her, Quint represents the larger problems she is facing with Miles. Moreover, Quint epitomizes all the hidden secrets—the hidden motivations—that she wants to understand by pressuring Miles to confess to her. She wants Miles to explain to her all those things that will bring him to safety. As she puts it, Quint's presence makes her feel as though she were "fighting with a demon for a human soul, and when I had fairly so appraised it I saw how the human soul—held out, in the tremor of my hands, at arms' length—had a perfect dew of sweat on a lovely childish forehead" (117). Even though Miles's eyes are "sealed" against seeing Quint, the governess believes that his very body responds to Quint's presence (120). Indeed, the "dew of sweat" she sees on Miles's face signifies that he understands the dangerous nature of his situation and his need to confess it to her (120).

When Miles finally confesses to taking the letter, the governess responds by drawing him close to her, an act that allows her to read more into his body. She notes that "I could feel in the sudden fever of his little body the tremendous pulse of his little heart" (117). As in Poe's "Tell-Tale Heart," the pulsing heart here signifies a certain kind of knowledge; in this case, however, Miles's heart does not drive the governess to confess the violent nature of her need to hear about Miles's actions, but acts as a sign that Miles is still in a position of safety. As long as his heart remains active, the governess seems to understand, Miles will be safe.

But Miles is not safe. As he begins to tell the governess about his actions—his own acts of telling, really—Quint draws ever so slightly closer to them. For the governess, Quint's face represents little more than the threat of cutting off Miles's confession, the very thing she has struggled so diligently to uncover. As the governess puts it, Quint's presence signifies a perverse desire to "blight [Miles's] confession and stay his answer" (119). But the governess never makes it clear precisely why Quint wants to prevent Miles from speaking to her. It is as though she believes Quint ultimately lies behind all of Miles's actions. Indeed, she calls Quint "the hideous author of our woe," as if he epitomizes all of the human evil that she or Miles may be capable of committing. Even worse, Quint's "white face of damnation" stands out to her as a threat against Miles's own possible innocence.

In the end, the governess, in the throes of the imp of the perverse, irrationally demands that Miles will not only see Quint but also name him for her. Only by naming Quint, the governess believes, will Miles truly confess all that he knows. In fact, she presses Miles to say his name by speaking around his name, which finally forces her to ask, "Whom do you mean by 'he'?" (120). Miles's response,

"Peter Quint—you devil," makes it clear to her that not only does he know the name, but he also recognizes the deeper connection to evil that he represents. Of course, the exclamation "you devil" probably refers to the governess herself (120). By naming Quint and insulting the governess, Miles comes to understand that he is caught between two kinds of threats to his safety. But, during the governess's own proclamation of victory over Quint, Miles dies. The governess notes that it took a moment to completely recognize that Miles was dead. She notes that "at the end of a minute I began to feel what it truly was that I held" (120). In her arms, Miles's body has gone limp and the governess knows that she no longer holds a boy in need of her protection. In her words, however, the governess simply writes, "We were alone with the quiet day, and his little heart, dispossessed, had stopped" (120).

Throughout this chapter, we have examined ways in which "The Fall of the House of Usher" helps us bring out new dimensions in *The Turn of the Screw*. Most connections between Poe and James largely distance them from each other; we argue, however, that their relationship has never been adequately developed. Our approach differs from that of others in that we have looked to find ways of reading James's famously vexing novella in light of Poe's psychological sense of what it means to be haunted. Our claim, then, is that both *Turn of the Screw* and "Fall of the House of Usher" develop the theme of haunting as a means of reading the self in the other, plunging into the shadowy unconscious, and projecting it onto the blank screen of reality. For Poe's narrator this process begins upon his first encounter with the House of Usher; for James's narrator the process begins when she first sees Quint. For the governess, that moment introduces her into a kind of hypnogogic state from which she never fully awakens. Like so many of Poe's troubled and obsessed protagonists—some even dogged by the infamous "imp of the perverse"—the governess self-destructs as she attempts to make sense of her life and how it impacts those of her young charges. In the end, both stories ultimately suggest that, while there is clearly more to our minds that we can know, we may prefer to remain ignorant of the very things we find.

CHAPTER 4

COSMIC "USHER": LOVECRAFT
ADAPTS HIS "GOD OF FICTION"

H. P. Lovecraft's devotion to Edgar Allan Poe was sometimes so strong that he once called him "my God of Fiction" (Joshi and Shultz, *Encyclopedia* 207). He may have been right. However, even Lovecraft would later admit that "there may be something rather sophomoric in my intense and unalterable devotion to Poe" (Burleson 214). Poe particularly meant a great deal to him at the beginning of his career while he was shaping his own voice. Indeed, as S. T. Joshi writes, Poe's influence may be identified as the one thing "that would definitively turn Lovecraft into the man and writer we know" (Joshi, *Life* 27). Lovecraft himself indicates, "Since Poe affected me most of all horror-writers, I can never feel that a tale starts out right unless it has something of his manner" (153). While readers of Lovecraft have long recognized Poe's influence, we argue here for a more extensive influence on not only the style of Lovecraft's tales, but also the nature of theory of fiction underlying them.

Given Lovecraft's indebtedness to Poe, we may be tempted to treat him solely as a doting disciple. But that is far from the case. Indeed, we suggest instead that Lovecraft read Poe in ways that taught him to read fantastic fiction in profoundly transformative ways. In "Supernatural Horror in Literature," Lovecraft gives readers a glimpse of just what he sees in Poe:

These bizarre conceptions, so awkward in unskillful hands, become under Poe's spell living and convincing terrors to haunt our nights; and all because the author understood so perfectly the very mechanics and physiology of fear and strangeness—the essential details to emphasize, the precise incongruities and conceits to select as preliminaries or concomitants to horror, the exact incidents and allusions to throw out innocently in advance as symbols or prefigurings of each major step toward the hideous denouement to come, the nice adjustments of cumulative force and the unerring accuracy in linkage of parts which make for faultless unity throughout and thunderous effectiveness at the climactic moment, the delicate nuances of scenic and landscape value to select in establishing and sustaining the desired mood and vitalizing the desired illusion—principles of this kind, and dozens of obscurer ones too elusive to be described or even fully comprehended by any ordinary commentator.

(45)

Lovecraft's evaluation of Poe focuses on several key factors. Probably the most important of these is his emphasis on Poe's skill with "the very mechanics and philosophy of fear and strangeness" (45). These mechanics, of course, are Lovecraft's theory of cosmic horror. In his essay "Supernatural Horror in Literature," Lovecraft outlines how to determine the effective employment of the weird. He writes that "the one test of the really weird is simply this—whether or not there be excited in the reader a profound sense of dread" (23). This dread, Lovecraft continues, should cause readers to suspend their sense of everyday life and begin listening for something like "the beating of black wings or the scratching of outside shapes and entities on the known universe's rim" (16). The true measure of dread comes from the degree to which those who experience it challenge their commonsense notions of the self, the world, and the universe. Without discounting Lovecraft's own contributions to his theory, we want to highlight that Poe's fingerprints are all over Lovecraft's theory of the weird. That he sees the weird in terms of audience reaction extends Poe's own famous emphasis on effect. As Poe writes, "I prefer commencing with the consideration of an *effect* . . . [and] consider whether it can be best wrought by incident or tone" ("Philosophy of Composition" 13). Of course, Poe goes on to describe his method in which all parts of the literary work are chosen only to reinforce the intended effect.

Lovecraft's mention of "the beating of black wings or the scratching of outside shapes" not only alludes to "The Raven" but provides a glimpse of how Lovecraft reads Poe (*Supernatural* 16). That is, he sees in his mentor hints of the inexplicable suspension of the laws of nature that underlie his theory of cosmic horror. In "Supernatural Horror in Literature," Lovecraft argues that weird fiction should disrupt one's sense of physical and mental security, persuading one that mankind represses the fact that human laws are constantly subject to destruction:

> The true weird tale has something more than secret murder, bloody bones, or a sheeted form clanking chains according to rule. A certain atmosphere of breathless and unexplainable dread of outer, unknown forces must be present; and there must be a hint, expressed with a seriousness and portentousness becoming its subject, of that most terrible conception of the human brain—a malign and particular suspension or defeat of those fixed laws of Nature which are our only safeguard against the assaults of chaos and the daemons of unplumbed space.

> (15)

For Lovecraft, weird literature invokes questions without answers, questions that frighten readers with the defeat of nature's laws (15). But Lovecraft wants more than just a "suspension" or even a "defeat" of the laws of nature (15). He wants to persuade readers that beyond human mortality, there are places where nothing makes sense. As Lovecraft suggests in "The Call of Cthulhu," "The most merciful thing in the world, I think, is the inability of the human mind to correlate all its contents" (139). To see more, to venture further, is to risk understanding things about human life that are too horrible even to consider.

One example of how Poe anticipates this dimension of Lovecraft's theory is in "The Black Cat." The narrator of "The Black Cat" finds himself up against inexplicable horrors and reaches out for help from his readers: "Hereafter, perhaps, some intellect may be found which will reduce my phantasm to the common-place—some intellect more calm, more logical, and far less excitable than my own, which will perceive, in the circumstances I detail with awe, nothing more than an ordinary succession of very natural causes and effects" (*Tales* 850). Likewise, the narrator of "William Wilson," unable to explain his fate in terms of natural forces, seeks an alternative explanation: "Have I not indeed been living in a dream? And am I not now dying a victim to the horror and the mystery of the wildest of all sublunary visions?" (427). In such passages Poe pioneers the defeat of cause and effect, and suggests "scratching shapes" outside the known universe. Along with Poe, Lovecraft is reluctant to count among the weird any tales that attempt to moralize on the world and its inhabitants. As he writes, "we may say, as a general thing, that a weird story whose intent is to teach or produce a social effect, or one in which the horrors are finally explained away by natural means, is not a genuine tale of cosmic fear" (*Supernatural* 16).

Another dimension of Lovecraft's theory of cosmic horror, or weird fiction, is its intention of trumping pleasure with fear. This aspect of his theory comes directly from what he listed as among his favorite weird tales, "The Fall of the House of Usher." Poe's setting itself manifests a kind of antipicturesqueness contrary to the Gothic tradition of writers like Radcliffe. In the opening lines of "Usher," Poe sets the pattern when the narrator comments about the house and its landscaping that "the first glimpse of the building, a sense of insufferable gloom pervaded my spirit . . . for the feeling was unrelieved by any of that half-pleasurable, because poetic, sentiment, with which the mind usually receives even the sternest natural images of the desolate or terrible" (*Tales* 397). Following suit, in the opening paragraph of "The Dunwich Horror," Lovecraft describes the countryside approaching Dunwich:

> When a rise in the road brings the mountains in view about the deep woods, the feeling of strange uneasiness is increased. The summits are too rounded and symmetrical to give a comfort and naturalness, and sometimes the sky silhouettes with especial clearness the queer circles of tall stone pillars with which most of them are crowned.
>
> (*Thing* 206–7)

Like Poe, Lovecraft is not going for a picturesque, cozy, romantic Gothic, but means to unsettle the reader's sense of the ordinary, the everyday, the real. Weird fiction must invoke lasting, visceral dread, just as "Usher's" narrator threatens readers with "the bitter lapse into every-day life—the hideous dropping off of the veil" (*Tales* 397).

Lovecraft believed that such dread can only be invoked by a peculiar kind of realism—a "scientific attitude" he admired in Poe, who "established a new standard of realism in the annals of literary horror" (*Supernatural* 43). Unlike the classic school of "realism" prominent in Lovecraft's time, cosmic horror grows out of the precise renderings of the inner, rather than outer, worlds of experience. In "Pickman's Model" Lovecraft illustrates such cosmic realism by commenting on the artist's inner visions as "the actual anatomy of the terrible" and the "hereditary memories of fright" (*Thing* 79). The test of such genius is, again, its effect on readers, whether it can stir in them "the dormant sense of strangeness" (79). Significantly, Lovecraft describes Poe's "realism" in much the same way Thurber describes his reactions to Pickman's art:

> The raven whose noisome beak pierces the heart, the ghouls that toll iron bells in pestilential steeples, the vault of Ulalume in the black October night, the shocking spires and domes under the sea, the 'wild, weird clime that lieth, sublime, out of Space—out of Time'—all these things and more leer at us amidst maniacal rattlings in the seething nightmare of the poetry. And in the prose there yawn open for us the very jaws of the pit—inconceivable abnormalities slyly hinted into a horrible half-knowledge by the words whose innocence we scarcely doubt till the cracked tension of the speaker's hollow voice bids us fear their nameless implications, daemoniac patterns and presences slumbering noxiously till waked for one phobic instant into a shrieking revelation that cackles itself to sudden madness or explodes in memorable and cataclysmic echoes.
>
> (*Supernatural* 43–44)

According to Lovecraft, Poe's work explores an unknowable power that is beyond us, that manifests itself inexplicably in our everyday world. This, for Lovecraft, is a realism synonymous with cosmic horror and the weird. Examples drawn from Poe include a black cat, a fiery horse ("Metzengerstein"), dead sailors on a ghost ship ("MS. Found in a Bottle"), a strange friend's house ("Usher"), a possessed daughter ("Morella"), or ourselves ("The Imp of the Perverse"). Beyond these terrifying vehicles for cosmic horror is the universe itself, defined by Poe in *Eureka* as the production of a God who creates beauty and harmony and then inexplicably destroys it. In fact, according to Poe's treatise, the current state of the universe is the ruins of a "big bang" that alienates us from each other and ourselves. Such titanic and horrific forces point toward the Lovecraftian universe of meaningless and unknowable horrors in which mankind finds itself a puny and helpless being. Through reading Poe as a cosmic realist, Lovecraft finds his fictional voice by developing the infinitely strange implications that make up what he names weird fiction. Indeed, Lovecraft would praise Poe as "the apex of fantastic art—there was in him a vast and cosmic vision which no imitator has been able to parallel" (Burleson 213).

Lovecraft's conversation with Poe, leading to the development of Lovecraft's theory of cosmic horror, includes multiple strands. Thus, Lovecraft's devotion led him to allude often to various of Poe's works in his own stories, in essence giving them Poe's stamp of approval by setting a proper weird mood of "fear and strangeness" (*Supernatural* 45). For example, in "The Horror at Red Hook" (1925), Lovecraft quotes Poe directly from "The Man of the Crowd," a tale of an encounter with an inexplicable and uncanny mystery: "The horror, as glimpsed at last, could not make a story—for like the book cited by Poe's German authority, *'er lässt sich nicht lessen*—it does not permit itself to be read'" (*Dreams* 118). Lovecraft explicitly borrows Poe's German source to bring out its more terrifying—because inexplicable—implications for a degraded part of Brooklyn: "What could he tell the prosaic of the antique witcheries and grotesque marvels discernible to sensitive eyes amidst the poison cauldron where all the varied dregs of unwholesome ages mix their venom and perpetuate their obscene terrors?" (118). It is as if the narrator were speaking directly to Poe, pointing out another cogent example of inexplicable horror in an urban setting.

In "At the Mountains of Madness," Poe is introduced into Lovecraft's own fictional universe, suggesting that the word *"Tekeli-li"* in *Arthur Gordon Pym* comes from "forbidden sources" used by Poe (*Thing* 331). That is, in a wonderful twist that reverses the direction of literary influence, Lovecraft suggests that his and Poe's fiction inhabit the same universe. At one and the same time Lovecraft is being playful, using Poe to create a moment of sublime speculation and is introducing Poe into his own world of strange and fearful cosmic monsters. Not content merely with conjuring up Poe in his stories or having a dialogue with him, here he purposely confuses the real Poe with the one he creates in his own image. That is, the dialogue defines Lovecraft as an extension of Poe—making them one.

But conversations go back and forth, and for Lovecraft, his tendency to conflate himself with Poe exacts a frustrating cost. While Lovecraft explicitly admired Poe and his techniques, relatively late in his career he sometimes voiced his frustration in the delayed discovery of his own original voice: "There are my 'Poe' pieces & my 'Dunsany' pieces—but alas—where are any 'Lovecraft' pieces?" (Joshi, *Life* 153). Importantly, Lovecraft is not seeking to get beyond or surpass Poe's influence, but wants to move from a place of merely receiving him to actually entering into a more advanced literary conversation with him so as to contribute to the cosmic horror project he felt they mutually shared. Though Lovecraft explicitly mentions or borrows from many Poe stories, we will show that his use of "The Fall of the House of Usher"— incorporating so much of Poe's arsenal of the weird—looms largest. Incorporated among his stories are various aspects of Poe's masterpiece: the strange atmosphere of the Usher house itself ("The Colour out of Space," "The Strange High House in the Mist," and "The Shunned House"), the focus on art ("Pickman's Model," "The Shadow over Innsmouth," "The Call of Cthulhu," and "The Picture in the House"), the outsider psychologically drawn into the "house" (*The Case of Charles Dexter Ward*, "The Haunter of the Dark," and "Innsmouth), Roderick Usher's fragile obsessions and fears ("Cool Air," "The Horror of Red Hook," and "Arthur Jermyn"), hereditary degeneration ("The Lurking Fear," "The Rats in the Walls," and "Innsmouth"), the return of the dead ("Herbert West—Reanimator," *Charles Dexter Ward*, and "Innsmouth"), and the ancestral estate ("Rats in the Walls," "The Thing on the Doorstep," and "The Shunned House"). This partial list begins to suggest how thoroughly Lovecraft dissected Poe's themes and images and used them as springboards to the creation of his own specific stories.

Generally, Lovecraft's conversations with "Usher" focus on the strong relationship between realism and cosmic horror in a search for an original voice. Through the increased surface "realism" of Lovecraft's approach to horror fiction, he hopes to explore new dimensions from "Usher's" hints about cosmic horror. This is made especially clear in the first paragraphs of "The Shunned House," wherein he engages Poe indirectly in a conversation about a certain strange house with a history of mysterious evil. The story begins as follows:

> Now the irony is this. In this walk, so many times repeated, the world's greatest master of the terrible and the bizarre [Poe] was obliged to pass a particular house on the eastern side of the street; a dingy, antiquated structure perched on the abruptly rising side hill, with a great unkempt yard dating from a time when the region was partly open country. It does not appear that he ever wrote or spoke of it, nor is there any evidence that he even noticed it. And yet that house, to the two persons in possession of certain information, equals or outranks in horror the wildest phantasy of the genius who so often passed it unknowingly, and stands starkly leering as a symbol of all that is unutterably hideous.
>
> (*Dreams* 90)

In effect, Lovecraft announces here the key to finding his own voice—to pick up where Poe left off. While Poe would explore the weird in a house he only imagines (Usher), Lovecraft contributes to the conversation with Poe by exploring the potential for cosmic horror through a specific house. In fact, it is the setting of cosmic horror in ordinary settings—rundown New England towns ("Innsmouth"), farms ("Colour out of Space"), or churches ("Haunter of the Dark")—that becomes an important distinguishing mark between Lovecraft's tales and Poe's, which are set in dreamlands "out of Space—out of Time." In a further nod toward realism, Lovecraft presents "The Shunned House" as something that actually happened, introducing the cosmic horror of "real" history. Indeed, this is an important step in Lovecraft finding his own voice since Poe rarely identified actual locations for his settings. As we will see throughout this study, by thus adding the mundane to cosmic realism as an additional source for the weird and uncanny, Lovecraft helps plot the course of twentieth-century Gothic horror fiction.

More explicit references to "Usher" appear in many of Lovecraft's stories, all part of his ongoing dialogue with Poe about cosmic horror. For example, in the last brief paragraphs of Robert Blake's "jottings" in "The Haunter of the Dark" (1935) as he faces his climactic dissolution, he writes of what's coming: "No light—no glass—see the steeple—the tower—window—can hear—Roderick Usher—am mad or going mad—the thing is stirring and fumbling in the tower" (*Cthulhu* 237–38). While the climax of "House of Usher" is obviously invoked here, Lovecraft has made what is coming more uncertain than the anthropomorphic Madeline Usher, amplifying the sense of dread in the narrator and the reader both. What's coming to kill Blake is an indescribable cosmic horror that no words can adequately embody. Like Usher himself, Blake becomes increasingly obsessed, his fear slowly increasing, until at his death he seems to have lapsed by some "profound nervous shock" (218).

In so invoking Poe here and elsewhere, Lovecraft turns Poe into an archetype of cosmic horror, a literary source, for him, on the level of mythology. Just as Greek and Roman mythology and the Bible have undergirded Western literature with their archetypal images and themes, so Poe's philosophy of creating effects in Gothic horror, images, themes, plot situations, and the like all become a mythology of horror for Lovecraft that is too foundational to be ignored. One might suggest further that many of Lovecraft's tales, focused as they are on the invocation of powerful, but sleeping "Old Ones," "Elder Gods," and "Deep Ones," are actually unconscious allegories of Lovecraft's invoking Poe—his own elder "God of fiction." Like Lovecraft's ancient, cosmic races of powerful others that once ruled the earth and seek to return and overwhelm mankind, Poe is specifically associated by Lovecraft with an "ultra-human point of view" (Burleson 214)— someone with more than mortal power whose influence can't be avoided. And as in Lovecraft's tales, the invocation of Poe becomes the horrific return of these sleeping, but not dead, forces, brought on by the investigations of an obsessed lunatic or a curious bystander. These probably unconscious Cthulhu "allegories" trace Lovecraft's apprenticeship relationship to Poe, and through such characters as Charles Dexter Ward, in the subtext of many of his stories, Lovecraft carefully studies Poe's "eldritch" tales to find the magic formulas for creating cosmic horror and uses these "spells" to spawn his own tales. In essence, like Victor Frankenstein, Lovecraft sews together his own tales from parts of the old—but not so dead—bodies of Poe's stories, more especially from "Usher."

I

Turning to "Pickman's Model" we find a prime example of how Lovecraft's fiction draws on his reading of Poe to develop its major themes and purposes. In particular, Lovecraft uses "Pickman's Model" to allegorize his own discovery of how Poe joins cosmic realism and Gothic horror in "Usher." In this story, Lovecraft introduces Richard Upton Pickman, a Boston painter whose skill centers on demonic portraits of fiendish ghouls. His friend, the narrator Thurber, explains why he is anxious about Pickman and his work, especially after Pickman's mysterious disappearance. After describing the horrific realism of Pickman's paintings, Thurber reveals that Pickman painted from a live model, a monster he kept in his underground studio. As in "Usher," "Pickman" is narrated by the friend of an eccentric, reclusive artist with a weird ancestry, who lives in a strange, secluded house full of his horrific art. Lovecraft develops an Usher-like atmosphere for Pickman's house by setting it in the decaying North End of Boston, which is so full of strange and awful things related to the witchcraft phenomenon that it is a place "overflowing with wonder and terror" (*Cthulhu* 82). Like "Usher's" narrator, who notes his awe at Roderick's unusual artistic genius, so Thurber is initially obsessed with Pickman's ability to paint horrific images. From there, the story progresses in dread and horror, climaxing in a cellar that, as in "Usher," encloses an inexplicable horror. In the end, as in Poe's tale, the narrator leaves and never returns, but has been forever changed by the fearful house and Pickman's strange behavior.

Read as a parallel to Lovecraft's relationship to Poe, Thurber becomes Lovecraft to Pickman's Poe—even feeling a similar "hero worship" for his artist friend and calling himself "very nearly a devotee" (*Thing* 80). In the story Thurber is introduced to new levels of horror in the art of Pickman and is moved to utter irrepressible screams—perhaps dramatizing Lovecraft's awakening through Poe "to every festering horror in the gaily painted mockery called existence" and "the solemn masquerade called human thought and feelings" (*Supernatural* 43). That Pickman may stand in for Poe is evident in Lovecraft's description of Poe and his art. Remembering that Lovecraft described Poe as having an "ultra-human point of view," Thurber similarly describes Pickman as not being "strictly human" (*Thing* 89). Further, having described several of Pickman's paintings as strikingly realistic—"I never elsewhere saw the actual breath of life so fused into a canvas" (87)—we remember Lovecraft's depiction of Poe's art: "Poe's spectres thus acquired a convincing malignity possessed by none of their predecessors, and established a new standard of realism in the annals of literary horror" (*Supernatural* 43). (Thurber's comment is also an allusion to Poe's "The Oval Portrait," a tale about the horrors of realism wherein a husband, painting a portrait of his wife, transfers her life onto his canvas, leaving her dead just as the painting is completed.) Like Lovecraft himself after his exposure to Poe's "realism," Thurber is permanently changed by exposure to Pickman's paintings. Lovecraft refers to Poe's expression of "cosmic panic" and "the master's vision of the terror that stalks about and within us and the worm that writhes and slavers in the hideously close abyss" (*Supernatural* 43). Just as Pickman "found a way to unlock the forbidden gate" (*Thing* 89), so Lovecraft describes how Poe "did that which no one else ever did or could have done," discovering "all phases of life and thought . . . equally eligible as subject-matter for the artist" (*Supernatural* 42).

More generally, "The Shadow over Innsmouth" (1937) serves as a strong example of Lovecraft's adaptation of the Usher formula by relying on "Usher" for its structure, unbalanced narrator, inexplicability, sense of dread, and gradual psychological decay. "Innsmouth" becomes a pastiche of concepts from and allusions to Poe's work, all set in a literary conversation over the ways and means of cosmic horror. In our discussion of "Innsmouth," we will analyze Lovecraft's conversation in a three parts manner, noting similarities to "Usher," innovations based on "Usher," and the overall significance of Lovecraft's achievement.

First, "Innsmouth" retells the "Usher" story of the apparent outsider who experiences an uncanny encounter with a weird place, only to realize, finally, that it is a reflection of himself, a hidden self that, up until then, has been deeply repressed. Thus, the tale unfolds as a journey into the unconscious shadow self embodied as a deteriorating architectural double. In fact, the focus of "Innsmouth" on the underwater origins and habitation of the deep ones who have infected the town's "people" with their worship of Dagon, as well as their DNA, reflects the depths of the unconscious that the story explores. As such, like "Usher," it is a story of psychic degeneration and decay. As the narrator approaches "rumour-shadowed Innsmouth" (*Cthulhu* 273) for the first time, he notes "crumbling" steeples, "sagging gambrel roofs," "wormy decay," "ruins of wharves," and "indeterminate rottenness" (273). In all that he sees in town, he feels, as Usher's narrator does, an inexplicable atmosphere of strangeness about the place, including in Innsmouth such anomalies as odd people and the absence of cats and dogs. All of this is the prelude to his final destination, the Gilman House, which in imitation of the introduction of the House of Usher, ends a longish, culminating sentence: "Then we rolled into the large semicircular square across the river and drew up on the right-hand side in front of a tall, cupola-crowned building with remnants of yellow paint and with a half-effaced sign proclaiming it to be the Gilman House" (275). As in the introductory passages in "Usher," the narrator finds the setting "getting more and more on my nerves," noting how the Usher-like "windows stared so spectrally that it took courage to turn eastward toward the waterfront."

The key moment for the narrator outside of the House of Usher is his uncanny reaction to the distorted image of the house in the tarn, a feeling that heightens his already strong feeling of horror. As a result, he is "oppressed" and experiences a "rapid increase of my superstition" (*Tales* 399). This sequence is important in anticipating the cellar entombment of Madeline and all of the horror that will be set in motion. Lovecraft's narrator has an equivalently unnerving experience when he *looks down* into the door of a church basement's "rectangle of blackness" and sees the impression of a deformed priest wearing—in a "touch of bizarre horror"—a tall tiara of "namelessly sinister qualities" (*Cthulhu* 275). As in "Usher," this terrifyingly uncanny moment foreshadows the climactic horrors to come when he is hunted down by such a figure as the priest he glimpses. Throughout the introduction the narrator's relationship to the town is anticipated in the "curious sense of beckoning" (273) he feels, and the "shuddering touch of evil pseudo-memory" (275). Here Lovecraft explicitly develops his narrator's prior relationship to the setting in ways that go beyond Poe's already uncanny approach.

In addition to these echoes of "Usher," other important allusions suggest the significance of the link between the tales. Before entering Innsmouth itself the narrator views a strange Innsmouth tiara at the Newburyport Historical Society, describing it in ways reminiscent of Poe's narrator's awed description of Usher's painting and improvised music. While Poe's narrator notes the "sulphureous luster" (*Tales* 405) Usher's "distempered ideality" threw over his art, Lovecraft's narrator speaks of the "weird . . . lustrousness" of the tiara (269). And in both stories the narrators comment on how difficult it is to describe what they are not permitted to see or hear, including the indeterminate sounds they hear that add to the growing atmosphere of dread.

The long climactic, almost apocalyptic, conclusion of "Innsmouth" connects to the ending of "Usher." In both there is the coming up to the surface horrific forces usually kept below the surface, suggesting repressed, subconscious knowledge. Just as Usher and his friend are terrified by the sounds of the impending appearance of the inexplicably alive Madeline, so Lovecraft's narrator hears the mysterious and horrifying slopping noises of the gill men in the Gilman House and outside. Like "Usher's" narrator, Innsmouth's narrator "gets away [temporarily] at a dead run" while the Devil's Reef is sunk by federal authorities in the similitude of the sinking House of Usher (268).

Having built his narrative upon the foundation of Poe's classic tale, Lovecraft develops it in original ways to emphasize his own brand of cosmic horror. One theme Poe develops in "Usher" is the return to the womb. The narrator, who had been Roderick's boyhood friend, spending much time at the Usher house as a child, is, in returning at Roderick's request, reentering childhood. The fears and superstitions he experiences as he approaches the house, and his imbibing of Roderick's shadowy theories of the sentient house and of a terror of fear itself, reinforce this sense of return. In addition, Madeline's death and entombment in the cellar doubles the narrator's return to the womb—in her case leading to a rebirth! Both the narrator and Madeline ultimately escape, she to a complete death with Roderick, and he to the countryside before the house collapses into the tarn. As we gradually learn in the course of the narrative, Lovecraft's narrator also makes a return journey, not just to Innsmouth, but to his hybridized biological genealogy. While he doesn't know it, his journey is one of a slowly dying human identity. His return to Innsmouth (a pun on "In its mouth?") is one of death and rebirth, ultimately leading to the watery womb of Devil's Reef. Unlike Poe's narrator, this one apparently doesn't escape, and in this is the crux of Lovecraft's innovation of the Usher formula. While Roderick and Madeline were tainted by their house and their blood, the narrator was only psychologically tainted. Lovecraft gives his narrator a biological corruption that can't be evaded. His entire experience, including his curiosity about seeing the tiara and Innsmouth itself, and then finding out all he can, comes from the pull of his blood. Furthermore, like certain primitive rituals in which the dead are reborn as animals—or with an animal's soul—Lovecraft's narrator will be reborn as a fish creature (Frazer 802). So while Poe's narrator collapses temporarily, and psychologically, into the house's spell, Lovecraft's narrator's collapse is psychologically, and biologically, complete.

Therefore, one of the significant aspects of cosmic horror by which Lovecraft seeks to go beyond Poe is to specify more precisely the horror of biological revulsion. That is, just as Whitman went beyond Emerson by balancing attention on both body and spirit, so Lovecraft adds a physical component to horror that Poe generally ignores. While Poe does include graphic violence in "The Tell-Tale Heart," "The Black Cat," and "Hop-Frog," most of such moments are brief, like the briefer cuts of violence in a PG-13 versus an R-rated film. Physical repulsion and fear of ancestral tainting in "Innsmouth" embody what Jack Morgan summarizes in his book *The Biology of Horror*: "Ours is a psychology correlative to and defined by our biological character" (2). The biological sources of horror are noted as the narrator describes his reaction to the tiara as located in "some image from deep cells and tissues whose retentive functions are wholly primal and awesomely ancestral" (*Cthulhu* 269). Soon after, when he boards the bus to Innsmouth, the narrator's view of the driver, Joe Sargent, sends over him "a wave of spontaneous aversion which could be neither checked nor explained" (271). Coming into town he also notices among the people "peculiarities of face and motions which I instinctively disliked" (274). Echoing his physical disgust with the apparent degeneracy of the people is the decaying and collapsing town itself: "pervading everything was the most nauseous fishy odour imaginable" (274). Thus, this sort of physical, biological horror response is not explored in Poe nearly to the degree it is in Lovecraft, who, in this case, does the master one better in terms of orchestrating novel effects on the reader. The inexplicable and the unnatural outside of the self is one thing; when it is inside you, that is another, exponentially ratcheting up the sense of dread and revulsion.

Reinforcing and expanding the biology of suppressed horrors, the narrator also invokes the title of a poem drawn from Poe's "Ligeia":

> The sight of such endless avenues of fishy-eyed vacancy and death, and the thought of such linked infinities of black, brooding compartments given over to cobwebs and memories and *the conqueror worm*, start up vestigial fears and aversions that not even the stoutest philosophy can disperse.
>
> (*Tales* 280) [Italics added.]

This allusion to Poe's "conqueror worm" becomes part of something more than death, something deep and horrific in the collective unconscious—at least in his narrator's. In "Ligeia," of course, the worm is conquered, apparently by Ligeia, who returns from the dead (either in actuality or in the mad imagination of the narrator). As such, the expression becomes a foreshadowing of the awful immortality of the deep ones who have also overcome the conqueror worm. But in the context of the "cobwebs and memories" in the above passage, it most importantly refers back to the "awesomely ancestral" (*Cthulhu* 269) "touch of evil pseudo-memory" (275) that his exposure to Innsmouth has awakened within the narrator—a worm in his Innsmouth heritage that he will not be able to repress or conquer.

Later in the story Lovecraft alludes to Poe's concept of the imp of the perverse. In explaining why the narrator didn't just leave town as he had planned, he suggests that "it must have been some *imp of the perverse*—or some sardonic pull from dark, hidden sources—which made me change my plans as I did" (*Cthulhu* 282; italics added). In terms of "Usher," this allusion to the imp of the perverse echoes Roderick's self-destructive behavior in knowingly entombing Madeline alive. Here again Lovecraft both invokes and twists Poe, who had explained the imp of the perverse as a psychological phenomenon—"a radical, primitive, irreducible sentiment" causing us to act "for the reason that we should *not* (Mabbott 1219–20). Lovecraft, on the other hand, adds the idea that perhaps this imp comes from "dark, hidden forces," that is, from somewhere perhaps outside of our purely psychological selves—ultimately originating as irrational forces from his hybrid blood. Again, Lovecraft widens the context of his predecessor's idea, in his conversation with his master about the further, horrific possibilities of one of his concepts. But Lovecraft doesn't stop there. Not content with merely a biological imp of the perverse, he posits an entire town in the grip of a collective imp of the perverse, not merely denying an inconvenient duty, but denying their humanity itself. Compared to Poe's tales of isolated psychological tragedy, this is horror of a much broader scope that anticipates and pioneers such collective horrors as Jack Finney's *The Body Snatchers* (1955) and Stephen King's *Salem's Lot* (1976).

Lovecraft uses the setting in Innsmouth itself to emphasize the physicality of his brand of cosmic horror. One of the ways he seeks to push "Usher" in new directions is to locate the inexplicable sources of horror within the mundane world. Nothing could be less exotic than Innsmouth, a rundown fishing berg; its only distinction is its crumbling architecture and depleted population. Here Lovecraft really pushes "Usher" and the Gothic, turning the mundane into something unusual and mysterious. But not only are the buildings deteriorating, the people themselves are also deteriorating. Their very features and skin are evolving, such that those in more advanced stages of the change can only be heard as they hide behind the town's crumbling edifices. This is a beautiful innovation on Poe's intricate network of doublings in "Usher." The narrator, the town, and all of its inhabitants are twins of each other, biologically amplifying the physical effects of the House of Usher on its last two residents. Such a move anticipates modern supernatural horror films such as *Poltergeist* (1982), set in ordinary suburbia. Innsmouth is presented by Miss Tilton, the curator of the Newburyport Historical Society, as merely "a community slipping far down the cultural scale" (270). Despite talk of pirate hoards and exotic peoples from China or Fiji, to the people of Newburyport, Innsmouth is merely an "exaggerated case of civic degeneration" (*Cthulhu* 268).

What is fantastic and weird about the town is mostly unseen and suggested—strange sounds from dilapidated houses, boarded up windows on upper floors, and the faintly repulsive and odd aspect of the thin populace. It has none of the dreamlike, unearthly setting of "Usher" that inexplicably creates feelings of "insufferable gloom" from its mere physical aspect (*Tales* 397). Not only does

Lovecraft step away from Poe, but he also steps away from a Gothic tradition that insisted on a sublime grandeur of place to increase its mystery and horror. He replaces the sublime with the shabby. In locating unimaginable cosmic horrors within this mundane setting, the shabby takes on a biologically repulsive aspect suggested by the worst smells of fish. Lovecraft's purpose is that the more we learn about the Innsmouth horrors the more terrible the setting becomes—a technique echoed later in Jack Finney's *The Body Snatchers* (1955), wherein the neglected yards and unrepaired streets come to represent the inhumanness of the pod people and make the town feel increasingly strange. The setting of "Usher" increases in horror mostly by what happens in the house, rather than by the house itself. Thus, Lovecraft pushes the possibilities for making a setting's terror increase, a technique he had used earlier in "The Colour out of Space." From this brief comparison of "Usher" and "Innsmouth," it can be seen how Lovecraft both relies on various narrative touchstones provided by Poe and seeks to expand them and push them in unexpected directions that contribute to the development of a more modern horror fiction.

Lovecraft explores the theme of writing and storytelling after the model of Poe in "Innsmouth." Poe's "MS. Found in a Bottle" is an early example, in which the tale is an up-to-the-moment report of a man's adventure, placed in a bottle and tossed into the sea just at the moment he and the ship enter a swirling vortex. Such a method gives the story intense immediacy—in fact, this tale won Poe $100 in a writing contest. Poe's *Eureka* also has a "bottled message" that is quoted extensively in the beginning, letting Poe lay out some of his ideas indirectly. Poe, in fact, addressed writing from many angles: satires such as "How to Write a Blackwood's Article" and "Lack of Breath"; stories whose focus is on the act of interpretation and the difficulties of reading such as "A Man of the Crowd," "The Murders in the Rue Morgue," and "The Purloined Letter"; tales that begin with a request for the readers to help the narrator understand the meaning of details he is about to relate such as "The Black Cat" and "William Wilson"; stories whose focus is on narration itself, including "The Oval Portrait" with its written narrative explaining a painting; and, finally, such tales as "Fall of the House of Usher," "Tell-Tale Heart," and "Pit and the Pendulum" in which a narrator is trying to recount incredible experiences. "Usher," like "Tell-Tale Heart," focuses on the utter lack of believability and the inexplicability of the narrative, raising doubts about the narrator's sanity. Roderick Usher himself, though not necessarily reliable, calls the narrator a "madman" near the tale's end. In all of this, Poe recognizes and explores the slipperiness of interpretation and, therefore, narrative itself. Often, as in "Usher" and "The Raven," the line between dream and waking, madness and sanity, is blurred.

Lovecraft also considers these issues in "Innsmouth," though, again, he tries to push them further by his more explicit approach. In the process of writing "Innsmouth," Lovecraft experimented in four drafts with different styles, seeking the "one best suited to the theme." He ultimately tossed these and "wrote in his accustomed manner" (Joshi, *Encyclopedia* 238). Yet, in fact, the final product seems experimental, presenting the details about Innsmouth and its inhabitants from several points of view. Through much of the story, the main narrator is merely a reporter of other people's stories about Innsmouth. The "shrewd" ticket agent gives an outsider's practical perspective, reporting the rumors and concluding that the real story is merely racism because of intermarriages in the town. The library provides statistical information and the county history seems "ashamed" of Innsmouth's presence in the county by giving it little attention. Miss Anna Tilton, Newburyport Historical Society curator, represents the cultural and religious elite, viewing the mysterious town with disgust for its paganism and cultural degeneracy. The young grocery boy in Innsmouth provides a practical, but limited, insider view of the town, supplying the narrator with a map and warning him of places to avoid. And finally, Zadok Allen tells an even more inside story of the horrors he'd seen first-hand since his youth, filling out the details the other stories had left out. Unfortunately, he is a longtime alcoholic whose story must necessarily be questioned.

These various versions are far more than merely a convenient and lively way to present the story; they provide a narrative crescendo leading into the main narrator's own harrowing experiences in a way that causes us to doubt the truth of his report. This is especially true when he tells us at the end that he himself has "acquired *the Innsmouth look*" and looks forward to dwelling with the Deep Ones "amidst wonder and glory for ever" (*Cthulhu* 317). Without qualifying his sudden change from repulsion to embracing the unimaginably repulsive community, we can hardly conclude anything else but that he is mad. From a skeptic's point of view, the narrator gets the Innsmouth story piecemeal, moving generally in the direction of more details, causing the narrator, even before meeting Allen, to report that "the town was getting more and more on my nerves" (280). He only talks to Allen after this because "some imp of the perverse . . . made me change my plans" (282), suggesting that he is losing control of himself and becoming obsessed with the Innsmouth story. His obsession makes him, of course, a prime candidate for Allen's story, which fills in all the horrific details that tie together everything he'd heard up to now. While the narrator tries to maintain an objective distance from the story during Allen's narrative, calling it an interesting but "insane yarn" (288), he is soon caught up in the terror: "Beginnin' to see hey?" (289). These passages function like the reading of *The Mad Trist* in "Usher." With its increasing hysteria, Allen's story, causing the narrator to "shiver with a nameless alarm" (289), leads directly to the climax. As he returns to the hotel, the narrator notes that Allen's story "communicated to me a mounting unrest which joined with my earlier sense of loathing for the town and its blight of intangible shadow" (294) and prepared him psychologically for his horrifying encounter—whether dreamed or real.

Through the use of multiple narrators, Lovecraft takes Poe's Usher formula several steps further, foregrounding the complexities and unreliabilities of narration, making it a story about storytelling and interpretation—in essence, a story about the inexplicability of the unnatural cosmic forces at the root of our existence. Setting his lengthy tale in mundane reality, juxtaposed with supernatural rumor and alcoholic ravings, we find ourselves "halting between two opinions," poised between what's real and what isn't. In short, Lovecraft finds his own unique way of creating the same mystifying effect as Poe does with Usher, though Lovecraft uses realism, in a somewhat more traditional sense, while Poe mystifies us with psychological realism in the context of a dream.

CHAPTER 5

HAUNTED "USHER": MOVING TOWARD ABSOLUTE REALITY IN *THE HAUNTING OF HILL HOUSE*

When critics turn their attention to Shirley Jackson's *The Haunting of Hill House,* they usually focus on its treatment of larger feminist or psychological questions. Tricia Lootens, for example, argues that Jackson's novel explores the destructive power of family life. According to Lootens, Hill House stands for the kinds of oppression that lead women like Eleanor toward destruction. Most importantly, Lootens implies that Jackson has the family in mind when she wrote that "no live organism can continue for long to exist sanely under conditions of absolute reality" (3). As Lootens puts it, "what Hill House reveals to its guests is a brutal, inexorable vision of the 'absolute reality' of nuclear families that kill where they are supposed to nurture" (167). Although we agree with much that Lootens asserts, we believe that her argument only captures a small part of Jackson's overall purpose. This is particularly true when Lootens suggests that Jackson's take on the family "touches on the terror of her entire culture" (167).

Other critical approaches to the novel equally overlook Jackson's development of the theme of absolute reality. Judie Newman, for one, suggests that the novel explores the pre-Oedipal relationship between mothers and daughters. For Newman, Jackson's novel offers a profound critique on Freud's male-centered Oedipal conflict. Other critics stress Jackson's Gothicism, but they narrow the focus on things like Jackson's exploration of the fragile state of "the disunified subject" (Hattenhauer 155). To be fair, such approaches may be said to touch on the notion of absolute reality quite faithfully. After all, questions of human development are clearly central to this novel from the very beginning. Moreover, each of these approaches seems to share an interest in the larger question of how Jackson treats the development of the self, particularly through her character Eleanor Vance.

Again, although the general tenor of these approaches contributes to our understanding of Jackson's novel, we feel that more needs to be done to explore Jackson's interest in "absolute reality" and how it shapes her development of Eleanor. Moreover, we argue that Jackson's initial juxtaposition of haunted houses with the concept of absolute reality needs further development. As the novel's first paragraph suggests, Jackson treats Hill House as a kind of character in the novel, a character that, even though it stands firm and upright, serves as the symbol of human madness. Indeed, when Jackson writes that "no live organism can continue for long to exist sanely under conditions of absolute reality," Jackson suggests that Hill House tests the limits of reality by allowing the mind to experience all of the horrors of consciousness without hope of relief. This is a concern her novel shares with Poe's own interests in the nature of dreams, reality, and madness.

Throughout his work, Poe repeatedly turned to the idea that the transition between the protected space of dreams and cold reality disrupts even the happiest of lives. In "Dream-Land," for example, Poe suggests that the return passage from the unimaginable land that lies "out of SPACE—out of TIME" (*Poems*, line 8) may only occur along a "route obscure and lonely" (line 1). Moreover, the traveler feels as though his or her every step contains both the memory of a dream world and the anxiety over mortal life. The result is the feeling that one's life is "haunted by ill angels only" (line 2). Similarly, in "The Fall of the House of Usher," Poe calls attention to the way the house itself seems to resist any conscious attempts to understand it. He speaks of the house in terms of the most stark reality, a place that lies behind the "hideous dropping off of the veil," or the "bitter lapse into every-day life" that leads to "an utter depression of soul" (397). Our view is that Poe's bleak conception of everyday life serves as a forerunner of Jackson's own notion of "absolute reality," the very condition that allows her to describe Hill House both as "not sane" and as a place where nothing "live" can "continue for long to exist sanely" (3).

Although it is true that Jackson never comments openly about her understanding and use of Poe, she was well acquainted with his work. As a little girl, Jackson often heard her Grandmother Mimi read aloud from her copy of Poe's works (Oppenheimer 23). The fact that Poe factors into Jackson's childhood is particularly relevant because Jackson holds a perpetual obsession with her childhood; she explores her childhood and adolescence in her first three novels. Even after her death, her relationship to Poe continues to be acknowledged. After all, Jackson posthumously won an "Edgar" award (the annual Edgar Allan Poe awards given by the Mystery Writers of America) in 1966 for "The Possibility of Evil" and was a 1961 nominee for her story "Louisa, Please." Moreover, some literary critics have begun to explore Jackson's connection with Poe by focusing on their use of the literary effects of mystification, mystery, and horror. Joan Wylie Hall, for example, sees a number of points of convergence between Jackson's short fiction and Poe's, noting that she shares with Poe an interest not only in Joseph Glanvill, but also in drawing on Glanvill's work to develop the themes in her own fiction. According to Hall, Jackson's use of Glanvill enables her to achieve "the same effect Poe does when he cites Glanvill" (Hall 8). She goes on to note that the appeal of Glanvill for both Jackson and Poe was the "linking of 'the rational to the irrational'" (8). Most importantly for our purposes, Jackson, like Poe, juxtaposes her own ideas about insanity with those of reality. In fact, she once commented that "no one can get into a novel about a haunted house without hitting on the subject of reality head-on" (Oppenheimer 226). Jackson's comment draws a strong connection between the two authors' interest in the nature of mortality, particularly on the subject of what constitutes a "haunted" house. Jackson explains that her interest in haunted houses really began when she felt like she had experienced one in real life. In her essay "Experience and Fiction," Jackson explains that she once "saw a building so disagreeable that [she] could not stop looking at it; it was tall and black and as [she] looked at it when the train began to move again it faded away and disappeared" ("Experience" 201). Later that night, however, Jackson "woke up with nightmares, the kind where you have to get up and turn on the light and walk around for a few minutes just to make sure that there is a real world and this one is it, not the one you have been dreaming about" (201). Jackson's experience points to her belief that a haunted house ought to strain one's sense of what is real. When she finally turned her attention to writing her novel, Jackson used her experience as a means of tracing Eleanor's own haunted journey into the unconscious while simultaneously trying to come to grips with her failed sense of self, something she felt was lost in the dreary and lonely years nursing her abusive, dying mother. Indeed, Eleanor is thus primed to journey into absolute reality.

Like "Usher," *Haunting of Hill House* begins with a journey that brings an unstable narrator to a remote and disturbing house that seems alive, and which becomes a virtual, but mysterious, character in the story. While Poe's narrator finds the effects of the House of Usher on him a problem "all insoluble" (*Tales* 397), Jackson's describes Hill House's inexplicability similarly: "No human eye can isolate the unhappy coincidence of line and place which suggests evil in the face of a house" (*Haunting* 34). Both houses radiate a gloom that pervades the surrounding landscape. Inside both houses the wood is dark, the ceilings are high, and the windows offer little light. In fact, both stories climax with apocalypses within and without the house, characterized by being the eye of a storm, wind inside the house, and the banging and grating of Madeline and Ethelred matched by the pounding and crashing on Eleanor and Theo's door when the house "went dancing" (205). Most important to establishing a connection between the two stories, however, is the relationship of the people to the living house. While Roderick feels from the house a "suppositious force" (403), Eleanor's psychological kinship with the house is ambiguous, complicated by the mystery of what actually happens in the house. Is the house actively haunting, perhaps possessing, Eleanor? Or are the strange happenings at Hill House the result of Eleanor's psychic projections? Like "Usher," *Haunting of Hill House* also tempts readers with many questions that it refuses to answer.

If we now turn to Jackson's descriptions of how she wrestles reality into fiction, we will find a significant clue to how she may approach adapting other texts to her own: "The only way to turn something that really happened into something that happens on paper is to attack it in the beginning the way a puppy attacks an old shoe . . . Shake it, snarl at it, sneak up on it from various angles" (Oppenheimer 211–12). Borrowing her puppy metaphor, we note that one bone of contention Jackson may have had concerning "Usher" is narrative point of view. While in several of his tales, including "The Tell-Tale Heart," "The Black Cat," and "William Wilson," Poe carves out new psychological territory for first-person narratives, "Usher" is told by a first-person narrator who mostly recounts Roderick Usher's activities and thoughts rather than his own. In addition to keeping the narrator in the shadows of the narrative, Roderick and Madeline, from realism's point of view, come across as symbolic stick figures, cogs in an infinite matrix of psychological doublings that precludes conventional character development.

With narrative point of view that grows out of character development in mind, probably the best indirect key to Jackson's rewriting of "Usher," if, indeed, she ever thought about it, comes as a story she remembers a college student writing about a beautiful quilt sewn by a woman in a small village that, during a raffle, is desired by several local women. In the end, ironically, the quilt is won by an outsider. She uses this "meaningless" but potentially effective story to illustrate how to write a short fiction:

> A bald description of an incident is hardly fiction, but the same incident, carefully taken apart, examined as to emotional and balanced structure, and then as carefully reassembled in the most effective form, slanted and polished and weighed, may very well be a short story.
>
> (Hall 118)

Jackson then goes on to show the various ways this "bald description" can become a story by fleshing out the characters and giving it a point of view that suggests emotional motivation. It is such realistic psychological motivation that is one important way Jackson differentiates *Haunting of Hill House* from "Usher." In fact, she not only takes "Usher" out of dream land and makes Eleanor's story a deeply intimate psychological study of deterioration but also rewrites the popular romantic Gothic of her own day in which the heroine usually *does* find the love Eleanor can only dream about at Hill House. The most significant difference this makes is based on Jackson's use of contrast in order to heighten the sense of the uncanny and the sheer terror of encountering

Hill House. "Usher" is written in an intense style that is so tightly focused that everything reflects everything else and motivation is vague—opening it up to endless interpretations while virtually defying definitive commentary. The oppressive tone is relentless with no attempt at providing readers with relief. Thus, unity of impression, a Poe hallmark, is well maintained here. Jackson, on the other hand, places the inexplicably evil and mysterious Hill House into our world—as if she moved the House of Usher itself into a modern setting. It is the contrast of worlds to which *Haunting of Hill House* owes much of its effect. Despite the guests with their petty problems, hopes, and fears, Hill House represents an unnerving absolute reality that never changes—a stark revelation of the inescapable chaos and evil just below our imagined "reality." Thus Jackson presents people as they might really behave in a Hill House—whistling in the dark with their jokes and make-believe, using science to try and measure the immeasurable, and seeking unlikely psychic solutions.

Another way to approach Jackson's notion of absolute reality comes from comparing the way she develops her novel's atmosphere to the way Poe develops the House of Usher's atmosphere. In particular, most critics highlight the way in which Poe doubles his descriptions of the House of Usher itself with the state of mind of Roderick Usher, not to mention the narrator who experiences an overwhelming "utter depression of soul" (397). Poe's atmosphere makes the House of Usher itself represent a complete refusal to explore its depths. In other words, the house represents a state of absolute reality, one that refuses to be understood according to conventional logic or reason. When the narrator approaches the house, for example, he comments on the fact that the house will not allow him to enter the kind of reverie typically associated with the contemplation of ruins. A romantic commonplace since the eighteenth century, the contemplation of ruins was meant to bring to mind a sense of the rising and falling of nations and peoples. The result was to be an odd form of melancholy, one that laments the fallen and one that celebrates the living. The House of Usher, however, will not allow for such feelings. As the narrator puts it,

> I know not how it was—but, with the first glimpse of the building, a sense of insufferable gloom pervaded my spirit. I say insufferable; for the feeling was unrelieved by any of that half-pleasurable,

because poetic sentiment, with which the mind usually receives
even the sternest natural images of the desolate or terrible.

(397)

Poe's statement suggests that the House of Usher refuses poetic
feelings of any kind. In other words, it suggests that there is nothing about the house that translates into metaphor or any other
kind of figurative language. Consequently, the house cannot be
understood according to conventional means of explanation. The
Usher house, like Jackson's Hill House, sits alone in a state of
what Jackson will later call "absolute reality."

If we turn back to Poe's description of the House of Usher, we
notice that the narrator seems to believe that the house can only
be understood in terms of an absolute reality. Preferring metaphor over realism, the narrator explains that his experience of the
Usher house is like experiencing a "hideous dropping off of the
veil" (397). In other words, the Usher house may be likened to a
moment in which all hidden things are brought to light. Such an
experience is "hideous" because all human protections—whether
conscious or unconscious—are suspended. In his tale, Poe's imagery of the veil suggests an encounter with the chaos of absolute
reality. As Richard Wilbur notes, "'The Fall of the House of Usher'
is a journey into the depths of the self" ("House" 265) as it dreams
itself into "the advanced state of somnolence, which immediately
precedes the mind's 'going under' into sleep" (*Poe* 26–27).

Being in a state of absolute reality, the House of Usher inspires
in Roderick a "highly distempered ideality [that throws] a sul-
phereous luster over all"—the results of a mind "from which
darkness, as if an inherent positive quality, poured forth upon all
objects . . . an unceasing radiation of gloom." Thus, Roderick's
guitar playing is a "perversion" (405), and his painting is full of
"ghastly and inappropriate splendor." Under these creations is a
"mystic current of meaning" (406) that points to their source in
absolute reality. Eleanor responds similarly to Hill House. Rather
than finding the hideout of smugglers with secret passages and
romantic chambers attractive, she is utterly repulsed, sensing it
is "vile" and "diseased" (*Haunting* 32–33). As she will soon dis-
cover, as the narrator had warned, "no live organism can continue
for long to exist sanely under conditions of absolute reality" (3).

One of the most complicated elements of Jackson's novel comes from the term "haunting" itself. Generally speaking, Jackson is quite reticent about the nature and the purpose of haunted houses. When she presents Hill House to the reader, it is unclear whether it is haunted or it is just a manifestation of pure evil. Longfellow once wrote that "all houses wherein men have lived and died are Haunted Houses" (E. H. B. 19). In the 1906 issue of *The Occult Review*, one writer, picking up on Longfellow's remark, explained that "wheresoever human spirits have lived on earth, their influence and thought will still linger" (19). But Jackson does not take that approach with her haunted house. Instead, she invites the reader to think about Hill House from the perspective of the novel's effect. To say that a house is insane, or that it is alive, is a contradiction of all we understand, but an idea Jackson actually believes. Describing Jackson's move into a house in North Bennington, Oppenheimer notes how she "was drawn to old houses, their history, their sense of other lives lived within. Such places had a presence in her mind—almost a personality, a potential for good or evil" (113). Unlike ghosts or dragons, which, given a fantasy premise, are easy enough to accept, a living/nonliving thing is an inconceivable concept. Talking cars and door knobs are one thing in a Disney animation, but a living house in a realistic narrative is another. It introduces a narrative problem, defying all expectations of realistic cause and effect, or of a world recognizable by readers. It forces a heroic act of suspending disbelief. Readers are distracted by questions such as how exactly does evil get into wood and bricks, or does evil itself "live" and have a consciousness? How do the moods and actions and tensions of a house's tenants become transferred into the structure and atmosphere of a house and continue to exist and affect others?

Thus, both *Haunting of Hill House* and "Usher" exist on an impossible premise that plays with and abuses the imaginations of their readers. The effect is one of such profound and puzzling vagueness, obscurity, and inexplicability that, if we continue to read, causes us to become mesmerized in wonder and awe. And here is the point. In such a condition, in a horror story, we are susceptible to experiencing an atmosphere of dread more palpable, because absolutely inexplicable, than otherwise possible. By defying our known rational laws, we are ushered into a world of psychic unease, paralleling that of the characters. In essence, we experience, as readers, a form of the uncanny as we see our own unease mirrored in the characters.

In *Haunting of Hill House* Jackson's use of this trope has a different effect than it has in "Usher." In Poe's tale the sentience of the house comes to us as only a belief of Roderick Usher's, one that the narrator dismisses—though his own powerful psychological reactions to the house upon his first encountering it somewhat suggest that he may be repressing his own feelings. But, in fact, if the House of Usher is alive, its primary effect seems to be on Roderick and Madeline. Eventually, the preponderance of evidence suggests that the house may indeed hide forces that are inexplicable. Jackson's novel, on the other hand, presents Hill House's consciousness in a more matter-of-fact way, noting its insanity, that it shutters, settles, broods, stirs, and waits. The characters quickly come to an agreement that Hill House is strange and that it may actually have some sort of life within it. Further, its effect on Eleanor is insistent and intimate enough to convince us that it is, indeed, after her. Her physical and psychological decline follows such a clear series of household occurrences that they become the central horror of the novel. Thus, the vague fears of sentience implied in "Usher" become in *Haunting of Hill House* the specific terrors of a house that is purposeful, evil, and clearly dangerous. Jackson's "effect" is more explicitly horrific, particularly in the realistic world in which Hill House anomalously exists. While "Usher" is a bit more of a distant nightmare from Neverland, *Haunting of Hill House* features a "haunted" house that seems to exist as a more immediate threat to our world.

I

With the absolute reality of Hill House established as the ultimate goal of Eleanor's journey, Jackson fleshes out Eleanor's psychological history with a dense literary context of journey motifs and allusions. This dimension of the novel may, in fact, have been somewhat influenced either directly or indirectly by Jackson's husband, Stanley Edgar Hyman, a prominent literary critic who taught a popular course in myth and ritual at Bennington College and who read Jackson's manuscripts as a sympathetic consultant. In fact, it was he who came up with the town's motto in "The Lottery": "Lottery in June, corn be heavy soon" (*Lottery* 297).

A friend of the Jacksons, Taissa Kellman, confirming Stanley's involvement in the creative process, remembers "sitting around listening to a lot of Shirley's stories being created, hacked out, fought out with Stanley, seeing a lot of things from around us being integrated into the stories" (Oppenheimer 102). As Eleanor journeys ever deeper into the absolute reality of Hill House and into her own mind, her quest for self is clearly signaled by the usual markers, including responding to the call, confronting a wicked ruler, leaving her native community, undergoing trials, facing the hideous monster, and battling the monster. We will track these narrative details mainly because it is through such conventional means that Jackson establishes the unconventional nature of Eleanor's journey. That is, Eleanor's journey is not really a quest so much as an escape, and her goal is anything but heroic or clear. In this section we will explore the several ways Jackson articulates the irrational, uncanny, and inverted character of Eleanor's journey. In addition to her ironic use of the stations of the traditional hero-quest story, Jackson takes us further into Eleanor's deteriorating mind through her similarities to Roderick Usher, Alice in Wonderland, Hugh Crain's design of Hill House, and the blurring of the narrator and narrative boundaries of the novel itself.

To begin, Eleanor's journey is signaled by her being "called" by Dr. Montague's letter, one calculated to "catch at the imagination of a very special sort of reader" (*Haunting* 5). Eleanor is indeed "special," set apart by both her years of caring for her ailing bully of a mother and her psychic sensitivity, a talent evidenced by the stones that pelted her house as a child. When called, as in the many stories that precede hers, her life is mundane and confining, and like so many classical heroes, she is being done out of her "inheritance" and rights by her usurping sister—in this case, a stand-in for the wicked ruler. Her sister, who let her do all the work with the mother, provides her with only a cot to sleep on and won't let her use a car that Eleanor half owns. For Eleanor, Montague's letter is an invitation to a new life, one in which she could make her own choices and be free: "I am going, I am going, I have finally taken a step" (15). Her first "steps," however, bring her to the "threshold" of her journey into a new life, which, as usual, involves obstacles and trials of interference bent on blocking her passage to Hill House. Her road trip to Hill House presents the fragility of Eleanor's grasp on reality, and therefore the irony of her heroic journey. While she is, in a sense, getting out into the larger world, her car is described as "a little contained world all her own" (16). Thus, Eleanor can't quite separate outside reality from her own imagination, an imagination that is quick to escape into a fantasy world. She imagines, for example, pulling over and chasing butterflies, following a stream, and then seeking shelter at nightfall at the hut of a woodcutter (17). Later she imagines herself wandering "into fairyland" as a princess where she will "live happily ever after" (20). She soon sees a picturesque cottage along the road and imagines herself living there as a fortune teller who brews "love potions for sad maidens" (23). All of Eleanor's fantasies anticipate how her mind often directs the course, and structure, of the novel. That is, the elements of the quest are just the way Eleanor would fantasize what she will later call her "adventure" (70).

It is important to note that along her path to Hill House, despite her fantasies, she is confronted with images of death and mundane meaninglessness. In her daydream of living out her life in the house with stone lions, she even imagines her own death, "When I died . . . " (18), and then goes on to describe stone pillars "leading away between them into empty fields" (19). While Eleanor recognizes that she is in "a time and a land where enchantments were swiftly made and broken," she doesn't calculate the actual distance between her fantasies and the absolute reality that "waited for her at the end of her day" (21). These death images, therefore, point to the irony of her hopefulness and punctuate again how her mind is dictating her destiny. Later, she finds the threshold into the alien world of Hill House blocked by a locked gate and a caretaker unwilling to let her in. Like her sister, Mr. Dudley enjoys his quasi-authority by stalling Eleanor with questions. This is a tough trial, having the potential to discourage one used to taking orders, not giving them. But she gets through Mr. Dudley by sheer will: "Unlock those gates at once," she declares, after enduring his stalling and his suggestion that she come back later (30). If we hadn't been reading too carefully, her journey thus far might seem to be a series of positive steps highlighting a growing assertiveness and leading to a new life in which she might even fulfill her fantasies of independence and happiness. However, as she is about to go through the gates, Dudley interjects an ominous foreboding that this journey will not foreshadow the usual happy, romantic possibilities of the female Gothic writers of the day: "You won't like it" (31).

Finally encountering Hill House itself, Eleanor now faces the hideous monster. Again her psychological instability tries to deny what she sees, first continuing with the romantic imaginings she'd indulged in while driving ("Journey's end in lover's meeting"): "Perhaps I will encounter a devilishly handsome smuggler" (32). But when she actually confronts the house for the first time, she changes her tune, echoing in her mind the icy foreboding of Poe's narrator: "Hill House is vile, it is diseased; get away from here at once" (33). Eleanor finds herself before something more than a house, but "a place of despair, more frightening because the face of Hill House seemed awake, with a watchfulness from the blank windows and a touch of glee in the eyebrow of the cornice" (34). What she feels in the house's despair is a denial of her hopefulness. But beyond her sense of the house's evil is her sense that it is actually alive, is "arrogant and hating," is "without kindness," and has an actual "countenance" that is "enormous and dark, looking down over her" (35). Further, in a narrative that blends seamlessly into Eleanor's own thoughts, the house is "without kindness" and "the house had caught her with an atavistic turn in the pit of the stomach" (35), making her journey to Hill House a circle back to the mother and the life haunted by death and guilt and a dependent helplessness she had hoped to leave behind. Interestingly, while on her journey to the house, thoughts of her mother didn't come; but immediately upon seeing Hill House, she begins to think again about her mother and mentions her frequently throughout her horrific stay. It is as if Hill House is a mirror of her own unconscious fears, an experience prefigured in the narrator's glance at the House of Usher's reflection in the tarn: "I gazed down—but with a shudder even more thrilling than before" (*Tales* 398). While Eleanor seems to have passed a crucial test of character in getting to Hill House, she fails the more important test of listening to her gut feeling to *"get away from here, get away"* (*Haunting* 35). Just as she'd done with her mother and sister, she resigns herself to an inevitable fate. This is emphasized in her new room, feeling not only "the pressing silence of Hill House . . . all around her," she feels actually "like a small creature swallowed whole by a monster" (41–42). Thus, she has come to that crucial stage of most heroic quests, inside the belly of the beast. In an important sense, this is also the beginning and end of her circular journey, as she becomes mired permanently in the psychological horrors of the house in a spiral of psychological battles that can only lead downward.

Eleanor's psychological disintegration is aptly prefigured in Poe's descriptions of Roderick Usher. Over the course of her futile journey toward selfhood, she passes through stages of hope and determination, to fear and gloom, and finally to insanity. Just as Roderick is described, Eleanor's strange behavior during the last two phases could also be characterized as "nervous agitation," "incoherence," "tremulous indecision," and "an anomalous species of terror" (*Tales* 402–403). Through much of the story, Eleanor is torn between feeling terrified by the house and hoping it will offer her a home. Some of this fear relates to thoughts of her mother, but mostly they come from the oppressive atmosphere of the house. In her new room she tries "to put her suitcase down without making a sound" (*Haunting* 41) and soon realizes that "she was afraid to go back across the room" (42). The middle of the book is punctuated by moments of intense fear that only loosens up as her mental grasp begins to slip. Also, like Roderick, Eleanor has a morbid "acuteness of the senses" that won't allow her to enter the library at first (*Tales* 403). Later, in her insane stage, she claims inhuman sensitivity of the senses: "I can hear everything, all over the house" (*Haunting* 206). (This is also an allusion to Poe's narrator in "The Tell-Tale Heart," who claims to have "heard all things in the heaven and in the earth" [*Tales* 792].) Her insanity, in fact, is also akin to Roderick's—cause and effect. Roderick claims that the house's sentience—the "kingdom of inorganization"—has a "terrible influence" on him and his family (408). Just so, Eleanor's insanity is the sign of her voluntary, but mad, "surrender" to the house that Jackson describes in her first paragraph as being "not sane" (*Haunting* 3). Like the House of Usher, Hill House exudes the darkness it holds within and claims those whose mental balance is fragile enough to resonate with the house's absolute reality.

During her battles with the house, she becomes an Odysseus without wax in her ear to protect herself from the siren song of Hill House—an island upon which she wrecks herself. The siren calls play upon her search for a self, a deep hunger indicated by her perpetual romantic fantasizing. Thus, the house's banging on her door, writing chalk and blood messages encouraging her to "come home," and holding her hand while a child weeps are all designed to fulfill her loneliness and her overwhelming sense that nothing ever happens to her. She is so well seduced by the house and her imagination that she begins to see herself as a returning, beloved princess. She imagines specifically her mother the queen waiting and weeping "for the princess to return" (20). Through thoughts such as these, Eleanor finds herself "disappearing inch by inch into this house . . . going apart a little bit at a time" (201). However much the house may scare her, it encourages thoughts that tempt her to "relinquish my possession of this self of mine, abdicate, give over willingly what I never wanted at all" (204). But like many a hero before her, she will ultimately refuse to return home, finding her fulfillment in Hill House itself. Ironically, her quest ends not with a reunion with the queen, but with an atonement with the father—that is, Hugh Crain. Thus, as with the House of Usher, so Hill House is a monster that psychologically eats its victims and slowly digests them.

In addition to "Usher" and the whole history of haunted house literature that Jackson draws upon, she relies on Lewis Carroll's *Alice's Adventures in Wonderland* (1865) and *Through the Looking-Glass* (1871)—more eighteenth than nineteenth century in style and concept—to further punctuate a number of things in the story of Eleanor's adventures in Hill House. Oppenheimer refers to the Alice books, in fact, as among Jackson's "favorite readings" (39), which she alludes to in order to reinforce the meaningless and irrational nature of Eleanor's journey. Eleanor's fairy tale imagination plays on the Alice stories and makes her experience at Hill House into an endless series of miscues and mystifying situations and characters. Among the most important functions of the Alice stories is to punctuate the inverted chaos of Eleanor's experiences, echoing the absolute reality that persistently defies her rational understanding. In fact, Eleanor, like Alice, thinks of her experience at Hill House as an adventure. While Montague is compelled into telling the history of Hill House by his "three willful, spoiled children" (*Haunting* 69), Eleanor thinks in her anticipation that "we have moved into another stage of our adventure" (70). Eleanor is often figured as a child or associated with children throughout the book. Several times she wants to cry, she is socially immature, and she is overly fearful of minor awkward or

challenging situations. Hill House itself reinforces Eleanor's connection to children, with its knocker of a child's face, the sobbing
children she hears in the house, and the story of Crain's young
daughters, including the blood-inscribed book Crain created for
Sophia. Like Alice in the latter book, Eleanor desires to find out
what life can be like somewhere else, and in terms of the many
inversions of Hill House (noted above), she might just as well
have gone through a mirror as travel by car.

Jackson draws on Carroll's influence early in the novel by
describing Eleanor's arrival at Hill House as a kind of Gothic wonderland. First is the description of Dudley, who smiles after non-
sensically stalling her entrance, and reminds Eleanor of "a sneering
Cheshire Cat" who may "keep popping out at me all along the
drive" (32). Second, after a conversation in front of a mirror,
as Eleanor and Theo take a walk on the grounds and note how
"altogether Victorian" the house appears (50), they hear something that Theo identifies as a rabbit. This series of allusions is
only the introduction to several more, including the fact that they
are all sleepy when they hear the Hill House's story, the nonsense
talk among the house's guests about their fanciful identities
("A courtesan, a pilgrim, a princess, and a bullfighter" [62]), many
inexplicable occurrences, the tendency to get lost in what Theo
calls "the crazy house at the carnival" (100), and Eleanor's annoy-
ance with Theo's rudeness (just as Alice is similarly annoyed by the
rudeness of the tea partiers). Furthermore, there is the chess playing as in *Looking-Glass,* Eleanor's feeling tiny in her room (as Alice
becomes tiny), and the continual search for self and a sense of
belonging as a play on Alice's continually trying to get along with
people and find her right size. The allusions to Carroll's text put
Eleanor's circular and confusing journey in perspective, becoming
a series of irrational inversions associated with Hill House. Rather
than the comic intentions of Carroll's book, Jackson's is about the
true horror of being psychologically lost.

Montague's insight into the impossibility of explaining Hill
House with our ordinary rational categories echoes to some extent
Julia Briggs's claim that one of the key features of ghost stories
is their "alternative structure of cause and effect" (123). In other
words, ghost stories operate against the commonsense notion that
everything can be (or ought to be) explained in terms that are
clearly understandable. Thus, the Alice stories are an appropriate

layer of the irrational for ghostly tales. For Montague, Hill House might be said to operate with what Briggs calls an "imaginative logic," one that may explain all the haunting, but does so in terms that maintain the likelihood of supernatural phenomena (125). According to Briggs, such ambivalence to scientific explanation characterizes ghost stories generally. To help explain this, Briggs suggests that Freud's notion that some modes of thinking have a kind of magical force that seems to control actions and events will serve as a useful analogy. As Briggs explains it, Freud's concept suggests that "thought itself is a mode of power, in which wishes or fears can actually benefit or do harm" (123). Again, Jackson, who dabbled in magic incantations, witchcraft, voodoo, and tarot cards, reflects her own eccentric sense of reality in *Haunting of Hill House*, likely accounting for much of its power. In fact, she even compared her writing to witchcraft: "You mixed a brew, threw in the people and incidents you decided on, and used your darker powers to charge the atmosphere with tension, control mood, set destiny" (Oppenheimer 43, 67, 101).

In addition to the fantastic Alice stories, Jackson constructs her story with a house that brings us back to Poe and the mystical and psychological connection between humans and their abodes. As mentioned above, Jackson, in fact, liked old houses: "Such places had a presence in her mind—almost a personality, a potential for good or evil" (Oppenheimer 113). Jackson warmed up for *Hill House* with *The Sundial* (1958), in which "the house itself began to move toward center stage," and she began to explore the "interchange between house and character" (Oppenheimer 217). In fact, Hill House, like the House of Usher, is defined by its psychological/social potentialities. First, as Montague explains during his tour of the house, Crain "made his house to suit his mind," which turns out to be an eccentric, as well as deceptive, series of wrong angles: "Angles which you assume are the right angles you are accustomed to, and have every right to expect are true, are actually a fraction of a degree off in one direction or another" (105). As Montague continues, he notes that "the result of these tiny aberrations of measurement adds up to a fairly large distortion in the house as a whole" (106). These distortions result in doors closing themselves and the inhabitants invariably losing their way. Crain was a religious fanatic with ambitious dreams of a dynasty centered in his showplace Hill House, but somehow something more of Crain's "sad and bitter" mind than strange angles worked its way into the house (75). The horrific hellfire book Crain made his daughter, *"for Her Education and Enlightenment,"* features graphic—near pornographic—depictions of the seven deadly sins and a covenant written in Crain's blood (167–68). If Roderick's guitar playing is the "perversion" by a "distempered ideality," Crain's book is a blasphemy (*Tales* 405). The book suggests that in some way Crain is responsible for, or at least contributes to, the house's evil. Theo calls him "a dirty old man," who "made a dirty old house" (*Haunting* 171).

Although Freud's theory of the uncanny does not claim to explain the existence of ghosts, it is especially relevant with a story like *The Haunting of Hill House*. After all, as we've noted, Jackson regularly attempts to describe the house in terms of a sick or diseased mind. When Montague explains the history of Hill House, he largely focuses on the seeming power of the house itself, a power that he can only compare to a human mind. Indirectly, Crain is compared to Dracula in allusions by Theo (48, 57), and in the conservatory Eleanor mistakes a statue of Crain for a dragon, and both Dracula and the dragon are images linked to the devil (108). But like Roderick, for whom darkness is an inherent quality that emerges in his art (*Tales* 405), Crain's darkness infuses his architectural design of Hill House. In the covenant, Crain reveals his distorted ambitions, encouraging Sophia to "have faith in thy Redeemer, and in me, thy father" and for her to view him as the "author of thy being and guardian of thy virtue" (*Haunting* 171).

Related to his ambitions of divine authority is another aspect of Crain's design of Hill House—concentric circles.

> Actually, the ground floor is laid out in what I might almost call concentric circles of rooms; at the center is the little parlor where we sat last night; around it, roughly, are a series of rooms—the billiard room, for instance, and a dismal little den entirely furnished in rose-colored satin . . . and surrounding these—I call them the inside rooms because they are the ones with no direct way to the outside; they have no windows, you remember—surrounding these are the ring of outside rooms, the drawing room, the library, the conservatory, the . . . and the veranda goes all around the house.

(100)

Symbolically, concentric circles are associated with the creations of God, the inner circle representing the "first cause" and the outer circles representing the radiating outward of God's creation (Chevalier and Gheerbrant 195–200). In terms of Crain, this symbolism suggests his twisted ambitions by inverting and distorting the divine meanings of the structure. Crain's structure is off, angles that deceive and unbalance and doors that shut by themselves to confuse, disorient, and trap. In Hill House, Crain's mind is the center from which the rest of the house radiates, "arrogant and hating, never off guard . . . only evil" (*Haunting* 35). In a sense, this house really seems "somehow to have formed itself" from Crain's dark Puritanism: it "reared its great head back against the sky without concession to humanity" (35). In fact, circles are often associated with the shape of the human head, a way to imagine Hill House analogous to way church structures display the image of the perfected man, Christ. However, within the belly of this architectural monster, one can neither find one's way—nor oneself. Rather than an image of radiating divinity leading through successive stages of perfection toward God at the center, Hill House is a vision of a Dantean Hell spiraling downward with all doors to salvation "sensibly shut."

This is the psychological predicament in which Eleanor finds herself. She's on a journey that keeps circling back to her mother, her own fears of inadequacy, and her loneliness. Again, Eleanor's story highlights another inversion of the structure of Hill House. While the outer circles in the classic concentric circle pattern normally suggest stages of spiritual progress, the individual moving toward completeness and perfection, Eleanor's circular journey is taking her through successive stages of psychological disintegration until she is cornered and has nowhere to go but to surrender herself to the house—to Crain. In a further inversion, while Jung finds in the circle archetype the image of the totality of the psyche, or ego, Hill House is defined by the fragmenting repression of closed doors and a distorted unconsciousness characterized by wrong angles. Rather than a house of order, as it pretends to be with its closed doors and linens "where they belong," Crain's structure is characterized accurately by Montague as "the uncharted wastes of Hill House" (64). That is, it isn't a structure at all, but a primordial, evil force masquerading as a house—absolute reality wrought in wood and brick. It is not the product of Crain's rational creativity alone, however, but the product of his insane, power-mad, self-righteous id. Lacking an explanation for Hill House, Montague is reluctant to call it haunted. Instead, he suggests that "any of the popular euphemisms for insanity" might be more exact (70). Indeed, rational explanations are finally impossible. "Some houses are born bad," Montague comments, reflecting back on an earlier comment that Hill House seems to have formed itself (70). "What [Hill House] was like before then, whether its personality was molded by the people who lived here, or the things they did, or whether it was evil from its start are all questions I cannot answer" (70).

One of the main effects of Poe's "Usher" is the inexplicable sense of the uncanny that accompanies the blurring of boundaries—between life and death, between different personalities, between sanity and insanity, and between dream and waking. Through such blurring, Poe creates a narrative dream land that haunts characters as well as readers. This reflects Jackson's own views of reality. As Oppenheimer comments,

> Shirley Jackson had been born with a terrifying gift: the ability to see. Straight down through the layers of appearance, of convention, of style, of hypocrisy—right into the nutty core of reality itself. And even beyond that, into the place where reality dissolved and became something very different.
>
> (17)

Throughout *The Haunting of Hill House,* Jackson repeatedly claims that Hill House cannot be explained rationally. Even Montague insists on the folly of trying "get things out into the open where they can put a name to them, even a meaningless name, so long as it has something of a scientific ring" (*Haunting* 71). With Hill House, no explanation comes close to putting everything together. Montague explains that those who have rented the house have always left early, despite their "effort to supply a rational reason for leaving" (72). Hill House defies rational explanation of any kind. Even with his own scientific pretensions, Montague feels that he cannot tell Hill House's tragic history without first filtering its reality by having a little brandy and enjoying some conversation about "music, or painting, or even politics" first (68). Moreover, both Theodora and Eleanor feel "drowsy" (68).

Even Jackson's descriptions of the scene suggest a kind of drowsy air: "Darkness lay in the corners and the marble cupid smiled down on them with chubby good humor" (68–69). Montague's delay in telling the history of Hill House has to do with his feeling that the story cannot be told with ease, nor can it be understood according to traditional or commonsense notions of cause and effect. Indeed, he insists that he will never be able to explain Hill House completely. He tells the others that "I will not put a name to what has no name" (74).

In *The Haunting of Hill House,* Jackson creates an uncanny effect as well by also ambiguously blurring boundaries, though she accomplishes this in a unique way within a more realistic context than "Usher." This realistic context involves the mundane details of the house's history, its inhabitants, and the knowledge we have of Montague and his guests/subjects. Hill House itself, for example, becomes a container of dread because the origin of its evil is uncertain. Is it a supernatural projection of the evil mind of Crain? As we've seen, there is plenty of evidence to support such a view. Or, is it a projection of the Eleanor's mind? There is evidence also to support this interpretation, particularly going back to the miraculous incidence of the stones pelting Eleanor's house. Her denials of it smack of repression: "That was the neighbors. My mother said the neighbors did that" (73). Montague blames the phenomenon on poltergeists: "They are destructive, but mindless and well-less; they are merely undirected force" (141). Perhaps Montague is right, or perhaps what he calls poltergeists are the uncontrolled projections of a tormented mind—which in the world of supernatural phenomenon should be no more unlikely than ghosts, cold spots, or poltergeists. After all, in her anger at Theo, she thinks, "I would like to batter her with rocks" (158).

Might not Eleanor have just as likely caused the pounding on the door, the writing on the walls, and the voices as anything else? For example, just before the chalk writing appears on the wall, Eleanor experiences a euphoric episode after hearing about poltergeists in which a "laughter trembled inside" and "she wanted to sing and to shout and to fling her arms and move in great emphatic, possessing circles around the rooms of Hill House" (141). Seemingly, the account of the supernatural may have triggered in her such a deep longing to stay in Hill House that she projected that desire in the wall message "HELP ELEANOR COME HOME" (146).

Later, when all are gathered in Eleanor's room during the second
door pounding episode, she is thinking, "How can the others hear
the noise when it is coming from inside my head?" (201). These
pounding episodes are especially linked to Eleanor as her mother
died because Eleanor failed to wake up when her mother pounded
on the wall in need of help.

In addition to the blurring of supernatural causation is the
blurring of the narration itself. While the narration is techni-
cally in third person, it is closely aligned with Eleanor's thoughts
in the manner of free indirect discourse. When not specifically
expressing Eleanor's thoughts, the narrator seems to express what
Eleanor may have thought. One particularly startling, and funny,
giveaway moment comes as Eleanor enters her room. The narrator describes Mrs. Dudley as "clean, her hair was neat, and yet
she gave an indefinable air of dirtiness, quite in keeping with her
husband, and the suspicious sullenness of her face was a match for
the malicious petulance of his" (36–37). Suddenly, the narration
comes to a screeching halt: "No, Eleanor told herself; it's partly
because everything seems so dark around here, and partly because
I expected the man's wife to be ugly" (37). Here it is as if Eleanor is eavesdropping on the narration and interrupting it to make
a correction. This, of course, relates to the idea that Eleanor's
unconscious is causing much of what happens at Hill House. In
this example, she even controls the text itself, haunting it, so to
speak. The narration's link to Eleanor's state of mind is shown
during the succession of quick, episodic chapters near the end
(chaps. 4–7), which echo in a changed narrative style the increasing incoherence of Eleanor's mind.

Throughout this chapter, we have emphasized Jackson's interest
in stretching the boundaries of reality. As Oppenheimer describes
it, Jackson's work often leaves the reader within an uncanny space,
a space that feels as though "the comforting limits of the real
world had dissolved, and the reader was left standing at a misty
crossroads, gazing into an abyss" (102). Although attempts to
clarify the boundaries between reality and fantasy are common in
literature, Jackson's efforts strongly resemble Poe's own interest
in describing a fantastic dream world that lies beyond the rational
limits of space and time. Moreover, Jackson's own life mirrors her
interest in challenging reality's limits. Indeed, Jackson repeatedly
claimed to have psychic experiences that led her to explore not only

the possibility of sentient houses but also the possibilities of power within witchcraft, voodoo, and fortune telling. But most importantly, perhaps, Jackson ventures deeply into her own mental life, which, somewhat like Eleanor's, felt outcast, and could become hysterical. In addition, especially when Jackson was young, she could see things no one else could see. Also, like Eleanor, Jackson was oppressed by a disapproving, perpetually correcting mother. But her darkest passage of the soul, in fact, came in the years just before writing *The Haunting of Hill House*, when she alienated herself from North Bennington over her campaign to have a cruel teacher removed from the school: "Her feelings of isolation and rejection would intensify, growing to alarming proportions . . . the sense of being surrounded on all sides by hostility would wear her down, finally leaving her helpless, nearly paralyzed, and close to madness" (Oppenheimer 216). From "Usher" she found the imagery of madness; from herself she learned its meaning.

CHAPTER 6

MATERNAL "USHER":
BLOCH'S *PSYCHO* AND THE BLOOD-
STAINED GODDESS OF DEATH

Although Robert Bloch's *Psycho* receives frequent mention in
horror criticism, it generally goes unexamined. Instead, most writers merely list Bloch's work alongside other significant treatments
of the serial killer theme like Thomas Harris's *Silence of the Lambs*.
This tendency to simultaneously recognize and ignore Bloch's
work is unfortunate. *Psycho* remains a strong example of plotting
and characterization, particularly as Bloch makes Norman Bates a
uniquely uncanny presence with his mysterious mother obsession.
No less a critic than Stephen King praises *Psycho* for its naturalistic setting and its development of the theme of the antihero
(*Danse* 84). Bloch, in fact, develops the antihero in unparalleled
psychological detail, linking him back to his Gothic antihero,
sister-obsessed predecessor Roderick Usher. In this chapter we
will explore how the antiheroic psychological journeys of Norman
and Roderick are linked by the mother as the Terrible Goddess
archetype. These issues are made more explicit when, near the end
of the novel, Lila Crane investigates the Bates house and makes
the important discovery of "the incongruous contents of Norman
Bates' library," including books on "abnormal psychology, occult-
ism, [and] theosophy" (200). Just as the books found in Usher's
library provide significant clues to better understanding the enig-
matic and eccentric host, Norman's library provides important

details about his complex personality and, coming late in the novel, signals revelations about to explode in the narrative. Norman's books point to different aspects of his psyche: some, like De Sade's *Justine, The Realm of the Incas,* and other books that Lila can only call "pathologically pornographic" (200), feed his most brutal instincts; others, notably his psychology and philosophy texts, suggest how desperately he is trying to understand and cure himself of problems he but partially comprehends. One of the books that he looks to for answers is Erich Neumann's *The Origins and History of Consciousness,* a mythological and evolutionary extension of Carl Jung's analytical psychology, tracing the parallel archetypal stages of the development of the individual and collective consciousnesses. Neumann describes how the son's unconsciousness is dominated by the mother and makes her a powerful block to the son's ego development. As Norman's mother side notes, "I know all about you, boy. More than you dream. But I know that, too—what you dream" (17). Hence, Norman's mother, in her repressive and harsh domination of his psyche, reveals herself to embody the Terrible Mother archetype (17).

Archetypes are central to any discussion of Jung's account of the development of the psyche. They function as the images of the unconscious mind that a culture collectively shares, most often expressed in cultural myths that are powerful dramatic stories expressing deep psychological insights into life. But beyond merely expressing our feelings about our experience, Jung argues that archetypes are instrumental in the developmental process itself. That is, young children project archetypes on family members and others just as they begin to perceive new aspects of their personalities, becoming one of the ways they define the world in which we live. Among the most potent of these projections of unconscious images onto actual people is the Terrible Mother archetype, a child's projection onto a personal mother. Also known as the Terrible Goddess, or Great Mother, archetype, she impedes the development of a fully independent consciousness (ego) in the child. Depending on the archetype's likeness to the personal mother, this psychological impasse can continue into adolescence, and even adulthood. The struggle to free the male ego from the powerful mother-obsessed unconscious is described by Jung in terms of the hero's journey. She becomes the psychological dragon that must be slain in order to free the self.[1]

Bloch regularly referred to his sense that the Oedipus complex provides a "valid answer" to Norman's behavior, particularly as it helps explain his relationship with Norma ("Shambles" 224). Norman even tries to tell Mother about Freud's theory with the hope that she will consider their relationship in that light; he even suggests that if Mother would only try to understand the Oedipus complex, their relationship would change. Furthermore, in Oedipal terms, Norman sees Mother's relationship with Joe Considine exactly the way he would a hated rival. Despite its obtrusiveness, and with all due respect to Bloch, his sense that the Oedipus complex would explain Norman Bates never seems quite convincing. Despite the clear allusions to the Oedipal problem in this text, we argue that it does not provide a deep enough explanation of Norman's complex relationship with his mother. While Freud is mentioned more overtly than the single allusion to Jung in Norman's library, this is easily accounted for by his readers' greater familiarity with Freud than with his one-time colleague Jung. Indeed, if one wanted to suggest deep psychological problems in a character, what more convenient shorthand than Oedipus is there? Finally, most of the explanations of this troubled relationship, including those Bloch himself provides, are not profound enough to understand precisely the workings of Norman's mind. Like his readers, Bloch would like to provide a pat explanation for the inexplicable, but he knows he can't. Our approach is not to find the final answer to Norman Bates, but to explore beyond where Freud's Oedipus complex takes us to explain his behavior and attitudes.

I

His imperative fixation with keeping alive the mother he murdered is the essence of Norman Bates. Neumann helps us understand Norman's state of development beginning at the creation phase, when the unconscious fetus develops as an appendage within the mother's body, making them essentially one. Following this blissful, warm oneness, the first trial for the child comes at birth, introducing to it an ambivalent world of danger, discomfort, pleasure, and pain (39). Even so, the infant is still under the protective care of the mother and is not at first capable of distinguishing itself from the mother—they are still essentially one. During this phase the infant's fragile ego gives in to the bliss of sleeping and eating, all associated inextricably with the Great Mother (43). However, when the child's individual consciousness begins to emerge, when it begins to separate itself psychologically from the mother, "the maternal . . . overshadows it like a dark and tragic fate. Feelings of transitoriness and mortality, impotence and isolation, now color the ego's picture" of the mother-world. At first the child surrenders itself to the Great Mother in an attempt to, in a sense, "return to the womb," but "this return becomes more and more difficult and is accomplished with increasing repugnance as the demands of its own independent existence grow more insistent" (45).

Applying Neumann's insights, we suggest that it is at this stage where Norman seems to have been arrested in his development—forever uncertain of his own place in the world and unable to insist on a complete break with Mother. While he continues to want to separate himself from her control and quit being a "mamma's boy," he finds the world too dangerous and terrifying to venture out into alone, even referring to himself as impotent. He feels so dwarfed and consumed by his mother that he feels helpless away from her. As Neumann puts it, the newly conscious ego "feels itself a tiny, defenseless speck, enveloped and helplessly dependent, a little island floating on the vast expanse of the primal ocean" (40).

According to Neumann, the archetypal hero's quest is to complete his psychological development, to differentiate himself from the mother and become an independent adult, making the hero's journey about the emergence of masculinity (137–38). But in Norman's case some impulse so deeply hidden in his unconsciousness that it can never be fully explained goes awry. This journey is never begun for Norman on a psychological level; rather, he kills his mother and her lover, literally, thus forestalling further emotional development. So he actually journeys backwards in an attempt to return to bliss of the womb by unearthing, preserving, and giving life to her body, allowing her dominance of his unconscious mind to be affirmed once and for all. Thus, Bloch has not only been influenced by Jung and Freud, he also enacts and literalizes their theories as his primary avenue into horror. In effect, Bloch imagines a purely psychological world as one that relies on violence. That is, he unfolds our collective unconscious archetypes before our very eyes, increasing the impact in the manner of "Usher," wherein Poe presents a world of shifting realities, irrational doublings, and inexplicable phenomenon in a veritable tour of the unconscious abyss.

Having failed in the imperative quest of his psyche, Norman recreates Mother as an idol and becomes, in essence, a worshipper of his personal mother, depicted in the novel like a "goddess of war," an archetype he projects on her that is associated with bloody sacrifices and feeding on corpses (54). This goddess was traditionally the center of fertility rites practiced in primitive cultures around the globe as drunken, sexualized orgies, which Norman re-creates in his alcoholism, reading of Inca sacrifices, and staring through his peephole and at his pornographic books (54–61). This goddess is also associated with witchcraft as described in Murray's *The Witch-Cult in Western Europe* (1921), a book Norman reads. At times witches worshipped a two-faced god (Janus) or mother goddess (Diana) that harked back to preagricultural fertility rites (12). Like the Devil, this goddess could raise storms, winds, and tempests, which might be alluded to from the stormy welcome Lila magically receives at the Bates' house (51–54).

Another dimension of Norman's worship of his mother as Terrible Goddess comes as Neumann harks back to Jung's discussion of the "battle for deliverance from the mother" in *Symbols of Transformation*. Here Jung characterizes the Terrible Mother as Hecate, spook goddess of the night and phantoms, sending out horrible night apparitions like Empusa, who "rushed out upon women and children from dark places"—not unlike knife-wielding, brow-beating Norma Bates (*Symbols* 369). Associated with these particular mythologies and related rites surrounding the mother-goddess archetype were devoted priests who cut their hair and transformed themselves into her—in essence sacrificing their own ego identities to her by actually becoming her and wearing her clothing (Neumann 59, 61, 78, 86, 160). Norman, from this perspective, behaves as a primitive, superstitious man who reenacts the impulses behind such ceremonial rites—as if he were enacting Neumann's descriptions as his script. By becoming Norma, with all of the bloodlust he has projected onto her, he ritually sacrifices his own, autonomous identity to Mother and, thus, remains part of her, attached within the womb. From this perspective,

Mary Crane, who arouses Norman, becomes a threat in at least two ways. First, she is a potential lover that would mean maturity, leaving Mother, and venturing into the dangerous outside world. Second, Mary is a rival mother, a Christian archetype who tempts Norman to be an unfaithful priest-son-lover. This tension can only be resolved by disposing of Mary in ritual sacrifice in behalf of the Terrible Mother Goddess. It does not seem coincidental that he happened, that day, to be reading about the violent sacrifices of the Incas.

Another dimension of the Terrible Mother that victimizes Norman is her ability to confuse the senses and drive men out of their minds. Just as the shaving of the head of Hecate's priests is a symbolic castration, so likewise "madness is a dismemberment of the individual" (61). In fact, as "the dissolution of personality and individual consciousness pertains to the sphere of the Mother Goddess, insanity is an ever-recurrent symptom of possession by her" (61). Neumann likens this phase with the mythology of magical transformations of men into animals: "the Great Mother is therefore the sorceress who transforms men into animals— Circe, mistress of wild beasts, who sacrifices the male and rends him" (61). Finally, the hero only emerges who overcomes the mother by overcoming fear of symbolic castration, which is a fear unconsciously associated with the female in general. The female is "synonymous with the unconscious and the non-ego, hence with darkness, nothingness, the void, the bottomless pit" (157–58)—that is, madness. Mother's power to confuse and madden Norman is clearly manifested in the trances he submerges into when he becomes her. While "Mother" kills Mary, Norman finds himself in a fugue state: "Every instant it was getting harder and harder to move even if he *had* wanted to. The roaring was steady now, and the vibration was rocking him to sleep. That was nice. To be rocked to sleep, with mother standing over you" (60). All of these manifestations of the Terrible Mother archetype point to Norman's double relation to his mother that is brought out several times in the book: (1) his need for her protection and continued presence, leading him to preserve her remains, and (2) his fear of her as an oppressive and overwhelming presence in his life that he surrenders part of his consciousness to but also wants to overthrow.

Norman's reading habits form a significant means of interpreting much of his behavior. Early in the novel, Bloch suggests that

Norman's reading of *The Realm of the Incas* is so focused that he does not notice the passage of time. This loss of time is significant because it demonstrates the highly literary quality of Norman's imagination, suggesting that the influence of the titles listed in his library is significant. As he reads of the Inca's "grotesque, but effective," habit of transforming enemy corpses into drums, Norman begins not only to "see the scene" but also to hear Mother's footsteps entering the room (11). This, in fact, is a striking recreation of the *Mad Tryst* sequence in "Usher," where the noises described in the book Roderick and his friend are reading are echoed in Madeline's grating and clanging escape from her tomb. Likewise, in Norman's mind, the texts he studies somehow bring Mother to life again and again. On the other hand, reading causes him to resist Mother, arguing with her about the meanings of the books. Whereas Mother has strong moral objections to much of Norman's reading, his interest in things like Inca rituals shows that he somehow finds a ritual pattern in the ways Mother appears and acts. Curiously, one of the things Norman seems to take from his reading about the Incas has to do with the ritual power of taking command of an enemy's dead body. In this context, it seems highly relevant for Bloch to cite a long passage from the book, which reads,

> The drumbeat for this was usually performed on what had been the body of an enemy: the skin had been flayed and the belly stretched to form a drum, and the whole body acted as a sound box while throbbings came out of the open mouth—grotesque, but effective.

(11)

By citing this passage, Bloch begins to establish one of the ways he will treat the theme of the body throughout *Psycho*.

This image of a fleshy drum perfectly embodies how Mother uses Norman to speak for her. In preserving Mother's body—the body he first killed, Norman is not much different from the Inca who transform bodies into drums. In Norman's mind, however, the beating of the drum represents Mother's irrepressible will, complete with infantilizing complaints about Norman's inability to function properly. But, as is so often the case in *Psycho*, Norman's relationship with Mother cannot be explained merely through an appeal to other texts. Were Norman really in charge of Mother, we could easily imagine him banging away at the fleshy drum that was once Mother's body. Bloch, however, constantly turns his reader's attention to the problems that come from applying any explanation to Norman directly. Even though Norman may have moments in which he feels power over Mother, he recognizes that every drum beat means that he, Mother's rescuer, falls under her power and authority every step of the way. Even though Norman may possess Mother's body, she remains the one who has the power to manipulate him, even to the point of taking possession of his mind and body. Indeed, Bloch notes that the drumbeat of Mother's voice begins to resonate with his own heart. "It was deafening him," Bloch writes, "the drumbeat of her words, the drumbeat in his own chest" (13). Norman quickly realizes that the beats themselves will eventually surround him, as though there were "no escape anywhere, from the voice that throbbed, the voice that drummed into his ears like that of the Inca corpse in the book; the drum of the dead" (15). Norman's belief that he hears the drumbeats suggests that he sees his body as something to be controlled, that the rhythmic beating of the heart and the music of the voice are somehow seen as external forces, shaped by an unseen hand, one that has taken control of things long ago. It is horrifically ironic that Mother figuratively plays Norman's body, since Norman is actually in possession of her dead body. It is this irony that helps plot the failure of Norman's psychological hero's journey—he has found the Holy Grail, Mother, but it controls and beats him.

In summary, Norman's library is important to understanding him and the sources of some of his thinking, though it seems to help *him* but little in terms of understanding himself. Instead, he finds both escape and descriptive patterns that only continue the drumbeat of Mother's thundering dominance—beats that explain partially, but never cure. While there is a touch of the rational hope in the Norman side of his personality for progressing toward full, independent ego development, Mother keeps him in check through harsh taunts, insults, and humiliation. Thus, Norman's imp of the perverse prevents the terrifying possibility of leaving Mother.

II

Mother's dominance of Norman takes still another literary turn, harking back to Bloch's own early obsession with Lovecraft. Like his mentor's weird tales of dormant elder gods who control and

possess weak mortals in order to wield lost earthly power, Norma
is a terrible elder god(dess)—Norman's unconscious mind—that
partially returns from the dead to ultimately possess Norman's
weak conscious mind totally. Poe, of course, also wrote of the dead
coming back to haunt the living, sometimes as a cat ("The Black
Cat"), a horse ("Metzengerstein"), or a woman ("Usher"). In an
essay comparing Poe and Lovecraft, Bloch finds Poe's influence
pervasive throughout his chosen field of fiction: "Lovecraft, like
every writer of fantasy and horror fiction subsequent to Poe, was
necessarily influenced by the work of his predecessor" ("Poe and
Lovecraft" 158). Bloch, in fact, is a devoted and enthusiastic fan
of Edgar Allan Poe. Demonstrating the degree of his own debt
to Poe, and more specifically "The Fall of the House of Usher,"
Bloch wrote "The Man Who Collected Poe," a tale in which he
slyly quotes sentences and phrases from "Usher" in toto, beginning with the hilariously derivative opening sentence: "During
the whole of a dull, dark and soundless day in the autumn of the
year, when the clouds hung oppressively low in the heavens, I had
been passing alone, by automobile, through a singularly dreary
tract of country" (*Complete Stories* 153). As was Lovecraft, with
whom Bloch corresponded as a young writer, Poe is an important
source of images and ideas that he creatively reworks in many of
his stories. Interestingly, Bloch really discovered his fascination
with horror when as a boy he saw Lon Chaney in *Phantom of the
Opera* (192), with its blatantly Poe- and Usher-esque elements: an
artistic, mysterious, and obsessive figure who inhabits a complex
old house with endless levels of cellars, along with a story full of
uncanny inexplicabilities. In addition, it has the famous Poe touch
of the Phantom's appearing at the grand masquerade ball as the
death figure from "The Masque of the Red Death." Obviously,
these images made an impression on the young Bloch that he never
fully left behind. Like Norman and Mother, Bloch both resists and
channels "old buddy Eddie Poe" in his writing (*Once* 271).

Like many of his contemporaries, including Jackson, Bloch
experiments with ways of bringing Poe's sense of the uncanny into
more realistic milieus. In his "unauthorized autobiography" Bloch
discusses the central importance in *Psycho* of "ordinary settings" as
a contrast to the dreamlike interior world of Norman's mind. To
make his novel fresh, Bloch notes that he gave "careful attention
to the details of ordinary existence in ordinary surroundings,

setting [the reader] up for the intrusion of the extraordinary" (231). This is important, of course, in masking the extent of Norman's fantasy world since we can't learn that he and his mother are one and the same until near the end. In fact, in the tradition of *Blackwood's Magazine*'s upgrade of traditional Gothic fiction into the realms of psychological realism, Poe's own psychological— sometimes scientific—realism set a pattern for his literary descendents that characterizes the many iterations of the Usher formula. As Lovecraft states, "Poe's specters . . . acquired a convincing malignity possessed by none of their predecessors, and established a new standard of realism in the annals of literary horror" (*Supernatural Horror* 43).

Psycho draws much of its basic imagery, structure, and characterization from "The Fall of the House of Usher." These elements include a stranger's arriving at an odd house off the beaten track at the end of a day's journey. The house, which is old and near a swamp, is virtually a preserved museum of the past that is unstable with its groans, creaks, and rattles that sound during a storm. In this old house are immured two strange people, a nervous man who reads books on fantastic and esoteric phenomenon and a woman who has an inexplicable mental hold on the man. She is eventually put in the cellar by the desperate man, but emerges again during a climactic storm and kills him. Thus far, this comparative summary accounts for characterization and imagery, and much of the plot structure. In terms of other literary tropes, a tendency to double each of the elements into an interlocking whole is characteristic. Just as "Usher" multiplies doubles, so *Psycho* spawns its own doubles: Norman with Mary, his mother, the house, and the motel. Also the house and motel, as well as Mother and house, reflect each other, providing multiple facets for elaborating the emotive and psychological aspects of the narrative. Bloch further emphasizes the double through his use of mirrors, particularly ones that display inner conflicts of identity. The precedent of course in "Usher" is the narrator's looking down into the tarn and being terrified by what seems to be an uncanny image of his own unconscious mind—"what *must* have been a dream" (*Tales* 400). For his part, Norman similarly finds terror in his reflection, never looking in a mirror unless shaving, because his mother once caught him looking at his naked body in the mirror and hit him hard with a hair brush. Mary looks in the mirror naked too—a mirror image of young Norman—finding a reborn self when she plans to return the money and dig herself out of the hole she's in. Ironically, of course, she is killed by Norman posing as his mother, who punishes Mary for his own crime.

Symbolically and psychologically, another level of uncanny similarities emerges between the two stories and among elements within each of them. In both stories, the tarn/swamp imagery reflects the protagonist's unconscious mind, linking it to the mother or other female archetypes. In mythology and folktales, such bodies of water as the strange tarn are places from which sirens, fairies, and witches arose and lured people to their death (Chevalier and Gheerbrant 585). Sumerian mythology traditionally links bodies of water with women, while Buddhism takes this association a dark step further, connecting such areas with sensual pleasure, becoming a deceptive phase of spiritual initiation (637–38). Neumann, whose Jungian book lies on Norman's shelf, links the swamp with the mother archetype that "begets, gives birth, and slays again in an endless cycle" (39). In this image, the paradoxical doubling of the mother archetype is displayed: the "good mother," who is "fullness and abundance, the dispenser of life and happiness, the nutrient earth," and the "evil mother," seen as "the bloodstained goddess of death, plague, famine, flood, and the force of instinct, or as the sweetness that lures to destruction" (39–40). In Martindale's archetypal reading of Roderick's ego development in "Usher," Madeline, "as evidenced by the inexplicable, numinous awe she engenders, is . . . a proto anima figure rather closer to the Terrible Mother than to the anima per se" (10). In brief, Madeline, as a force in Roderick's unconscious, causes him to regress into a state of hypersensitivity associated with sensory deprivation, which is counterbalanced with the therapeutic stimulation of the narrator's arrival. Ironically, however, as Madeline "dies" and is buried (repressed) in the cellar, Roderick becomes listless and more unhappy than ever until he wills her back so she can take over his conscious mind completely, signaled by their burial in the tarn (10). In this scenario both the tarn and the cellar are equated as symbols of the dominant female dimension of Roderick's unconscious.

This fearful mother image, embodied here by Madeline, comes from a number of Poe tales, including "Ligeia" and "Morella," which show a protagonist obsessed with a powerful woman who in knowledge and wisdom is far superior to him and who must be overcome through death (as in the hero's quest described by Neumann). As precedents for Bloch, these disposed-of women are never really overcome, but continue to terrify, obsess, and fascinate the protagonists who bring them back to life in a visionary way. This aspect of Poe also influenced Lovecraft, whose elder gods, like Poe's powerful women, are overwhelming in their strength and influence and are both feared and worshipped in their ability to possess minds, even when "dead" or dormant.

Norman himself struggles to make sense of Mother's power over him. Throughout the novel, he wavers as to her true nature. A good example of this comes through Norman's swamp vision, which Bloch explores more completely than Poe does in the narrator's experience with the tarn in "Usher." *Psycho* follows a similar, though more explicit, symbolic logic, linking the swamp with both Norman's unconscious mind and his mother—ultimately becoming one and the same. After Norman disposes of Mary's body, he has an extended fantasy in which he sees Mother drowning in the swamp. Norman imagines that Mother had "blundered down the bank in the darkness and she couldn't get out again" (76). Completely stuck, all Mother could do was to thrash against her fate. While he watches her drown, Norman begins to see Mother, not as a dying woman, but as an object of sexual desire. He notices that as "her hips were sinking under, her dress was pressed tight in a *V* across the front of her thighs." At the same time, Norman tells himself that because "Mother's thighs were dirty," he "mustn't look" (76). But Norman, who senses that he must repress his feelings for his mother, transforms his sexual anxieties into a wish for justice. Bloch writes that Norman "*wanted* to look, he *wanted* to see her go down, down into the soft, wet, slimy darkness" (76–77). Norman transforms his forbidden feelings for Mother into a desire to be free of her by watching her drown. "Let her drown in the filthy, nasty scum," Norman tells himself (77). At the same time, however, Norman sees Mother sink further, the muck now beginning to cover her breasts. As Norman looks on, he again struggles with his constant anxiety over the meaning of Mother's body. He considers that "he didn't like to think about such things, he never thought about Mother's breast, he mustn't, and it was good that they were disappearing, sinking away forever, so he'd never think about such things again" (77).

But Norman's wish is also combined with his fear of life without his Mother's nurturing breasts. Despite his constant fears and anxieties, Norman needs Mother to remain unchanged, to remain an object that mingles feelings of fear and desire with a constant need for protection.

So strong is his attachment to Mother that Norman replaces her drowning image with a vision of himself sinking into the swamp. As he rapidly descends to his death, Norman begins to consider that Mother is really the only one who can save him. Bloch describes Norman's near-death even more vividly than he discusses Mother's near-drowning. He writes that "the foulness was sucking against his [Norman's] throat, it was kissing his lips and if he opened his mouth he knew he'd swallow it, but he had to open it to scream, and he *was* screaming. *'Mother, Mother—save me!'*" (78). Norman's pleas for help coincide perfectly with his newly found insight that it was Mother all along who saves him from the swamps of evil and immorality, the swamp that now represents Mary Crane. It was Mother, he reasons, who saved him from Mary's seductiveness and "the perversion of her nakedness" (77). Mary, according to Norman, deserved to die because she represented one of the most powerful threats against Mother—infidelity. Norman tells himself that "so what Mother had done was to protect *him*, and he couldn't see her die, she wasn't wrong. He needed her now, and she needed him, and even if she was crazy she wouldn't let him go under now. She *couldn't*" (78). As Norman hopes, Mother not only rescues him but also tucks him safely into bed, leaving him to conclude that no matter what Mother does (or who she kills), he will protect her.

Not surprisingly, Norman's fantasy goes back to Freudian insights. In an early treatment of the Oedipus complex, Freud suggests that fantasies of rescuing one's mother "takes on the significance of giving her a child or making a child for her" (393). In Norman's case, however, he cannot rescue Mother from the swamp because he begins to see himself as the drowning object—a death wish, perhaps. Even though Freud's conception should help us interpret Norman's rescue fantasy as a symbol of Norman's Oedipal desires, Bloch's shift from Norma to Norman as the victim suggests that something else is at work than a classical Oedipal struggle. As Freud puts it, "a man rescuing a woman from the water in a dream means that he makes her a mother, which in the light of the preceding discussion amounts to making her his own mother. A woman rescuing someone else (a child) from the water acknowledges herself in this way as the mother who bore him" ("Special Type" 394). Not only has Mother given birth to Norman, she now also has a greater control over his life by being the only one who can truly rescue him from himself.

Although Freud's interpretation is useful, we suggest that another psychological dimension of the swamp vision also needs to be explored. In fact, an Oedipal explanation only scratches the surface of the confusion of Norman's unconscious mind revealed in this fantasy. Since the swamp serves as a symbol for the unconscious itself, it relates to both Norman and Mother. Moreover, Mother and Mary are linked to the swamp through both their sexuality (what Norman calls "dirty") and their deaths. Mother is also linked to Norman's unconsciousness through the swamp—at once an emblem of the nurturing and terrifying tomb. Thus, these passages suggest the doubling patterns common in "Usher." Within this novel's "ordinary existence," Norman's mind is as much a dreamy psychological quagmire of fluid doubling as "Usher." In burying Mary in the swamp, Norman tries to repress both his sexual desires and his mother's homicidal dominance, and by wishing Mother into the swamp during his "dream" he reenacts his murdering her years ago. But in addition to suppressing his guilt, wishing her into the swamp denies how much a part of his sexuality she is—linking her again with Mary. In fact, swamps are often traditionally associated with sensual pleasure. This is evident as he explicitly links his arousal toward Mary and his mother by calling them both "bitches," his code word for women who simultaneously aroused and "perverted you" (60) and then "laughed" at one's "impotence" (57).

According to Jung, male sexuality is bound up with the mother because of her powerful presence in the unconscious. As he writes, "therefore, the simple relationships of identity or of resistance and differentiation are continually cut across by erotic attraction or repulsion" (*Archetypes* 85–86). That is, one is both attracted to and repulsed by the mother sexually, complicating the establishment of a separate autonomous identity. Norman's fantasy of himself sinking into the swamp instead of Mother reveals his own self-loathing death wish—one that will be fulfilled when Mother takes over psychologically in the end. This reenacts Roderick's death wish in burying Madeline alive. But his sinking into the swamp, described as "kissing his lips" (78), is also a sexual union with Mother—one he both fears and desires. This sequence displays the confused combination of Norman's feelings about Mother as dangerous, nurturing, and sexually desirable. His rescue vision, therefore, plunges him further into his mother complex than ever before, foreshadowing the final dissolution of his own identity.

Another central symbolic and psychological image in both "Usher" and *Psycho* is the house, often emblematic of the center of the world (Chevalier and Gheerbrant 529). The House of Usher certainly fulfills such a view, being hermetically sealed as the only world the family has known. Relative to this, houses are often symbolic of the inner being, or states of the soul—cellars, for example, representing the unconscious—while some see the house as feminine, that is, a sanctuary suggesting the protection of the womb (530–31). In "Usher" Poe treats the house as symbolic of the human body and mind, as suggested in its "vacant eye-like windows" (397) and more particularly in "The Haunted Palace." In that poem its "banners yellow" and "pearl and ruby" door suggest Roderick's hair, lips, and teeth, while the fantastic forms within represent Roderick's disordered mind (406–7). The feminine side of the Usher house is its link to Madeline, revealed in the narrator's similar intensity of emotion in reaction to her as to the house, as well as her entombment in the cellar, which is commonly an emblem of the womb or of the female nature of the unconscious. Furthermore, the parallel questions about the sentience of the house and whether Madeline is actually alive or not link them. Thus, Roderick, feeling oppressed and controlled by the house, seeks relief by entombing and repressing Madeline—a symbol of the house as synonymous with the psychological oppression of the Terrible Mother. The house's "terrible influence which for centuries had moulded the destinies of his family" shows its function to be that of the all-powerful unconscious mind, even to the arrangement of its stones and fungi (408).

The house in *Psycho* provides a powerful composite image of the Mother, as well as Norman as "mama's boy," and of his unconscious mind, especially as it wavers between personalities. As Mother, the house is virtually a museum of her earlier years—as it/she was when Norman fixated on her. As such, it serves as a symbol of Mother as protective womb, the safe place that

Norman refuses to abandon despite his mother's death. When Mary suggests to Norman that he can't act like a little boy the rest of his life, he says that despite what the psychologists say, "I have a duty toward my mother" (43). Such is his excuse for what even he seems to recognize, at least partially, as abnormal behavior. The fact that there were no personal mementos in Norman's room suggests that he has so thoroughly given his life over to his mother that he virtually has no life of his own. In fact, since Norman has not successfully separated himself from his mother, the lines between them remain as blurred as they were in his infancy. He keeps her room immaculately clean, and her clothes preserved as carefully as he has preserved her body. The book gives the impression that in the house Norman and Mother get along better than they do when he "strays" at the motel, where the inner conflicts between sides of Norman's psyche seem to erupt—where Mother catches him reading "trash" and using his peephole. This perpetual incapacity to choose full consciousness is, in "Usher" terms, the great fissure running along the walls of Norman's fragile ego, making him a mere reflection in the mother tarn. He cannot fully exist apart from his mother. Norman is the potential hero who refuses the call of his masculine ego consciousness to venture forth and destroy the hold of the Terrible Mother Goddess (or dragon) on him.

For Lila's part, the most powerful reaction she felt upon entering Norma Bates's room was that "*it was still alive*" (202) like the House of Usher itself. Her sense of unnatural life and "of dislocation in time and space" refers to more than merely its old-fashioned décor. Indeed, "it was still the room of a living person"—but not in the usual sense. What Lila senses, of course, is Norman's living unconsciousness and its power to keep alive the past. Reminding herself that there were "*no ghosts*" (203), Lila feels a palpable presence that she cannot see—but can hear without knowing it. Throughout her tour of Norman's house/mind, a thunderstorm rages, echoing Norman's determination, as Arbogast learned, to preserve his schizophrenic fantasy world at any cost. As in "Usher," the house is a living embodiment of a mind. While Roderick tells the narrator about the terrible influence of the centuries-old house on the family (408), the narrator describes Roderick himself as having a "mind from which darkness, as if an inherent positive quality, poured forth upon all objects of the moral and physical universe, in one increasing radiation of gloom" (405).

Hence, Poe makes it ambiguous whether the house is the cause of Usher's madness and gloom, or vice versa.

At the climax of the story, when Usher is troubled by his sense that Madeline was buried alive, a strange storm gathers outside, reflecting his torment and abject fear. It is here, in terms of the relationship between man and house, subject and object, that Bloch adds an important touch to the idea of the sentient house. While the uncanniness and horror of Poe's tale rests on its clearly ambiguous relationships between characters and things, Bloch discounts the supernatural explanation outright. Despite Norman's book on witchcraft (201) and his belief in magic (190), the world of *Psycho* is our own ordinary, mundane world of natural cause and effect. The sense of the supernatural, and the uncanny, is found in the mysterious, and ultimately inexplicable, depths of the unconscious mind. Here, indeed, time and space are dislocated, cause and effect are cancelled out by "magic," and the fierce desires of our archetypal projections, fixations, and complexes rule supreme.

Among the most mysterious attributes of the mind is its ability to balance opposites, to see double. Just as the mother archetype is split between loving life-giver and threatening death- bringer, so the climactic storms in both stories are based on conflicting archetypes. Scientifically, thunderstorms are themselves the products of powerful opposites encountering each other in the atmosphere. They occur where high humidity meets atmospheric instability, high amounts of condensation forming within an unstable air mass that causes powerful air currents to flow upward. On the positive side, storms herald the fertility of the land and the preservation of life—causes for celebration. They have also suggested the presence of a higher power and revelation. On the negative side, however, storms can be destructive and imply the anger of God and the subsequent punishment of his children (Chevalier and Gheerbrant 941–42). On the psychological level, of course, storms suggest the torment of the human soul, the mind swirling in angst, guilt, anger, revenge, or indecisiveness. In "Usher" Roderick and Madeline are the opposing atmospheric forces that unleash powerful destructive energies, initially "killing" Madeline, and then bringing her back from the dead—though it is uncertain how, or if, these things actually happen outside of the troubled imaginations of Roderick and the narrator. The "Usher" storm suggests these opposing perspectives, described by the narrator as "a sternly beautiful night, and one wildly singular in its terror and its beauty." But this tempest was anything but usual: the clouds didn't pass away and they glowed "in the unnatural light of a faintly luminous and distinctly visible gaseous exhalation which hung about and enshrouded the mansion" (412). The unnaturalness of the light, with its source about the mansion itself, of course, points to its unnatural origins in the mind—or in this case, two primary minds. This storm represents both the anger and revenge of the prematurely buried Madeline rising from the tomb, and the terror of her guilty brother, whose eyes evidenced a "species of mad hilarity" (412). In *Psycho* the storm similarly represents Mother, her rage at the intruder, and also her rage at Norman for repressing her in the fruit cellar. Like Madeline, she is about to resurrect herself and destroy the son who is her double.

III

Psycho focuses on difficult psychological questions that revolve around the concepts of personality, the human psyche, and family relationships. More specifically, *Psycho* turns on the impossible question of who Norman Bates really is and to what extent his personality depends on his dark conception of Mother. By the novel's climax, we learn that the name Norman Bates simultaneously refers to three people—Norman, Norma, and Normal Bates. These names, Bloch suggests, serve as the signifiers that try to name all the components that make up a single, lonely and overweight man with a deeply ingrained mother complex. Norman's psyche, like his uncanny names, remains, throughout the novel, unable to reconcile its contradictory elements. As David Punter writes, "the novel largely centers on the problem of Norman's divided psyche" (92). According to Punter, the psychological complexities of Norman's mind render questions as seemingly simple as why did Bates kill Mary Crane nearly impossible to answer. What's more, *Psycho* concludes by providing the reader with a psychoanalytical narrative that attempts to make sense out of Norman's personality and behavior. Punter rightly points out that one of *Psycho*'s unique features lies in the fact that it "contains its own psychological explanation" (92). This comment refers to the conclusion of the novel in which

Sam Loomis summarizes for Lila Dr. Steiner's psychoanalytic position on Norman's murderous behavior. According to Punter, Steiner's explanation makes the novel difficult to interrogate because it only seems to offer certainty to a rather difficult problem. Indeed, in the end, Steiner's psychological explanation for Norman's behavior almost works against the mystery and horror of the novel as a whole, pushing it into the realm of the weird. Lila's reaction suggests even further decay of the horror, claiming that Steiner's report helps her feel sorry for Norman. From this point of view, *Psycho* invites readers to consider two contradictory problems: first, the problem of recognizing that an average man is a brutal killer, and second, understanding such behavior to the point of empathy. As Punter puts it, the novel may be explained as "a drama of the vicissitudes of the psyche entrapped in a wish to be loved" (96). In other words, Norman acts from a fragmented psyche, one that compels him to violence because it may serve as a means of healing (96). Faced with such a reality, Norman lives in a permanent binary state, one in which "there is only absolute power or absolute powerlessness" (106). As he recognizes, he must "put Mother where she belonged," but to do so requires that he, too, must be put away (63).

Although we agree with Punter's analysis, we believe that there is another element of Norman's behavior worth exploring. While Punter dwells on Norman's perpetually restless mind, there is a side of him that recognizes the need for stability, order, and control. The best evidence of this point of view appears most strongly in the novel's fifth chapter when Norman faces the problem of cleaning up Mary's bloody and beheaded corpse. The question we want to answer is, why does Norman spend so much time cleaning up Mary's remains? We argue that it is at this moment that Norman begins to recognize that he must choose between the mess Mother has made and the mess that he has made. In other words, Norman's cleaning begins to show the complexity of the battle that takes place in his mind. We begin to see the ways Bloch opens up Bates's two sides—the largely unremarked upon orderly side that wishes to keep things in their place, and the overly developed destructive side that wants to destroy everything that may threaten Norman's safeguarding of Mother.

At first glance, Norman's cleaning hardly seems worth careful consideration. Norman obviously has to clean up the body to cover up the evidence of his crime and to protect him and Mother from arrest and incarceration. Our claim is that Norman's cleaning demonstrates his latent understanding that he needs to bring order to the conflicting parts of his mind. Bloch opens chapter 5 by pointing out that Norman needs to clean himself up. As he writes, "his clothes were a mess. Blood on them, of course, and water, and then he'd been sick all over the bathroom floor" (63). But Norman immediately recognizes that his mess is not "important now. There were other things which must be cleaned up first" (63). These "other things" that Norman cleans first refer to the mess Mother left behind after beheading Mary Crane in the shower. Reflecting on this problem, Norman begins to tell himself that "this time he was going to do something about it, once and for all. He was going to put Mother where she belonged. He had to" (63). Bloch's language is telling—Norman recognizes that there is an at least symbolic relationship between his cleaning up after Mother and his need to control her. In fact, Norman recognizes that his relationship to "all the panic, all the fear, all the horror and nausea and revulsion, gave way to this overriding resolve" (63).

By cleaning up after Mother, Norman not only puts away the evidence of a crime, but he also attempts to bring under control the erratic and dangerous parts of his mind. Significantly, Norman's resolve causes him to feel "like a new man—his own man" (63). Throughout the chapter, Bloch makes repeated descriptions of Norman's careful cleaning, which he does with such resolve and determination. As he cleans up Mother's clothing, Norman pauses long enough to reflect on his need for priority. He notes that there is "no sense stopping to wash up now—that could wait until the rest of the messy business was completed" (67). Although Norman's determination to clean will not bring the results he desires, his temporary sense of being his "own man" helps us see the connection between his sense of control and his need for a well-ordered environment (63).

If we turn briefly to Mary Douglas's book *Purity and Danger*, we may begin to place Norman's actions within a more ritualized context. If we only read cleaning in terms of hygiene, Douglas suggests, we miss the ritual significance of cleaning completely. As she argues, "uncleanness or dirt is that which must not be included if a pattern is to be maintained. To recognize this is the first step towards insight into pollution" (50). According to Douglas, "dirt is essentially disorder" (2), or matter out of place. When we engage in cleaning actions, Douglas continues, we do so as a means of "positively re-ordering our environment, making it conform to an idea" (3). By connecting the symbol of dirt to our idea of order, Douglas suggests that cleaning has a ritual dimension, one that she links to the difficult task of making sense of "disparate experience" (3). Returning to Norman's decision to clean up after Mother first, we see its significance in trying to bring order to the disparate parts of his fragmented psyche. Punter was right—*Psycho* is a novel that is essentially about control. What he missed, though, was the importance of achieving that control through the ordering of the physical environment. After all, the state of the physical environment—as Poe taught so well in "The Fall of the House of Usher"—is what best represents the workings of the mind itself. By choosing to clean up after Mother first, Norman demonstrates his belief to the point where his personality will dominate over hers. Indeed, the idea of defeating mother invigorates to the point of feeling "like a new man—his own man" (63). With the resolve to clean up Mother's mess—and thereby to "put Mother where she belonged"—Norman reveals a side of his behavior that can have control over his own mind and body (63).

IV

In his book *Using Murder,* Philip Jenkins demonstrates that *Psycho* serves as a significant development in the history of fiction that deals with serial murder. Jenkins points directly to Bloch as an example of an important author who "mine[d] the history of American serial murder for fictional themes" (83–84). As Jenkins suggests, Bloch held a strong interest in serial killers, with a particular fascination for the theme of the ordinary "man next door" who turns out to be a brutal killer. Much of Bloch's fiction is concerned with trying to make sense out of the different ways people turn criminally insane, especially people who seem otherwise normal. Such stories serve as parallel examples of the question that Bloch originally asked as the premise of *Psycho*—namely, what would it feel like to realize that an ordinary-seeming person was really a brutal killer? Bloch's treatment of "the killer as psychotic" was so well done in his early novel *The Scarf* that he even received praise "in a professional psychiatric journal" (84). In part, *Psycho* represents Bloch's interest in the ways we learn to recognize, and thereby name, the monsters that lurk within our society. In his essay "The Shambles of Ed Gein," Bloch reminds his readers of Lovecraft's well-known notion that "the true epicure of the terrible" is more likely found in the "lonely farmhouses of backwoods New England" than in faraway strange places (*Quality* 216). For Bloch, however, Lovecraft could never have conceived of an Ed Gein, "the gray-haired, soft-voiced little man who may or may not have been a cannibal" (218). Norman Bates is a gambit by Bloch to take a fictional psychotic further than either his mentors, Poe or Lovecraft, go. Ed Gein becomes the prototype, not only of the most horrifying serial killer to date, but of the utter inexplicability of such a personality.

Despite all attempts to explain why Norman kills, finally we can only contextualize, speculate, and puzzle over it. While Bloch provides Dr. Steiner's psychoanalytical explanation for Norman's behavior, Steiner's comments never offer any final conclusions as to why Norman murdered Mary. Indeed, Bloch never explains why Norman is driven to killing, later admitting that he wrestled with "the ticklish question of what made him tick" ("Shambles" 224). He finally determines that "the Oedipus motif seemed to offer a valid answer, and the transvestite theme appeared to be a logical extension" (224). Bloch's explanation notwithstanding, the Oedipus complex hardly explains "the matter of motivation" (224). Although they certainly have explanatory power, Oedipal struggles hardly come to terms with Norman. As he writes, "the real chamber of horrors is the gray, twisted, pulsating, blood-flecked interior of the human mind" (224). Can psychoanalysis explain Norman Bates? Bloch's answer, of course, is a highly qualified yes: one knows to look inside the human mind, but one may not completely understand how.

Norman Bates represented for Bloch an opportunity to explore the ways in which human beings define and recognize the monsters among us. In other words, Norman Bates was dangerous, not just because of the killer hidden behind his innocuous façade, but also because nobody understands how to recognize him as a monster, even after his capture. In other words, Bloch sees characters like Norman Bates as people who skirt definition. Roderick

Usher, too, skirts definition. After all, he is a nervous eccentric who simultaneously loves his sister and then knowingly buries her alive. Bloch shares this interest with Poe, who, in stories as "The Tell-Tale Heart," tries to imagine a murderer drawing on Enlightenment rationalism to explain his actions. The result, of course, is a horrific irony, one that cannot be understood easily. The fact that madness can masquerade as sanity remains puzzling. To explain his point, Bloch often turned to Ed Gein. As Bloch writes, "what interested me was this notion that a ghoulish killer with perverted appetites could flourish almost openly in a small rural community where everybody prides himself on knowing everyone else's business" (224). Moreover, Gein "was—by his own admission—a ghoul, a murderer, and a transvestite. Due process of law has also adjudged him to be criminally insane" (218). And yet, Bloch points out that "for decades he roamed free and unhindered" (218). Indeed, Gein was "a well-known figure" in his small community (218). Sometimes he would even joke about the real crimes he committed, though nobody ever took him at his word. Bloch's descriptions are harrowing, particularly in the way they juxtapose blatant human evil with everyday acts of kindness. As a result, Bloch seems to realize that one can no longer hold to any authoritative ideas about what constitutes a murderer. Bloch's point, we suggest, is that the means we use to make sense of human behavior are insufficient for recognizing the monsters in our midst.

V

Ironically, just as Norman creates a monster out of Mother, so the public turns him into one. Bloch explains that the story of Norman Bates appeared all over the major news outlets. He writes that the media "worked up a sweat over the 'house of horror' and tried their damnedest to make out that Norman Bates had been murdering motel visitors for years" (149). However, *Psycho* never achieves a cathartic resolution. Bloch shows that attempts to explain Norman Bates will constantly fail. Bloch demonstrates how the name Norman Bates finally becomes used to name a monster rather than a man. He does so by showing how the media takes something awful and makes it into something even worse. Along such lines, Ingebretsen suggests that monsters often serve ideological purposes, ones that come with preformulated narratives. He writes that even the "telling of the monster, caught up in ideology, can only be spoken in formulas that preexist it, despite the promise of uniqueness the monster brings, which, finally, undoes the monster more than any stake or exorcistic rite. Formulas of horror, sentimentality, and spectacle must be called upon to complete the story so monstrous that language itself leaves it untold" (41). Hence, so great was the outcry over Norman Bates that "they called for a complete investigation of every missing person case in the entire area for the past two decades and urged that the entire swamp be drained to see if it would yield more bodies" (149–50). People want to know how to explain the monster and so the stories escalate to match the monstrosity. Bloch cynically writes that the called-for aggressive investigation is motivated by politics and that the constant rumors did everything they could to tie themselves to Norman (150). The hardware store increased in business, and the motel itself saw lots of interested people driving by.

By the end of the novel, any rational explanation of Norman's behavior fails entirely. He has become so consumed by Mother's voice that he no longer recognizes himself as Norman Bates. As he sits in his cell at the mental hospital, Norman sees that "there always *had* been one person, and *only* one" (157). But that person was not Norman Bates. Instead, Norma Bates has finally asserted herself so strongly that she has complete control over Norman's mind. She reflects that "it was so much better to be this way; to be fully and completely aware of one's self as one *really* was. To be serenely strong, serenely confident, serenely secure" (157). Thus, like the Ushers, who have become one and disappeared into the tarn, Norman has, so to speak, returned to the womb and reattached himself to his mother, burying his own ego in the swamp of his Mother-controlled unconscious.

Just as is true for "Usher," *Psycho* is ultimately an inexplicable narrative construct of blurred boundaries that defies language itself to explicate in paraphrase. Despite Bloch's emphasis on ordinary realism as his narrative mode, the novel merely creates a new language for entering the unconscious and irrational realms of dreamland. Finally, all of the books of psychology, science, primitive rituals, witchcraft, and so forth that are tantalizingly alluded to in the book become Bloch's way of telling his readers that they are on their own. However, we can take comfort in the fact that the reasons behind Norman's killing Mother and Mary is not the point, anymore than understanding why Roderick buries his beloved sister Madeline alive is the point. The real point for Poe, and Bloch, is the effect of such inexplicably horrific actions and their fallout on the reader. Neither *Psycho* nor "Usher" can be primarily read as a case study for Freudians or Jungians, though they can provide helpful psychological contexts. Despite the horrific implications of Bloch's novel, particularly of his main character, with the horror comes a sense of awe and wonder that monsters generate, that makes us want to read and gossip about them. Alfred Hitchcock once explained that he learned from reading Poe that fear is an emotion that is fun to experience when you know you are safe. What he left out is that facing the inexplicably horrible, especially when safe, is also fun—for its own sake. Hitchcock, in fact, always claimed that his adaptation of *Psycho* was his "little joke"; perhaps it was Bloch's little joke first.

CHAPTER 7

EVIL "USHER":
ROSEMARY'S BABY, POP CULTURE,
AND THE EVILS OF CONSUMERISM

In his book *Nightmare on Main Street,* Mark Edmundson suggests that American culture is deeply divided between the dark, brooding spirit of the Gothic and the optimistic, hopeful spirit of the American Dream. Edmundson captures this dichotomy effectively by pitting Ralph Waldo Emerson against Edgar Allan Poe to determine which of their voices will best speak for American culture. Edmundson explains his choice by reminding us that "ours is the culture that produced both 'Self-Reliance' and 'The Fall of the House of Usher'" (5). Edmundson's comment is intriguing—after all, America seems to have wrestled with both angels of optimism and demons of despair for generations. How else do we explain the anxiety of the New England Puritans who walked in fear of having one foot in heaven and the other in hell? Such questions help us speculate on the larger problems raised by American culture's tendency to offer both a grand Dream and an awful Nightmare. As Edmundson suggests, what kind of a nation can successfully contain within its borders such extremes of optimism and despair? Or, to return to Poe, what if there is no way to clean up the wreckage left behind by the House of Usher? What if our national house, like Usher's house, can only be held together by a tenuous fissure?

Although Edmundson captures the darkness inherent in Poe's work generally, we disagree that Poe's vision is one of total despair. Instead, we see Poe's work as a struggle against the kind of darkness and destruction suggested by "The Fall of the House of Usher." We turn, therefore, to Ira Levin's novel *Rosemary's Baby* as a means of addressing not only how it relates to "House of Usher," but also how it imagines negotiating the pressure of an entirely Gothic world. Indeed, *Rosemary's Baby* asks readers to imagine that the foundations of Poe's house now lie beneath an apartment complex in 1960s New York and that the crashing house will also bring about an apocalyptic transformation of the world. To put it another way, Levin's novel underscores Edmundson's description of the Gothic as not only "unsentimental, enraged by gentility and high-mindedness, [and] skeptical about progress in any form," but also that it is finally "antithetical to all smiling American faiths" (5). In *Rosemary's Baby,* Levin freely explores the total darkness and despair that, for Poe, is more likely the stuff of nightmare than reality. After all, if there is any smiling in *Rosemary's Baby,* it appears only on the mouths of the chanting cultists whose cries of "Hail Satan" hold little hope of a faithful future.

Levin, perhaps, also smiled; after all, his delineation of a cultural crisis in mid-1960s America, which he tied closely to his plot, makes *Rosemary's Baby* considerably more than the standard Gothic horror fare. In fact, Levin ushers in a renaissance of American Gothic horror that echoes the social and political upheavals of the period and helped create the market for the Stephen King phenomenon. *Rosemary's Baby* opened a natural new direction for horror fiction by updating Gothic conventions, particularly those that involve the devil's incarnation in the modern world. Of course, there had been devil-centered stories for decades, including popular films such as *The Bad Seed* (1956) and *The Curse of the Demon* (1957)—even the comedy-musical Broadway hit *Damn Yankees* (filmed in 1958) took a stab at the demonic. *Rosemary's Baby,* in turn, has spawned a legion of spin-offs—including *The Other* (1972), *The Exorcist* (1973), *It's Alive* (1974), *The Omen* (1976)—and introduces a rebirth of Gothic horror tales set in the modern world. This rebirth was furthered by Roman Polanski's effective film adaptation of *Rosemary's Baby* (1969).

Set in mid-1960s New York City, *Rosemary's Baby* tells the story of the young married couple Guy and Rosemary Woodhouse who rent an apartment at the seemingly elegant, but very Gothic, Bramford (The "Bram") apartment complex despite being warned of its weird and violent history by Rosemary's old friend Hutch. Shortly after moving to the Bram, Guy and Rosemary quickly find Hutch's warnings partially fulfilled in the suicide of a young woman named Terry who lived with the kindly couple Roman and Minnie Castevet. To put quickly what becomes evident gradually, Roman Castevet entices Guy into a modern-day Faustian bargain that requires him to turn over Rosemary so she can be used to give birth to the Antichrist and bring about the end of the world. In exchange, Guy is promised that he will become a successful actor. Consequently, Guy willingly drugs Rosemary who is subsequently raped by a monstrous incarnation of the devil during an evil ritual in the Castevets' living room. Following that awful night, Rosemary finds herself pregnant and Guy lands successful acting parts. The rest of the story develops the travails of Rosemary's pregnancy, including her discovery that the Castevets and her obstetrician are actually cultists. Her delivery of the son of Satan (or "Andy") on June 25, 1966, horrifically inverts the date of the traditional birthday of the Christ child on December 25. The novel ends as Rosemary decides against killing her baby and herself and determines instead to raise Andy with the hope that her loving influence will counteract his more devilish side.

Among the more prominent contributions critical readers note about *Rosemary's Baby* is its perceptive, often ironic, depiction of its times. In particular, several critics turn a watchful eye on *Rosemary's Baby* to explore its relevance to both feminism and religious liberalism. Others examine the novel within the Gothic tradition, particularly in the way it develops prior tales of monstrous children such as "The Great God Pan" by Arthur Machen, "The Dunwich Horror" by H. P. Lovecraft, and *The Midwich Cuckoos* by John Wyndham. Still other approaches to *Rosemary's Baby* comment on Levin's use of satanic lore, not to mention the rise of death-of-God theology in the 1960s.[1]

What such readings generally miss is Levin's broader concern with evil in the modern world, a concern he used to shape his novel both morally and aesthetically. We argue that Levin's depiction of satanic cults comments both on the shallowness of the world and on the banality of evil. Levin's novel seems especially insightful in light of its overall indictment of human beings as mindless consumers who seem capable only of seeing satanic plots in light of how they impact their personal lives. To put it another way, *Rosemary's Baby* is more invested in questions concerning America than in providing another tale of a classical satanic plot that involves things like ancient runes, unreadable texts, and implausible monsters. In this chapter, we will explore these concerns and tie them back to how Levin's novel draws on Poe's "House of Usher" to deepen his commentary on the cultural and social climate of the 1960s.

Levin's interest in the Gothic begins with his early fascination with Edgar Allan Poe, who influenced both his mystery writing and, as we argue here, his horror writing. Most of Levin's critics conspicuously overlook Poe's shadowy presence behind *Rosemary's Baby,* particularly its treatment of fallen humanity. Even Douglas Fowler's otherwise meticulous work only hints at Poe's influence. In fact, Fowler seems determined to demonstrate that Levin avoided certain old-fashioned, mysterious descriptions in his novel, the kind "traditionally done in purple inks on loan from Poe" (13). Moreover, Fowler writes that Levin's novel barely escapes "sounding like a parody of 'The Fall of the House of Usher,'" and notes that what little of Poe there is in the novel was "smuggled in under a plain brown wrapper" (13). We disagree. Instead, we suggest that Levin's novel extends the microcosm of Poe's House of Usher into a look at the role of evil in the macrocosm of the world. In other words, *Rosemary's Baby* makes explicit the nightmare that Poe symbolized through his depiction of the dark destinies of Roderick and Madeline Usher. Reading *Rosemary's Baby* through the lens of "Usher" will provide a means of tracing the implications of imagining an apocalyptic annihilation in a contemporary setting. One of the crucial components Levin uses to ground his vision of evil in *Rosemary's Baby* lies in his Usher-esque structure that suggests the horrible end to a hopelessly deteriorated reality. Like "Usher," *Rosemary's Baby* is apocalyptic, suggesting the end of a decaying and dying world. In "Usher" the world is represented by the falling and lifeless house, landscape, and family. *Rosemary's Baby* creates a world that is also lifeless and running down, one that no longer has faith in higher things. With the birth of the devil's child, evil symbolically inherits this mundane earth.

In *Rosemary's Baby* several elements echo "Usher," including the opening focus on an old, decaying, and strange "house" inhabited by weird people that sits at the center of a spiritual wasteland about to collapse. In Poe's story, the House of Usher itself becomes the central feature of inexplicable horror beginning with the narrator's detailed introduction to his feelings upon first encountering it. He is unable to explain rationally why or how the house seems to cause an "insufferable gloom" to infect him, and, like the guilty center of a depressed and troubled soul, only allows him to feel that "every-day life" is a "sickening of the heart—an unredeemed dreariness" (*Tales* 397). Like the House of Usher, the Bramford apartment building seems to belong to another time and, similarly, has horrific associations. Levin describes it as a rather different sort of House of Usher by presenting it from a particularly ominous point of view. First, like the House of Usher, it has a dark history that their friend Hutch fills them in on. He tries to actually dissuade Rosemary and Guy from renting in what he calls a "danger zone" (23). He summarizes its evil history, including such infamous residents as the cannibal Trench sisters who killed and ate small children, the mysterious Keith Kennedy, and the Satan-conjuring Adrian Marcato. On the one hand, Hutch gives a most plausible explanation for the Bram's exorbitant number of deaths and wicked tenants by describing it as "a kind of rallying place for people who are more prone than others to certain types of behavior" (21). On the other hand, Hutch adds that there may be "things we don't know . . . [by] which a place can quite literally be malign" (21). Hutch notes other "less spectacular irregularities" such as that "there've been more suicides there, for instance, than in houses of comparable size and age" (21). Since Rosemary and Guy are skeptical, Hutch concludes with some advice to Rosemary: "And don't go wandering through the halls introducing yourself to all and sundry. You're not in Iowa" (25). This allusion to *The Wizard of Oz* ("We're not in Kansas anymore") strikes a final chilling note of the fantastic. Like Dorothy in Oz, or Alice in Wonderland, Rosemary's home in the Bram compels her to embark on a strange journey that defies all her common-sense assumptions about what is and isn't possible—just as does "Usher's" narrator.

Yet Rosemary and Guy's mundane point of view does not really make the Bram seem the traditional "bad place" of horror fiction. Through their eyes it seems merely a token Gothic presence. Though in reality it is the appropriate atmosphere to house its coven of witches, it sits in the modern world as glaringly and absurdly out of place as Edward Scissorhands's Gothic mansion in modern suburbia. From the moment the Woodhouses are shown the apartment, the mood is light. Noting that the man showing them around is ominously missing fingers, Guy jokingly "made a leering vampire face" (6). Later, as they are taken along dark hallways where various evidences of decay are manifested, Guy, rather less than awestruck, satirically comments on the patched carpet (7). Again, after they learn the gloomy news about the previous tenant's recent death, Rosemary is soon "giggling" at the fact that the kitchen is "as large if not larger than the whole apartment in which they were then living" (8–9). Thus, at each opportunity to create an atmosphere of dread, Levin shifts gears and turns it into a joke. Unfortunately, Guy and Rosemary both see the Bram as a haunted carnival ride whose corny "horrors" are merely laughable.

Nevertheless, the Bram has some legitimate horror effects for the modern couple that make it increasingly Usher-esque. But though Levin disperses our supernatural dread somewhat, he subtly sounds ominous notes for the reader to ponder. For example, Rosemary hears chants through the walls late at night that blend with her own dreams. This is typical of the atmosphere of the Bram—suggestive, mysterious, unsettling, but never blatant until the end. Another quiet aspect of the Bram's evil is its association with repulsive smells and tastes, particularly the silver ball of tannis root and the herb shake Minnie delivers to Rosemary daily. Later, too, Rosemary finds herself "chewing on a raw and dripping chicken heart—in the kitchen one morning at four-fifteen" (178). Such strange behavior is tied directly to the Bram, as is Rosemary's incessant and unnatural pain during her pregnancy. Among the chief horrors Rosemary faces is her increasingly troubled relationship with Guy, whose inexplicable changes in behavior threaten their marriage. All of this builds slowly for the reader on guesses and intuitions only, but cumulatively create a definite sense of the Bram as a unique kind of bad place, primarily through what is suggested, suspected, and almost evident.

The Bram is defined in part by its essential contrast to the mundane world of empty consumerism. Even the Gothic horrors of the Bram have been reduced to consumable artifacts for aspiring yuppies who line up on a waiting list to get an atmospheric apartment. Entering this world is Rosemary, a lapsed Catholic from Omaha, Nebraska, just the type of newly secularized urbanite that Vatican II hoped to reinterest in the church. She is presented as an outsider whose family back home has all but disowned her for marrying the agnostic (and Protestant) actor Guy Woodhouse. Guy is a comfortable liar who twists the truth to accomplish any end that seems important at the moment, including the move into the Bram. Even Rosemary admits that she likes Guy's lying attitude: "And yes he might lie now and then; wasn't that exactly what had attracted her and still did?—that freedom and nonchalance so different from her own boxed-in propriety" (123). In other words, she marries Guy, in part at least, because she admires his relaxed respect for traditional mores and aspired to be like him. Therefore, as in all of the "Usher"-inspired texts we've examined in this study, the main characters seem psychologically prepared for the house into which their destiny brings them. Just as Marcato's evil ambitions drew him to the Bram, so Guy's modern ethics prepare him to quickly abandon all moral concerns, including the sanctity of his wife, in order to make a pact with the devil to further his career. Evil, in this case, is near-perfect self-centeredness. He thus collapses into the house's evil willingly, joining the counterculture coven whose values fly in the face of the dominant culture. Rosemary will capitulate a bit more slowly, making the collapse complete when she decides to love her child despite everything. In the end, the Bram's living presence overwhelms her.

In "Usher," Poe develops the theme of collapse from the beginning. Just as the narrator's mood darkens and fades into the surreal gloom of the Usher estate, so he soon finds the tottering Roderick seemingly on the same verge of collapse as the house. Roderick's poem, "The Haunted Palace," makes the connection between the house and its residents explicitly. Madeline, too, seems overpowered by the melancholy atmosphere and is buried alive in the bowels of the House of Usher's living death. Finally, of course, the theme of collapse is both physical and psychological as evidenced by the physical collapse of Madeline on the insane Roderick even as the house itself sinks into the tarn. Like the House of Usher, the

Bram, in fact, does seems alive—as an acquaintance of Rosemary's raves, "All those weird gargoyles and creatures climbing up and down between the windows!" (16). The Bram becomes associated with Rosemary's dreams, a kind of architectural unconsciousness from a century of evil from which her own unconscious mind becomes indistinguishable. On one occasion, when Rosemary is falling asleep, the sounds of Minnie Castevet's voice transform into the voice of Rosemary's harsh, former Catholic school teacher, Sister Agnes. The blend of Rosemary's memories and the voice through the wall suggests a connection between Rosemary's guilt at her lapsed faith and the Bram's designs on her. Like the House of Usher, the Bram is necessarily associated with the people in it—in this case, it is full of witches. Later, while she is being raped by a leathery-skinned incarnate devil, Rosemary slips into a dream state that combines her own religious guilt with the devastating loss of President Kennedy, a death that many associated with an important loss of leadership that might have staved off the more terrible results of the Vietnam War and the struggle for civil rights.[2]

As with the House of Usher, too, the inhabitants of the Bram will eventually collapse psychologically and morally into it. Guy, like Roderick, sacrifices his wife for selfish purposes. While Roderick buries Madeline alive, Guy, the consummate consumer, sees Rosemary as currency to pay for what his vanity craves—fame and glory as an actor. But like Roderick, once Guy has done the deed he becomes troubled, moody, and nervous, withdrawing into his own world. The scene in "Usher" when they carry Madeline's body down into the cellar tomb is reflected in *Rosemary's Baby* when Rosemary is taken from her apartment through the adjoining closet between the apartments into the Castevets' to play her role in the intended ritual. Rosemary's dream during the rape sequence, in which she is only half awake, seeing actual reality as well as her dream images, nicely echoes the "Mad Trist" passages in "Usher," wherein events in the story of Ethelred are reflected in the apparent sounds of Madeline's escaping the tomb. The effect in "Usher" is to blur the line between reality and dream, and in *Rosemary's Baby*, too, they are blurred, just as Rosemary's faith has been buried in her unconscious and mainly surfaces in her dreams. During the rape she is visited in her dreams by the Pope, who symbolizes her guilt for not going to see him preach at

Yankee Stadium that day, just as the "Mad Trist" becomes a maddening catalyst to awaken Roderick's guilt. Finally, like "Usher," the climax of physical and psychological collapse is an apocalyptic flurry in which the real meaning of Rosemary's pregnancy is revealed. The postapocalyptic deadness and sorrow of "Usher's" setting and people quietly resonate in *Rosemary's Baby*. Both are stories of the end of time, so to speak, of worlds that have died on the vine. Even as radically as Levin has literalizes the evil lurking in the shadows of Poe's tale, there is still enough of the vestiges of a morality abandoned to give spiritual poignancy to this modern horror story about a world in which God seems dead indeed.

Turning back to "House of Usher," we also perceive a strong sense of the preapocalyptic gloom of a dying world. Broadly speaking, the notion of apocalypse is a culmination of the misdeeds of mankind since the biblical fall of man, a fall to which Poe himself alludes in the title of his famous tale. Poe's own end-of-the-world setting begins in the "autumn of the year" as "the shades of evening drew on," and thereby emphasizes the sense of endings, in terms of both oncoming death and the impossibility of lasting joy (*Tales* 397). The narrator not only can't enjoy a romantic sentiment in beholding the house and estate of Usher, but feels "an utter depression of soul . . . a hideous dropping off of the veil" (397). The strong sense of absence is disturbing. From the "vacant eye-like windows" (397), which admit only "feeble gleams of encrimsoned light" into the house (401), to the obvious infertility of the rank sedges, white trunks of decaying trees, and the "deficiency" of the Usher progeny, we see that, like Eliot's "Wasteland," there is clearly no god in residence. Not only is the dreariness spiritually "unredeemed" (397), but the whole had "an atmosphere which had no affinity with the air of heaven" (399). Even the "specious totality" of the house itself and the fissure zigzagging through it are, in their inverted reflection in the tarn, witnessing this setting as the inverse of Eden—or the end result of the fall that happened there. Depression and terror have replaced the possibility of joy, peace, and love.

Among the more salient clues to Poe's use of this dark mood are the several religious-themed books he mentions in Roderick's library—Gresset's "Vert-vert, the Parrot," an allegory of man's frailties; Machiavelli's *Belphegor,* about damnation and hell; Swedenborg's *Heaven and Hell,* about mystical religious experiences; and *Vigiliae Mortuorum secundum Chorum Ecclesiae Maguntinae,* used by the Catholic Church for services with the family of the deceased to pray for their welcome into heaven. This latter text, which was Roderick's "chief delight," suggests perhaps that he found temporary solace in the hopeful prayers therein. But not all the textual allusions in "House of Usher" point to a universe consumed by meaningless darkness and despair. Roderick's horrible guilt at burying Madeline alive suggests that there yet remains a moral structure to his thinking that allows his actions to be understood as evil choices. For example, Poe alludes to Psalms 139:7 ("Whither shall I flee from thy presence?") to suggest that Roderick's guilt over his actions parallels those of the psalmist who fears God's judgments against him. Further, Poe alludes to the destructive power of God's wrath in Ezekiel 43:2 ("His voice like a noise of many waters") to describe the sound of the house's final descent into the tarn.

Poe extends his allusions to biblical passages by using "The Haunted Palace" as a kind of prophetic parable about the ultimate fall of the house and its inhabitants. While most of Poe's interpolated poems within tales are only vaguely or indirectly related to the stories themselves, "The Haunted Palace" is a straightforward encapsulation of the tale in moralistic imagery that hints at a core cause of the condition of the House of Usher and its inhabitants. As a loose allegory of the fall of man, Poe's parable concerns the failure of an ideal when "evil things, in robes of sorrow, / Assailed the monarch's high estate" (ll. 33–34). The poem begins by describing the Eden-like setting ("in the olden / Time long ago" [11–12]) of the palace: "In the greenest of our valleys, / By good angels tenanted" (ll. 1–2). Just as "a river went out of Eden to water the garden" (Gen. 2:10), so through the palace door "came flowing, flowing, flowing, / And sparkling evermore, / A troop of Echoes . . . " (ll. 27–29). After "evil things" (Eden's serpent) insinuate themselves within the palace the poem describes its fallen state of sorrow ("I will greatly multiply thy sorrow" [Gen. 3:16]), desolation ("thorns and thistles shall it bring forth to thee" [Gen. 3:18]), and death ("for in the day thou eatest thereof thou shalt surely die" [Gen. 2:17]). Like "Usher" itself, the poem's upper current deals with psychological deterioration, while biblical imagery creates an undercurrent that suggests the moral underpinnings of the minds' "well-tunéd law[s]" (*Tales* 407).

"The Haunted Palace" rightly characterizes Roderick as an inverted Adam figure dying within a fallen world rather than being born into a newly created one. While Adam uses his creativity to name the cattle, fowls, and beasts (Gen. 2:20), Roderick "poured forth" darkness "in one unceasing radiation of gloom" by creating perversions of known musical styles and painting oppressive, gloom-ridden pictures (*Tales* 405–6). Madeline, likewise, represents an inverted Eve figure whose allegorical "rib" is suggested by the fact that she, impossibly, is Roderick's identical twin. But their fall, unlike that of Adam and Eve, is into complete darkness, at least as long as Madeline represents a living corpse that fills the narrator with "dread" at the sight of her (404). In this Eden, Madeline's death must occur twice, first when she is entombed by Roderick and his narrator friend and second when she falls into the tarn with Roderick and the house itself.

Functioning thematically like "The Haunted Palace," Levin's use of New York City in 1966 as a setting is crucial to considerations of good and evil and their effects in the novel. While vibrant and upbeat on the surface, the soul of the country is bleak and vacuous, every bit as spiritually decayed and depressed as Roderick's "mansion of gloom." This is a postlapsarian time of the upheaval of traditional values and boundaries, typified by the popular, iconoclastic phrase, "God is Dead." This is echoed in the novel as Guy cynically reacts to Mrs. Castevet's remark that the Pope will postpone his visit to New York until the newspaper strike is over by saying, "Well . . . that's show biz" (70). Roman Castevet adds that "every religion" is really about show, "pageants for the ignorant" (70). On the social front, anarchy emerges as politics turns unruly with marches, protests, sit-ins, riots, and the burning of draft cards, flags, and neighborhoods. In terms of religious authority, during an era when Catholics were leaving the church in droves, the church finds itself in an increasingly chaotic and secular consumer world in which, as John Lennon iconoclastically states, the Beatles are more popular than Jesus. Ultimately, as Levin reminds us in *Rosemary's Baby,* this is an era where it seems that God is not only dead, but irrelevant. Youth, too, are rejecting the traditional moral values of the dominant culture, including sexual restraint and respect for adults. Nowhere are these attitudes better epitomized than in the rock culture whose holy coordinates are knowingly dubbed as "sex, drugs, rock and roll."

But beyond being a mere subculture, rock was well on its way to becoming coequal with the dominant hegemony as boundary lines begin to blur. In short, what is right and wrong in mid-1960s America becomes as hard to distinguish as what is and isn't real in "Usher."

The results of decaying mores are made clear by the novel's allusions to popular culture. These allusions become significant metaphors of Levin's sense that the contemporary world provides more commodities than opportunities for transcendence. Though he mentions popular books, films, and music, Levin particularly highlights the world of theater that Guy hopes to conquer. Like the inexplicable world of "Usher," the popular dreamworld of Broadway musicals and movies is central to Rosemary and Guy's consciousness, and they have little else, other than each other, to hold things together. Importantly, the two plays most mentioned are *Luther* and *Nobody Loves an Albatross*, invoking religion, and, indirectly, "The Rime of the Ancient Mariner" and its depiction of sin and hell. In addition, several of the plays alluded to serve as ironic counterpoint to the story—*Wait Until Dark* foreshadows Rosemary's horrific fears, *Mrs. Dally* concerns a woman's unhappy married life, and *Come Blow Your Horn* is about amoral types like Guy. Levin's point is not that these productions of popular culture are weak and shallow inherently, but that this world—and the ambition to conquer it—has replaced and destabilized the real world.

Like Poe, Levin uses the novel's setting to set the stage for his meditation on the problem of evil. *Rosemary's Baby*'s sense of evil suggests that while men and women may be free to choose, they are inclined to choose evil more often than good. Thus, Levin's so-called modern world is, in reality, as blasted and morally decaying a world as that surrounding the Usher house. This brings the issue full circle, but now puts evil squarely in the lap of humankind. But evil is an invisible reality, a theater where everyone, like Guy, acts according to their selfish interests. Evil is only fully recognized by Rosemary because her baby is threatened by the plot of those around her. In other words, in *Rosemary's Baby*, the problem of evil isn't theoretical, but is a practical problem indeed, one that for Rosemary is up close and personal.

Such a world, wherein boundaries of all sorts are becoming slippery and blurred, constitutes a major contribution from "Usher" to *Rosemary's Baby*. In "Usher" blurred boundaries are central to the tale's effect of dreamlike inexplicability. For example, the boundary between human and inanimate objects, like Roderick and his house, is blurred, as is that between living and nonliving things brought out by the house's sentience. Furthermore, the narrator blurs the line between consciousness and dream in the beginning, while Madeline's behavior makes life and death indistinguishable. Finally, the line between sanity and madness is uncertain throughout "Usher," maintaining an uncanny atmosphere in which reality is impossible to discern. Sigmund Freud helps us recognize that the uncanny produces its unusual effect precisely because it blends our sense of both the familiar and the unfamiliar. For example, Freud refers to the unnatural "impressions made on us by waxwork figures" because of the feeling that they are at once like us and not at all like us (135).

Turning to one of Levin's more striking descriptions of Guy Woodhouse as a wax image, we see the extent to which Levin draws on the power of the uncanny to make readers uncomfortable with the events in his novel. We begin with the question that Douglas Fowler raised in his book on Levin: "What kind of person would allow the Prince of Darkness to use his wife as a mother for the Anti-Christ?" (36). To respond, we suggest that Levin provides us a glimpse of Guy's character in the moment when he first realizes that Roman and Minnie have somehow blinded his rival Donald Baumgartner to make good on their promise of supernatural success. As Guy hears the news of Baumgartner's tragedy, he simply sits there, silently holding the phone, saying nothing, doing nothing. As Levin describes him, Guy "was pale and dummy-like, a Pop Art wax statue with real clothes and props, real phone, real can of paint remover" (Levin 91). By comparing Guy to a Pop Art figure, Levin pictures his character as a lifeless object, a mere representation of a man who, though surrounded by real objects, has nothing real about him. Guy is here reduced to a signifier of a man with no perfectly corresponding signified that will help us make sense of who he is. This is particularly true given Guy's willingness to sacrifice Rosemary to the Castevet's satanic plot. To return to Fowler's question, "What kind of a man would sacrifice his wife to the Prince of Darkness?" the answer now seems more obvious than before—a man who only sees other people as empty bodies that can be twisted and tortured for his own gain.

We may further explore Levin's allusion to Pop Art sculpture if we turn to the work of the American Pop artist George Segal. In his 1961 sculpture *Man at a Table,* Segal created a plaster statue of a man sitting at a plain table with nothing in front of him. His facial expression shows no discernable emotion and his hunched-over posture suggests a passive acceptance of his lonely, alienated condition. Though this image does not correspond exactly to Levin's description of Guy, the comparison is nevertheless apt because it can help us understand the power of Levin's use of his Pop Art metaphor. Commenting on Segal's sculpture, the art historian Wayne Craven claims that "the personality of the individual is eliminated as Segal's figures become symbols of 20th-Century man caught in the social and psychological web of his own making" (659). Similarly, Levin turns Pop Art sculpture into a metaphor for Guy's loss of all the things that made him unique both as a man and a husband. Now he is only an actor, a man willing to exchange his wife's body and soul for success. Like Pop Art, Guy exists only for the purposes of display. He now represents only the external features of a man, while internally he is soulless and morally directionless. The result is an uncanny play between presence and absence.

After Guy agrees to use Rosemary to bring forth the devil's child, he increasingly lies to Rosemary about where he's going and what he's doing, becoming more of a phony and more of an actor. Eventually, Rosemary begins to suspect that Guy's feelings for her are not motivated by genuine feelings of love; instead, Guy's life as Rosemary's husband becomes little more than a distraction between his endless stream of auditions, callbacks, and rehearsals. Even worse, following Rosemary's violent rape, Guy explains that the consequent scratch marks on her body are the result of his own passionate lovemaking to her while she was asleep. Outraged by this claim, Rosemary recoils from Guy, shocked by the idea that "Guy had taken her without her knowledge, had made love to her as a mindless body . . . rather than as the complete mind-and-body person she was" (Levin 115). Guy, now little more than a shell of a man, seems only capable of seeing other people as exchangeable bodies, bodies that can be bent, blinded, and betrayed according to his personal needs. Even though Rosemary has a distant memory of being raped, she cannot trust Guy's love for her following his claim that he had sex with her without her knowledge or consent. She considers that "no motive and no number of drinks could have enabled him to take her that way, taking only her body without her soul or self or she-ness—whatever it was he presumably loved" (115).

Turning to "House of Usher," we note that one of the uncanny dimensions of Poe's story for readers is their reaction to the narrator. The longer he is with Roderick, and begins to become more his double, readers increasingly feel an uncanny distance from him—that is, the same "utter astonishment . . . and dread" he'd felt about Madeline. Thus, while he often sounds somewhat reasonable (questioning Roderick's theory of sentience), he also presents alarmingly ambiguous and inexplicable information quite blandly (as in the *Mad Trist* episode). Rosemary, too, does not remain untainted by her association with Guy or her setting. Thus, Rosemary's complaint about her body being made love to without her soul is somewhat ironic, because her own personhood is being called into question as well. The image of her as a "mindless body" echoes the image of Guy as a Pop Art statue. She is so caught up in her own obsessive consuming that she too is centered on the mere appearance of things. Levin frequently reminds us of Rosemary's passion for upscale apartments, nice furniture, hip clothing, and her flirtation with contemporary religious skepticism. Moreover, she regularly asks Guy to lie when it benefits them. Early in the novel Rosemary praises Guy as a "*marvelous* liar" (4). Guy has, in fact, become such a compulsive liar that Rosemary can no longer read him accurately, choosing to accept for a time the fabric of illusion he enacts for her. The most disturbing illustration of Rosemary's failure to read Guy comes in the aftermath of her rape. Feeling "a disturbing presence of overlooked signals just beyond memory, signals of a shortcoming in his love for her," she is too slow to put the pieces of the conspiracy together (115). While she is not as far along the path of self-deception as Guy is, she is clearly moving in the same direction. Her self-deceptive journey ends with her choice to raise Andy as if he were not only the product of a rape but also the child of an incarnate devil.

One of the most controversial problems in readings of *Rosemary's Baby* concerns its seemingly negative perspective on religion, particularly Catholicism. No doubt, some readers saw the novel as blasphemous, even dangerous, for those weak in the faith. Some critics have even taken Roman and Minnie at their word and declared that all religions are a sham. For example, Ronald Ambrosetti argues that Levin's novel deserves a place alongside existentialism as a popular statement about the possibility of a world without God. In particular, Ambrosetti claims that Levin exposes the mythological core of religion by showing the ease with which people like Guy and Rosemary move from Christianity to Satanism. While Ambrosetti is certainly right that human beings refine and reshape "traditions and symbols," we disagree with his overall sense that *Rosemary's Baby* demonstrates this shifting from one belief to another so casually (140). The religious issue at the heart of the book is not merely their shifting, but what people are willing to shift to when faced with a world without God. This is clearly the sense of the world of "Usher" as well as *Rosemary's Baby*. In his own godless world, Roderick's future is defined not by hope but by an unnamable fear, the tale's psychological focus suggesting that reality is as chaotic as a bad dream.

A most disturbing component of *Rosemary's Baby* for more religious readers is the constant exclamation that "God is Dead," a theology that briefly flowered during the 1960s. If anything, devil cultists' shouts of "God is Dead" bolster Levin's critique that popular culture is little more than an endless exchange of meaningless ideas and phrases. Even those who espoused the death-of-God theology recognized that their claims were about the problem of understanding transcendence within the limits of mortal language. Thus, "God is Dead" suggests religious forms without spiritual substance—like a Pop Art church.

In this novel, religion has died in the sense that it no longer holds credibility in a world that can only see religious pageantry in terms of "show biz." When Rosemary's baby—"Andy"—is finally born, the reader expects some kind of grandiose event, something that presages the end of the world. But Andy's birth clearly provides more whimper than bang. An early review of the novel complained that "the ending of [the novel], though inevitable, is flat" (Fowler 41). Similarly, Fowler raises the question whether "there really [is] any way for Levin's ending *not* to be flat and anticlimactic?" (41). Our view is that the novel ends appropriately because its anticlimactic feeling draws out quite powerfully the overall consumer-driven theme of the novel by presenting the son of Satan not as a powerfully immanent presence but as an easily commodified version of the devil himself. Indeed, there is nothing particularly convincing about Andy other than his symbolizing the banality of evil in the modern world, a baby devil complete with horns, tail, and weird eyes. In this sense, Andy is not real at all; instead, he is little more than a mockery of the very idea of the profane, just as his presence alone is supposed to mock the sacred. *Rosemary's Baby* is a novel, in part, about the very flattening of the division between the sacred and the profane. Moreover, Andy is consumed at the very end of the novel in a way that is entirely mawkish and mundane.

The last scene in the novel, for example, features a Japanese cultist who "slipped forward with his camera, crouched, and took two three four pictures in quick succession" (302). The image of this man taking pictures of Andy helps demonstrate that *Rosemary's Baby* is invested in a satire of consumerism. One wonders what value his pictures of Andy will have on the market, especially since potential viewers will only recognize him by his audience-friendly yellow eyes, budding horns, and sharp claws. Whatever dark intentions Levin initially imagined, his novel ends with the whimpering cries of a baby that is little more than a harmless creature—or, as King describes him, "the comic-book version of Satan, the L'il Imp we were all familiar with as children" (283).

Despite its satanic premises, *Rosemary's Baby* rarely invites the reader to feel drawn to the power or influence of evil itself. As Noël Carroll argues, horror fiction's appeal cannot be explained solely on the grounds of a fascination with evil. Such explanations only apply to a few cases, and even those are questionable (Carroll 168). *Rosemary's Baby* is no exception. Levin himself confesses that he was "stuck with Satan" as the father of Rosemary's child because John Wyndham already wrote the definitive paternity-by-aliens novel *The Midwich Cuckoos* (Levin 306). If we take Levin at his word, evil was less a thematic necessity than a part of his overall concern with the astonishing effect of some kind of alien birth. If anything, the effect of Levin's plot on the audience is more significant than its meditation on the problem of evil. For Levin, the mainspring of evil is best seen in a post–World War II America characterized by affluent consumerism.

Levin's insight into the nature of evil provides new answers to old questions about "The Fall of the House of Usher." The theme of human motivation addressed in our discussion of Guy's puzzling inclination to sacrifice Rosemary reminds us of the relationship between Roderick and Madeline Usher. Indeed, similar concerns may easily be raised concerning Roderick's own strange behavior—after all, what kind of brother buries his "beloved" sister alive, especially when he knows that she suffers from a condition that masks death? This question has puzzled scholars and readers for more than a century and lies at the heart of many discussions of "Usher." Roderick's strange behavior, after all, may suggest that he suffers from a complex array of guilty feelings that stem from his plot to facilitate Madeline's death in some way. Such behavior, particularly given Roderick's own fearful dread of the future, implies some awareness that his plans are evil. On the other hand, his sincere and tearful anticipation of her death—he buries his face in his hands and sobs when he sees her—shows that he is torn about his plans. Could Madeline—Rosemary-like—be intended as a sacrifice in a mad, desperate, last-minute appeal to ancient and pagan gods to bring back fertility and life to the Usher house and its sterile family line? Certainly, Poe's tale is primarily designed to produce a dreamlike effect on readers that is fundamentally inexplicable. But in order to give it dimension and suggestiveness—the "undercurrent" that he claims is necessary in "The Philosophy of Composition"—we feel encouraged to follow up on Poe's hints at exotic possibilities that give the dream an atmosphere of true dread and horror.

From this perspective, we may tentatively claim that Roderick feels compelled to commit the great sin of the ancient world—idol worship and sacrifice to foreign gods. Certainly, ancient Israel sacrificed animals for atonement in order to be reconciled to their god. But who is the god or goddess Roderick would sacrifice to? We can only speculate on ways to answer this question. Nevertheless, Roderick's obsessive hinting that the House of Usher is a conscious, powerful entity that controls his family's destiny seems suggestive. As the narrator put it, Roderick was "enchained by certain superstitious impressions in regard to the dwelling which he tenanted," which he believed had a "supposititious force" that had an influence "over his spirit" (*Tales* 403). Moreover, Roderick clearly believes in the house's "sentience," as evidenced—in his mind—by the arrangement of the stones and the inverted image in the tarn—all of which had had a "terrible influence" on the Usher family time out of mind (408). Since the Usher line is so depleted, we wonder whether human sacrifices have happened here in the past—a kind of traditional, ceremonial rite of sacrifice that delays an inevitable fall. The narrator reports that the family vault, where Madeline is entombed, was used "in remote feudal times" for the "worst purposes of a donjon-keep" (410). It is possible that the narrator doesn't know the half of it, and that Roderick is actually renewing an ancient family practice in his mad superstitious desire to save the House of Usher—and himself. It is further possible that Roderick needs to escape his incestuous relationship with his sister and find a more wholesome partner by which to reinvigorate the Usher line.

Rosemary's Baby inverts our image of "Usher" and opens up new ways to read it. By importing Poe's Gothic underworld into his novel, making *Rosemary's Baby* a tarnish reflection of "Usher," Levin invites us to contemplate "Usher" from the perspective of a modern world in psychological and moral decline. Thus, like the tarn's reflection in "Usher," a darker, more thrilling horror is created. From this point of view, Roderick Usher's behavior becomes subject to unsuspected motivations that add to the tale's horror. Thus, Roderick, like Guy, is seen as a liar who tells the narrator that Madeline is dead when in fact she is in a catatonic trance. The narrator, with Roderick, then becomes an accomplice to treating Madeline, like Rosemary, as merely an object, a body to be manipulated according to whim.

To conclude, we return to our earlier discussion of the problem raised by Edmundson concerning the twin poles of the American Dream/American Nightmare. If Edmundson is right, the angels of optimism and the demons of despair have been wrestling for generations without any hint of a permanent victory for one or the other. In *Rosemary's Baby,* the match is finally called on behalf of the demons, anticipating subsequent examples of triumphant evil in popular films like *The Ring* based on Koji Suzuki's novel. But Levin's novel should not be read as a celebration of the triumph of evil. Instead, it explores a kind of afternoon Gothic, a moment that exploits the uncanny moral complacency of a modern world that imagines human beings as Pop Art figures mentored ironically by kindly, selfless, and satanic cultists. The result is an apocalyptic fantasy that shows us the world dying with a routine whimper instead of an Usher-esque bang. Indeed, Levin's tale suggests that the modern world—represented by the Bram—may finally find a place in the tarn next to the already-collapsed House of Usher. But the Bram will collapse under the weight of innumerable consumables. In this sense, we may read *Rosemary's Baby* as a kind of cautionary parable about how vapid and secularized consumerism masks the deeper demonic threat poised to bring about the end of the world. Finally, Levin's tale is particularly striking in the way it draws on Poe's influence to underscore the uncanny, yet mundane, nature of that final descent.

CHAPTER 8

CEREMONIAL "USHER": THE INITIATION OF JACK TORRANCE AND THE FALL OF THE OVERLOOK HOTEL

Stephen King's *The Shining* draws on many texts and styles to weave its tale of the potential and real tragic horrors of modern family life, but what animates all of these elements of King's novel, raising important questions about King's purposes, is its ancient structure of initiation into the mysteries of a cult god originating in Egypt and further developed in Greek and Roman cultures. Although we borrow our idea from Barton Levi St. Armand's classic essay on Edgar Allan Poe, we believe that *The Shining* bears an uncanny resemblance in both structure and theme to the overall ritual structure Armand sees in "Usher." As in "Usher," *The Shining* traces a family's ritual journey into hell, adding to Poe's concept a terrifying naturalism. In fact, the phases of this ritual journey become a metaphor for the disintegration of Jack Torrance's dark unconscious. Indeed, by the end of the novel, he can only be described as a monster who looks like Jack but has lost all sense of what Jack was. In other words, the descent into evil has its own markers and milestones. We will trace Jack's ceremonial collapse into the Overlook Hotel, both in terms of how he has been prepared and chosen as an initiate, and in terms of the associated pageantry, trials, and tortures of his downward descent. Throughout this process he is led by various guides, who promise him the treasures and gifts through union with the hotel's cult god.

In his article "The 'Mysteries' of Edgar Poe: The Quest for a Monomyth in Gothic Literature," Armand highlights the way "The Fall of the House of Usher" features strong suggestions of ancient Egyptian initiation patterns and rituals. Tracing the Gothic-Romantic thirst for novel exoticisms, he notes that "the most avant-garde of the Romantic revivals when [Poe] was writing ["Usher"] in 1839 was the Egyptian mode" (69). He notes various initiation phases in the tale, including contemplation, purgation, a journey through the higher and lower regions, and the climax of union and rebirth (81). Thus, the narrator's depression at beholding the House of Usher and its environs represents the soul's helplessness without the promise of salvation. As in Thomas Moore's *Alciphron,* in which the hero is searching for the secret of eternal life, so the desolate inmost mind of Poe's narrator is made evident in his descriptions of decay and melancholy. Like the dark thoughts of death Moore's central figure experiences when viewing the pyramid tombs of Memphis, so the House of Usher "is also as mummified as the corpse of any embalmed pharaoh" (79). Roderick becomes the neophyte narrator's guide through the Isis rituals of Usher, through the subterranean regions, vaults, and crypts within the house. Osiris-Usher thus introduces the uncomprehending narrator into the mysteries of the house—including its sentience, its esoteric library, the death of Isis-Madeline, and the inexplicabilities of her resurrection in the climax. Roderick teaches his old friend of aspects and principles of the initiation's mysteries through music, painting, and studying books on journeying into the underworld (82). The tale of *The Mad Trist* becomes the "pageant or dumb show of the trials and torments that the questing aspirant has to endure" (88). The trials of earth (Madeline), and fire and water (Roderick and the narrator in the storm), lead to the climactic union and rebirth. In the end, from Armand's perspective, Madeline's death grip of Roderick, and their collapse with the house into the tarn, becomes a transcendent new genesis rather than an apocalypse.

While we agree with Armand's basic premise that Poe wrote "The Fall of the House of Usher" with some awareness of Egyptian rites, and that "Usher" has a kind of ritual structure, we find Armand's emphasis on a monomyth—including its emphasis on the search for eternal life—less convincing given the tale's bleak narrative surface. What makes "Usher's" initiation rituals relevant to *The*

Shining, we suggest, comes from their shared ritual structure, one that inverts the goal of eternal life into what becomes primarily a journey into a hellish underworld of the mind. Although there are redemptive elements in both "Usher" and *The Shining*—the narrator and Danny escape destruction and may have learned valuable lessons through their experience—the predominant *effect* of both stories concerns the dark, the violent, and the inexplicable and uncanny blurring of boundaries between dream and reality.

Just as Armand highlights "Usher's" ritualistic subtext, so we approach *The Shining* as an inverse ritual, one that introduces Jack into the hellish world of the Overlook Hotel. In King's book, Jack is served by a host of departed fellow sinners in a hierarchal order of revelers at a perpetual masked ball that has been going on since midnight of August 29, 1945. Somehow, the hotel has imprinted this moment in its very architecture, becoming itself a thing of evil, animating fire hoses and topiary animals, and weirdly "initiating" those who've died within and without its walls—like the bath suicide in room 217, the "hungry boy-thing that had been in the concrete ring," and Delbert Grady, the previous caretaker who killed himself and his entire family (*Shining* 430). In his own quest to associate with the ghosts of the Overlook Hotel, Jack, in a sense, seeks transcendence and a place of honor in the revelry cult of Horace Derwent—the Bacchus of the Colorado Lounge. Unfortunately for Jack, the Overlook does not make friends for the gods—it makes monsters. Jack's destiny, therefore, is not to go through a refiner's fire, but to "be bent and twisted until something snap[s]" (278). While Jack's descent into madness and evil touches many of the phases typical among the initiation patterns, his initiation is into the Overlook Hotel itself, an inversion of the ancient religious rites, taking him from the potential Elysian Fields of a happy family life and productive writing and teaching career (the American Dream) to a hell paved by Roderick Usher of self-loathing, paranoia, denial, and murder—the heart of his very dark shadow self.

According to what is known of the Egyptian Isis mysteries, the broad pattern largely followed later in Greece and Rome, from which much of our information has been gathered, begins with the selection of a worthy neophyte. After a careful preparation of contemplation and purgation that included instruction and fasting to purify the mind, the neophyte is ushered into the temple, where he sees a dramatic presentation of the life of the goddess or god the ritual centers on, views sacred objects and partakes of sacred food, and is ceremonially cleansed. He is then taken on a journey through Hades—that is, through a series of rooms and passageways below the temple that are set apart for these rites. During this journey's series of tests of endurance, the neophyte sees apparitions and visions and endures physical trials—including talking statues and other mechanical contrivances such as mock earthquakes created with false floor—and overcomes the fear of death. Spence describes the dramatic flavor of these trials by citing an inscription found on the ruins of one the temples: "Whoso shall pass along this road alone, and without looking back, shall be purified by fire, water, and air; and overcoming the fear of death, shall issue from the bowels of the earth to the light of day, preparing his soul to receive the mysteries of Isis" (206). Having endured a simulated death, the neophyte receives a password that leads him to the Elysian Fields, emerging a new being, reborn in friendship with the deity.

In *The Shining*, Jack and Danny's initiation journeys take place in the Overlook Hotel, a place Stuart Ullman protectively venerates as a kind of temple, but is, in reality, a classic King bad place. From the perspective of the Torrance family ordeal, however, the Overlook more specifically becomes an inverse temple dedicated to the ongoing wickedness of its ghost god, Horace Derwent. His name, of course, is a play on Horus, the ancient Egyptian god with the falcon head whose names means "high" or "far off," appropriate to the Overlook's remote setting. Horus was associated symbolically with the dead, the funerary rites, and the renewal after death. From the beginning, readers have little doubt that the Overlook represents complete evil. As one critic writes, evil in King's fiction tends to appear as "something negative, barren, weakening, a principle of death" (Magistrale 65). Moreover, evil in King's fiction "isolates, disunites, and tends to annihilate not only its opposite but itself" (65). This description captures precisely what the Overlook Hotel offers to Jack. Indeed, we could almost map out step by step the ways in which Jack follows these different aspects of evil all the way to the annihilation of the self. Though he doesn't see it right away, Jack's fascination with the hotel's ongoing masked ball—not to mention the abundant food and drink—can only end with an invitation to be trapped forever within its ghostly walls. Like the narrator in "The Fall of the House of Usher," Jack has unknowingly prepared himself to merge with a setting that seems to be waiting, and watching, for him. Indeed, both men comment on "how much [the windows of each place] seemed like eyes" (279). Jack is especially prepared for initiation into the Overlook because of his general lack of self-control, particularly as it contributes to his violent temper and his heavy drinking. In his own way, his violent alcoholic past echoes that of the thugs who were given to revelry, debauchery, and murder at the hotel. While a pure mind was the necessary qualification for the neophyte of Isis, the corrupted, and corruptible, mind is the requirement of Derwent and his own underworld "high priests." Like Eleanor in *The Haunting of Hill House*, Jack's unfulfilled past makes him yearn for recognition and prepares him to desire a new "home" among a ghostly company. Among the Egyptian neophyte's requirements for the ritual was a preparatory fast to cleanse and purify the mind so that he can receive the sacred rites properly. In an ironic inversion of that ritual, Jack abstains from alcohol for several weeks, but with all the pressures his employment and family problems have created, he comes to the Overlook desperately thirsty. Jack's demons begin to awaken from the moment he enters the hotel, signaled repeatedly by his customary alcoholic gesture of wiping his lips and compulsively chewing Excedrins, suggesting a nervousness akin to Roderick Usher's.

As with the holy neophytes, Jack has need of a guide in his initiation into absolute evil. In fact, during the course of his descent, he meets with several important guides: Watson, who sparks Jack's curiosity about the hotel's checkered past; Grady, a previous neophyte who becomes a model for Jack of how to rise in the phantom organization; and most importantly, his father's ghostly and homicidal voice reverberating in his mind. Who better to guide him through his descent into Hell than the one who initially prepared him by his abusive example of family terror? He beat his wife mercilessly in front of the children and treated the children with the worst kind of unpredictable behavior—a playmate one moment and a brutal drunk the next. Upon arriving at the Overlook, Jack's mad unconscious self, presided over by his father, begins to emerge and dominate. In the dark, cobwebby cellar among mounds of dusty, rat-infested newspapers and hotel rubbish—the very image of his dark unconsciousness—he finds the scrapbook "with white leather covers, its pages bound with two hands of gold string that had been tied along the binding in gaudy bows" (154). It is at this point that Jack's initiation officially begins as a card flutters out of the scrapbook: *"Horace M. Derwent Requests the Pleasure of Your Company At a Masked Ball to Celebrate the Opening of THE OVERLOOK HOTEL"* (155). Jack's imagination begins to connect immediately with the hotel as he pores over the sordid and colorful history in the scrapbook's newspaper clippings and photographs—repeatedly wishing he "had a drink" (159) while reading Horace Derwent's history. So drawn in is he during this initial engagement with the scrapbook that when he sees photographs of the decaying hotel in the late 1950s, it "wrenched Jack's heart" and he now "understood the breadth of his responsibility to the Overlook. It was almost like having a responsibility to history" (159).

At this point Jack's initiation has advanced to the stage where he is allowed to view the Overlook's most sacred writings and other objects—the scrapbook, invitation, and other memorabilia. In ritual terms, Jack has experienced the equivalent of the dramatic rendering of the "representation of [the] myth of the god," or "Tradition of the Sacred rites," a crucial part of the Isis preparatory rituals (Spence 204). In "Usher" the narrator is similarly informed about the history of Roderick Usher in Usher's improvised song, "The Haunted Palace." By committing his heart and mind to the secrets of the Overlook's history, Jack is now prepared for his descent into Hell and the trials that await there. Wendy's later interruption of him reading the scrapbook emphasizes how quickly he becomes alienated from his family. He guiltily lies to her, hides the scrapbook, and accuses her in his mind of trying to smell liquor on his breath (165). Thus, he has already joined the ranks of the hotel's ghosts, though he doesn't yet know it, making the Overlook as much his psychological home as the House of Usher is Roderick's. In *The Shining,* King's House of Usher is reimagined to symbolize the decaying sense of American culture in the late twentieth century. Whereas Poe used his tale to comment on the state of one family, King invites a broader sample of the American population to stay within the walls of the Overlook Hotel. After Jack reads the scrapbook, he begins to aggrandize its history. As he tells Wendy, the hotel itself "forms an index of the whole post-World War II American character," an index that points directly to overwhelming evidence that the American Dream is little more than a nightmare (186). In terms of Jack's psychological journey, the fact that he is more fascinated than appalled by the corruption, drugs, vice, robbery, murder, and suicide he reads about in the scrapbook demonstrates as well as anything else the dark kindred nature he shares with the hotel.

To refer to Jack's kindred nature to the Overlook suggests that the hotel has a nature, and like the House of Usher is somehow alive. In fact, an important way King draws on "The Fall of the House of Usher" is through his development of both the symbolic nature of haunted houses and his shared interest in the possibility of sentient houses. Poe famously introduces this concept in "Usher" by suggesting the "sentience of all vegetable things" as a scientific possibility (*Tales* 327). Not only does Roderick accept the belief that life is literally all around him, he also argues that his own home somehow shares its life with him. According to Roderick, "the conditions of the sentience had been here . . . fulfilled in the method of collocation of these stones—in the order of their arrangement, as well as in that of the many *fungi* which overspread them, and of the decayed trees which stood around—above all, in the long undisturbed endurance of this arrangement, and in its reduplication in the still waters of the tarn" (327). In other words, the House of Usher mirrors the very patterns of life itself. It almost follows nature in that each of the components of the house lives off the others. Even more startling, Roderick suggests that there is such a significant relationship between the life of the house and the lives of the Usher family that they are forever intertwined. As Poe relates it, "the result was discoverable . . . in that silent, yet importunate and terrible influence which for centuries had moulded the destinies of his family, and which made *him* what I now saw him—what he was" (327). As both family and living presence, the House of Usher shapes, even controls, the destinies of those who descend from its loins and reside within its walls. The connection is so strong, in fact, that the house shares the same fate as Madeline and Roderick. Like the house, this set of doomed twins literally collapse into death and destruction.

Unlike Roderick Usher, however, Jack Torrance initially struggles to accept the possibility that the hotel may be alive. Instead, he constantly wavers between his sense that the Overlook wants to use him to find Danny and his commonsense notion that such desire from the hotel would be impossible. Yet, there are passages in the novel where Jack will begin to feel that all the events Danny reports are real, only to turn almost immediately against his son in a blind rage. It is as if he wants the Overlook's mysteries to himself, not wanting to share them with Danny and Wendy, perhaps sensing that he is in competition with Danny for the hotel's rewards. Jack speculates that "maybe the Overlook has something" (263), that the hotel somehow collects "the residues of the feelings of the people who have stayed here. Good things and bad things" (264).

To move toward a symbolic death and achieve rebirth in the ancient mystery cult involved a process of trials and tests just as it does in King's *The Shining*. As a recovered scrap of these Egyptian rituals indicates, he who proceeds "must travel many avenues of hazard, of painful detours through the shadow-world, until at last a marvelous light appears before it and it approaches a higher sphere" (Spence 197–98). The ritual light at the end of the journey, a signal of rebirth, will become here the boiler explosion in the Overlook that brings bright death and destruction, the symbolic embodiment of the creeping eruption of Jack's unconscious. Among the things the Egyptians experienced during this descent into Hades are "apparitions" or "mysterious visions, terrifying in their portent," which "stalked the footsteps of the [initiates] through the shrine" (198). In addition to the masked mystery cult guides and "the hissing of serpents and the howling of wild beasts," the statues that surrounded "the novice became animated, speaking and admonishing him" (229). Certainly, Jack experiences analogously inexplicable apparitions and horrors along his journey, including the impossibly living wasps, the moving topiary, and the woman in room 217. This and other supernatural occurrences seem intended to convince Jack of the reality of the spirit realm within the Overlook, a reality he is prone to resist for a time, thinking that he is merely imagining things, that his mind is slipping. He finds such rationalizations more difficult after he experiences the reality of the woman in room 217 because of Danny's corroborating experience. But he tries to live in denial, such that when he finds the snowmobile battery that would enable the family to leave the Overlook, he is frustrated and resorts to an insanity plea to rationalize staying: "It was an hallucination, no different from what had happened yesterday outside that room on the second floor . . . a momentary strain, that was all" (278).

The last, and perhaps most essential, component of his initiation into evil is Jack's relationship with his dead father, a relationship that inevitably reminds us of *Psycho* and Norman Bates's relationship with his dead mother. In both cases, the sons are haunted by dead parents that exert a continuous and powerful controlling influence over their unconscious minds. In addition, both sons find themselves arrested in their psychological development, leaving them helplessly guided by growing impulses to commit murder in the name of the parent. As we discussed in our chapter on *Psycho*, the archetype of the Terrible Mother is bound up with Norman's sexuality and sense of identity to such an extent that he can't overcome his need to remain attached to her in their original oneness. The situation with the father as an archetype is different. According to Erich Neumann, the unconscious should be read as having a "bisexual" nature, one "possessing masculine and feminine symbolic qualities" (170). But while the mother side represents instincts and nature, and embodies everlasting and unchanging principles divorced from peculiar cultural conditions, the "archetypal image of the father . . . is conditioned less by his individual person than by the character of the culture and the changing cultural values which he represents" (171–72). Rather than instincts and nature, the fathers represent law and cultural order, handing down the highest collective values of civilization (172–73). They are the "guardians of masculinity and the supervisors of all education," certifying the coming of age (173). In Jack's case, his father was such a dysfunctional and brutal tyrant, whose sense of law and order revolved around his alcoholic, paranoid whims, that Jack's progress into masculinity became distorted. Indeed, the heart of Jack's personal struggle has to do with how he will handle himself as a father. This decision is crucial to his position within the hierarchy of the Overlook Hotel, which represents the most extreme and violent version of patriarchy. In the Overlook, men rely solely on brutality to enforce their will. Jack is constantly bombarded by both the hotel's notions of masculinity and his own unconscious struggle with his father's own voice that constantly belittles him. In this sense, King's novel reflects a concern about the potential abuses of certain masculine roles, particularly those that demean others through drink or inherent brutality. We suggest further that in *The Shining*, as Anne Williams suggests about Gothic discourse, King challenges extreme versions of masculinity, depicting Jack's father actually "outside the Law of the Father"—that is, the conventional patriarchal laws. Although *The Shining* is not considered King's most strikingly feminist work, Jack's struggle with his father's voice suggests an interest in coming to terms with conventional masculine roles and how they impact family life, particularly when abused. With Jack's death and Danny's understanding of Jack's struggle against evil, the destruction of the Overlook Hotel also leads to the "Fall of the House of the Father" (175–76). In other words, King's novel focuses on the apocalyptic nightmare that follows familial patterns of abuse.

Jack's unconscious relationship with his father embodies another aspect of Poe's psychological art in "Usher" and elsewhere—the inexplicable imp of the perverse. Like Poe's character in "The Black Cat," in which Poe first defines this concept, Jack has an uncontrollable temper and an unyielding thirst for alcohol, both expressly related to his psychological state. Moreover, King's reflections on Jack's violent actions, not to mention his suggestion that some elements of human behavior lie beyond human agency, bring to mind Poe's definition of perverseness as the "unfathomable longing of the soul *to vex itself*" (599). According to Allan Lloyd-Smith, Poe's presentation of perversity constitutes his "great contribution to psychological acuity" (114). Lloyd-Smith's claim invites us to turn our attention toward the fundamental problem of human nature as inherently unstable. He argues that Poe transforms "the perverse desire to vex the self into the central motivation of his characters, removing the clutter of eighteenth-century rationalist reflection and commentary so that the self-damaging impulse stands out in sharp relief and beyond explanation" (114). Reason, in other words, will not save a person from the causes or the effects of the imp of the perverse. As Poe has it, perverseness is "an innate and primitive principle of human action" (*Tales* 827). Though he does not call it perverseness, King's descriptions of Jack's behavior point to a rationale similar to Poe's concerning a primitive desire to act contrary to one's best self. Like Poe, King connects our fears to our most "primitive level" (*Danse Macabre* 4).

We are given a glimpse of Jack's perverseness through his memory of breaking Danny's arm. Thinking back on that moment, Jack attempts to distance himself from his violent actions by describing them almost as if they were separate from him: "It was all hard to remember through the fog of anger" (16). Moreover, Jack didn't even hear his wife calling out to find out what happened because her voice was "faint" and "damped by the inner mist" (17). The awful sound of Danny's arm snapping "through the red fog" of Jack's anger is loud enough that he begins not only to realize what he did, but also to recognize "the dark clouds of shame and remorse, the terror, the agonizing convulsion of the spirit" that were beginning to descend (19). In other words, Jack begins to understand that he has acted contrary to his own soul.

Another manifestation of Jack's perverseness, as in Poe's the "Black Cat," comes from his alcoholism. From the beginning, Danny senses that his father's struggle with alcohol is tearing him apart psychologically, making it the "Bad Thing" (27). Indeed, Danny senses that his father craves the Bad Thing psychologically, with a "constant craving to go into a dark place and watch a color TV and eat peanuts out of a bowl and do the Bad Thing until his brain would be quiet and leave him alone" (27). Clearly, Jack finds solace in drinking, a kind of solace that would shut off his turbulent mind for a while. But what is it that Jack wants to quiet down in his mind? We argue that one of the things Jack is trying to forget is his own tendency to desire the Bad Thing—that is, to rely on the very thing (alcohol) that will vex his soul in order to calm his soul. The problem plaguing Jack the very most is his self-destructive sense that he is nothing, an idea compounded by his inability to maintain a happy and solvent home. Therefore, his perverseness manifests itself as a desire to free himself, even if violently, from his family obligations. In King's hands, perverseness looks more like the nagging fear that there is nothing more to live for, that his family would be better off "if he left" (27).

Jack's drinking becomes a psychological oasis from the inner conflict he feels between receiving and resisting his father's legacy. As Jack's journey continues, the imp of the perverse, now recognizable as the previously unconscious presence of his father, becomes ascendant and, despite his love for his family, fuels Jack's violent desire to destroy his family: "The wanting, the *needing* to get drunk had never been so bad. His hands shook. He knocked things over. And he kept wanting to take it out on Wendy and Danny. His temper was like a vicious animal on a frayed leash" (36).

As is always the case with the imp of the perverse, Jack distances himself from his own unmotivated actions, frequently reflecting on his actions as things that happen to him, thus denying that he is a rational agent of any kind. This is one of the most frightening things about Jack. Nevertheless, in the scene where Jack pulls the magneto off the snowmobile for the simple reason that he doesn't want to leave the Overlook just yet, he shows most strongly the influence of perverseness. For one moment of perfect sanity, he realizes that "it wasn't Danny who was the weak link, it was him" (278). He recognizes clearly the evil of the house and its plot against him and his family, and the fact that the hotel doesn't want them to go. But then, just as suddenly as his sanity emerges, it disappears: *Except he still didn't really want to go*" (281). King can provide no explanation beyond the simple fact that Jack's perverse will must do what is contrary to his own better thinking. In such a moment, the fine line between perverseness and possession is impossible to distinguish. Just as his perverseness has made him call Ullman and gloat over his plan to write an exposé of the Overlook, so he throws away the magneto key and dooms the family he loves to a long, waking nightmare.

Such denials of his fading rational self soon becomes uncontrollable rage when in a trance he hears his father's voice coming out of the radio: "You have to kill [Danny], Jacky, and her, too" (227). Jack's father's voice becomes not merely an inner voice, not merely a supernatural trick played on him by the hotel, but "the voice of the Ghost-God, the Pig-God, coming dead at him out of the radio" (228). *"You're dead, you're dead,"* he shouts as he smashes the radio to bits, unable to deny how compelling the voice is as the voice of a god. This incident sheds new light on Jack's initiation. His father becomes the face of god, a kind of Osiris figure along his journey with whom he merges and as whom he will be reborn. But this incarnation will hardly appear as a divine being of glory—instead, he will appear as a tarnished deity, the god of all abuse, vengeance, and murder. Derwent is merely the chief guide, like his divine Egyptian namesake, who leads him to his terrible psychological destiny. Like the hotel's evil that is lit up by Danny's shine, or the dormant wasps, so Jack's father comes back from the dead to possess his son, stinging him with memories and feelings of uncontrollable rage. In reviewing the history of the evils of Derwent, Jack's own inner demons are awakened, becoming an outward manifestation of the inner spectacle of his father's horrifying deeds. Jack's father has been the unknowable, inexplicable part of him that has motivated all of his drinking and rage before even coming to the Overlook, the "broken switch" on which Jack, in "passive mode," blames all of his problems (107–8). In a very real sense, his paranoid father has been initiating him all of his life; Jack's experiences in the Overlook are merely the accelerated finishing touches on his dark destiny.

Even with all of his unfortunate qualifications, Jack remains a rather poor initiate. Throughout the novel, he wavers between accepting the Overlook's summons and abiding by the love he feels for his family. This is partly complicated by Jack's career stresses, causing him to see everything in terms of his writing career. His first impulse when he learns the mysteries of the Overlook Hotel is to write an historical exposé of the hotel's seedy underbelly, the very material that is meant by the hotel to entice him to murder his family. Thus, his ambitions are obstructing his dedication to the hotel. Only when he can admit the transcendent dimension of the hotel does he drop the idea of writing a book and dedicate to the work Derwent, and more importantly, his father, has for him to do—to kill his family. From this point Jack learns to apply his father's hateful words to his own family. These words become for him the solution in his struggle to be free from guilt and self-loathing. As he walks through the hotel chanting phrases like "You have to kill him," "Give him his medicine," and "Cane him within an inch of his life," these phrases become all powerful, and, as with the ancient initiates, serve as the "words of power" that are revealed along the journey to enable progress in the initiation. Then, indicating how completely the son has merged with the father, Jack's own concerns begin to emerge in his father's voice: "Because a real artist must suffer. Because each man kills the thing he loves. Because they'll always be conspiring against you, trying to hold you back and drag you down" (227). Note how in his own way Jack's father, as one of the archetypal "fathers," cites a set of perverse cultural laws that Jack must adhere to if he is to be reborn as a real man.

The Isis initiation rituals end after the symbolic death and resurrection of the neophyte enable him to leave Hell and enter the Elysian Fields. This would happen with a sudden burst of blinding light from the midst of darkness, again accomplished by some mechanical means unknown. As Moore expresses this transition in his *Alciphron,* a poetic account of a neophyte's experience, the entry into the Elysian Fileds was glorious: "But, when I woke—oh the bright scenes, / The glories that around me lay— / If ever yet a vision shone / On waking mortal, *this* was one" (292). King's dark horror drama of the Torrance family also ends, if not happily, then happier than it might have. Jack comes out of his possession by the hotel just long enough to say goodbye to Danny: "Doc," Jack said, "Run away. Quick. And remember how much I love you" (*Shining* 428). In addition, of course, Danny, Wendy, and Hallorann escape—eventually healing physically and psychologically. This hopefulness for the future is signaled as the boiler, like Jack, finally explodes and destroys the Overlook in a burst of flame and smoke. Presumably, as in the House of Usher's climax, even the ghostly inhabitants go down with it.

However, *The Shining*'s ritual climax is characterized not only by the presence of Roderick Usher, but by that of the Red Death. King calls much attention to "The Masque of the Red Death" directly by a long epigraph and by alluding to it throughout the novel. In fact, "The Masque of the Red Death" seems so prominent that some writers have claimed its deep significance for reading *The Shining.* As Indick writes, Poe's story serves as an "inspiration for and encapsulation of" the novel as a whole (19).

Importantly, Poe's tale has a ritualized narrative structure, highlighted by the collective initiation of Prince Prospero and his dreamy court into death through a series of colored, brazier-lit rooms, created, like the Isis rituals, with startling lighting effects that play on the emotions of the initiates—particularly, of course, the great sounding clock in the ominous seventh room. *The Shining* echoes this approach by featuring a dramatic series of spaces through which Jack and Danny pass along their journey: the playground, the basement, room 217, and the Colorado Lounge with its own great clock. An important use King makes of Poe's imagery is the Overlook's masked ball. While reading an invitation to Derwent's 1945 masked ball that fluttered magically into Jack's hand, he hears in his mind, *"The Red Death held sway over all!."* Interestingly, Jack comments: "What left field had that come out of? That was Poe, the Great American Hack. And surely the Overlook—this shining, glowing Overlook on the invitation he held in his hands—was the farthest cry from E. A. Poe imaginable" (155). Where, indeed, did it come from? There is, of course, a literary playfulness here—since the phrase must have leaped into King's head before Jack's, and seems a humorous way to call attention to Poe's irrepressible influence—from one hack to another. King thus dares us to see connections with Poe's world and the Overlook—not such a far cry from each other. Poe's voice, it is implied, haunts all Gothic horror fiction—that's the left field where it came from. As the climax gears up, Danny also hears Poe's words, leading him to summon Dick Hallorann with his "psychic gun" (314).

"The Masque of the Red Death" concerns the mad Prince Prospero who recasts the usual carnival celebrants by inviting the aristocracy to the carnival instead of the common people, leaving them outside to face the Red Death plague destroying the area. Through Poe's tale of costumes, revelry, and debauchery, King introduces the carnivalesque into *The Shining.* An important contribution of Bakhtin's to our understanding of the novel is his reading of Rabelais, in which Bakhtin sees in Rabelais's comic violence, exaggeration, shape-shifting, and bad language a literary incarnation of the freedom embodied in the Renaissance carnivals. Bakhtin saw the carnival as a unique space and time in which the oppressed are freed from the power of the state and the church, in which the individual joins with a collective body (and bawdy) that defies the usual cultural standards and distinctions. Through the wearing of costumes and the donning of masks, the individual changes identities and is reborn. Thus, the carnivalesque (the carnivalizing of normal life) is literature that reshapes and upends social standards through ritual spectacles, comic verbal compositions, and abusive language. That is, it is iconoclastic, freeing the imagination to see beyond the barriers, hierarchies, and restrictions of society. King, who cultivates the art of humorous and shocking profanity and presents ritual spectacles of horror by magnifying and re-creating them, celebrates the liberation of the imagination in a genre characterized by breaking through barriers and taboos (see Holland-Toll). *The Shining* is no exception and centers on a character that is all about the struggle between self-restraint and letting go, whose insanity meter continually creeps up as his personality is absorbed into the collective mind of the Overlook Hotel. Thus, as "Usher" provides *The Shining* with the initiation structure, so "The Masque of the Red Death" provides the subversive nature of the initiation into unrestrained, self-indulgent revelry. This is where King subverts Poe—or, uses Poe to subvert Poe—and the Egyptian initiation structure of "Usher." Rather than moving toward deification, Jack aspires to hold a position among the evil shades of the Overlook not unlike a "carnival king." As distinct from the funereal atmosphere of "Usher," the pageantry of his initiation is clearly carnivalesque, with the masks, confetti, and phantom alcohol in the timeless party in the Overlook's Colorado Lounge.

Therefore, unlike the natural and spontaneous iconoclastic glee of the classic carnival, this exclusive highbrow carnival is an orderly "dream" with rules, elaborately designed and colored rooms, and a clock that keeps very good time. In essence, Prospero creates a counterfeit dream atmosphere to escape the reality of the plague year. In addition, "there were much of the beautiful, much of the wanton, much of the *bizarre*, something of the terrible, and not a little of that which might have excited disgust" (673). Prospero and his crowd represent the evils of the world, and they are eliminated in a just apocalyptic ending wherein, ultimately, the "the Red Death held illimitable dominion over all" (677). King relates Poe's tale to Derwent's exclusive set of warped ghosts that now dreamily haunt the Overlook Hotel and want Danny's power to increase their own. Like Poe, King juxtaposes the carnivalesque atmosphere of the masked ball with the increasingly destructive power of death. In this case, Jack serves as a one-man Red Death of social values who inverts social mores by trying to kill his wife and son. During the climax, Jack ultimately fails in his major test—that of killing his family. Drinking himself into a near stupor, courtesy of the Colorado Lounge masked ball, he is overcome by Wendy and locked up in the pantry. This leads to the part of the ritual known as the "Osirian tribunal," wherein the neophyte's worthiness is judged. In this case, Grady guides him through this process with ghostly sarcasm: "I see you can hardly have taken care of the business we discussed, sir." "You let them lock you in?" "Oh dear. A woman half your size and a little boy? Hardly sets you off as being of top managerial timber, does it?" (383).

But like the hotel itself, Jack has become an irrational and uncontrolled destructive force that is psychologically impotent and physically incapable of completing his mad initiation. Wendy herself recognizes Jack's fusion with the hotel. Hearing him yelling and howling in the distance, Wendy "was hearing the lunatic, raving voice of the Overlook itself" (411). Not even human anymore, Jack has become "the *thing* that was after [Danny]" (italics added) and the *it* that "slashed out [at Danny] with the scarred hammer" (426). He has virtually collapsed into the hotel, becoming one with it. After the thing that was Jack smashes his own face repeatedly with the mallet, another strange manifestation of the imp of the perverse, Danny sees "a strange, shifting composite, many faces mixed imperfectly into one. Danny saw the woman in 217; the dogman; the hungry boy-thing that had been in the concrete ring" (430). In other words, Jack has psychologically merged with his shadow self, the raving archetype of his father. Still at war with himself, Jack becomes everyone else, an empty shell to be possessed by the house and its legion of inhabitants at will. Again we are reminded of the end of *Psycho*. Like Norman, Jack's identity crisis resolves in the annihilation of the host personality. When Jack faces Danny, for example, he "looked uncertain, as if not sure who or what it was" (427). Finally, just as Norman collapses into his mother in the end, so Jack's own ego disappears completely. The initiation into evil and death is complete as Jack is inversely reborn into the underworld of the darkest corners of his own unconscious mind. Ironically, he ultimately cannot prevent the boiler from blowing, and, like Prospero's uninvited, final guest in Poe's tale, brings death to the Overlook Hotel and its evil reveling.

We have seen so far that Jack experiences his initiation on two levels: the first centers on Derwent, including the book he hopes to write about the hotel, and the place he desires in his masked court; the second initiation is his merging with his father, becoming high priest to his father's model of complete autocratic rule, and meting out the final, apocalyptic, punishment to those perceived to be subverting Jack's will. But there is another level on which his initiation occurs, the one from Danny's perspective, representing Jack before he was corrupted—that part of him in which there is a shred of hope. Jack perceives Danny's parallel journey through the hotel as a threat, as if Danny were competing with him for the hotel's favors and rewards. This competitiveness causes Jack to deny Danny's repeated supernatural encounters at the hotel. In nearly every case, Jack interprets Danny's experiences in light of how they take the hotel's attentions off him. In particular, Jack refuses to accept that Danny encounters, and is nearly killed by, the ghostly woman in room 217. He understands that Danny is afraid of ghosts, but chooses to reject the possibility that they can leave actual fingerprints on his son's neck. He tells himself that Danny must have made the marks himself while under the influence of the house's long and possessive memory. Even worse, Jack tries to write off Danny's experience through an irrelevant appeal to Freudian dream theory, transparently rationalizing Danny's experience through double-talk.

From Danny's own perspective, his experience is very different from Jack's rationalizations. In fact, Danny begins having trials before he ever sees the Overlook Hotel, in his psychic experience of his parents' marital struggle, his father's inner demons, and the frightening trances that take him through dreamlike journeys into horrific future possibilities. We argue that King sets up Danny's own psychological journey to echo other stories of childhood initiations into adulthood. These intertextual parallels include "The Book of Daniel" and Faulkner's "Barn Burning."

Ultimately, the success of Danny's journey into adulthood through patient endurance of his various tests and trials enables him, like his namesake, Daniel the Prophet, to grow up pure and psychologically whole. For example, Daniel and Danny are similar in being visionaries, prophets, and possessing purity and divine power. The allusion to Daniel accounts for things like the topiary lions, the bloody "writing" on the walls, and the apocalyptic nature of the story of a family and a hotel that are in their last days. Danny's "shine" is equivalent to Daniel's prophetic power, enabling him to view the future, including horrific visionary warnings of the Overlook Hotel, and to see what others don't see at the hotel. Just as Daniel the Prophet reads other's dreams, so Danny can read minds. He understands his parents, for example, sometimes better than they understand themselves. While the topiary lions are indeed dangerous, scratching him during his escape, he is essentially unharmed by them. And like his biblical namesake, Danny is a lone beacon of purity and innocence, making him the object of persecution, in his case by his jealous father and by the ghosts of the Overlook Hotel, which want him dead so they can add his unusual mental gifts to their collective mind. Finally, just as Daniel faces his king, Belshazzar, and pronounces his doom,

so Danny faces the thing that was his father and sets him straight
about how the hotel lies, unveiling its true nature and sins, and
warns that because they forgot the boiler, "*It's going up! It's going
to explode!*" (430). Like Daniel, Danny survives a wicked dynasty
that seemed to have the upper hand.

According to Edward Ingebretsen, the biblical imagery of the
apocalypse has much in common with the Gothic. In his book
Maps of Heaven, Maps of Hell, he claims that "a map of Heaven
could only be constructed, as it were, by inversion, beginning
with Hell" (ix). Ingebretsen's concern largely develops around
the uncanny parallel between the Gothic and the Theological, one that demonstrates their shared interest in mystery and
apocalypse. The ritual components of "The Fall of the House
of Usher" suggest the possibility that the Theological and the
Gothic share a concern with eschatology. Indeed, both "Usher"
and *The Shining* emphasize an apocalyptic fall with little promise
of a renewed Heaven and Earth. By highlighting the shared ritual
context of both works, we suggest that they turn on the question
of final things, particularly as they relate to the death or survival
of the family. Ingebretsen also suggests that "Gothic and theo-
logic epistemologies ritualize mystery as the great secret, whose
gradual revelation, in however complex ways, functions as the
sacrament of Judgment and Revelation" (197).

William Faulkner's "Barn Burning," an additional initiation
intertext, helps King define Danny's growth through the novel,
providing an additional complexity to Jack's story by pointing to
Danny's own initiation. While Jack, whose alcoholism and violent
temper is witness to his excesses in embracing the horrors of the
Overlook, Danny shuts his eyes to the horrific visions that confront him from Tony and the hotel. Danny's point of view also
provides an innocent perspective on the carnivalesque dark side
of Jack, a point of view that parallels the story of Sarty, the young
son of a white trash sharecropper whose fierce pride becomes a
violent hatred. The father hates those who have the wealth and
position he lacks, leading to planned altercations with his land-
lords that justify him in burning their barns. The story is told
through Sarty's innocent perspective. Torn between defending
and loathing his father, he increasingly senses the injustice of his
father's actions and attitudes until, in the end, he warns a farmer
of his father's impending barn burning, leading to the father's

death. Sarty then moves on, leaving the family and its corrupt excesses behind. "Barn Burning" and *The Shining* are both about massive cultural changes in which corrupt lifestyles are indicted, wherein the boys are left to choose a better way for their future. Like King's story, Faulkner's story is about cultural decay and decline, and about the subsequent onset of a new social/cultural order. Both Sarty and Danny are harbingers of change in rejecting the corrupt and outmoded social structures they are expected to accept and forward. If Jack hadn't died at the end of the novel, Danny might well have followed his powerful example of drinking and brutality—just as Jack had followed his father's. In the end, Danny is able to overcome the weight of his past and move on, suggesting a new start for the worn-down Torrance family. For Sarty and Danny, their fathers' behavior is as inexplicable to them as Roderick Usher's is to the narrator. In a sense, Sarty and Danny, like "Usher's" narrator, both escape the sinking of the worlds they grew up in that have become ripe for apocalyptic destruction. Thus, these source texts are initiations, like "Usher," that take these young men down into the underworld of a depraved reality, displaying the corruptions and horrors of those worlds and enabling the boys to be reborn as they escape their once-dark fate.

Danny is another boy who idolizes his father, despite his abuse and alcoholism. Jack's death ends the generational cycle of failure and unhappiness. The hotel, which embodies all that Jack represents in the world, wants Danny. This parallels Sarty's father and the white trash South that "want" Sarty and will corrupt him if not stopped. Jack is too far gone, too mentally unstable, has done too much to escape the lure of the Overlook's offers of power, position, and freedom. While Danny is centered in love and forgiveness, Jack can only lash out—at Danny, George Hatfield, and even the wasps that sting him ("They would pay for stinging him" [115]). The hotel offers Jack reasons to blame his family for his lack of success. Since the hotel wants Danny because of his gift, it attacks Jack in order to get to Danny. Ironically then, Danny is the cause of his father's ultimate downfall, just as Sarty is responsible for the death of his father. While Jack carries the weight of the past inside, Danny carries the future. Like the "Usher" narrator, he is ultimately able to walk away from the site of inexplicable forces and madness to watch it collapse under the weight of its evil. Jack, on the other hand, has become like Usher, a victim of the house he embodies and must die with it.

While Danny's initiation parallels Jack's experiences with the woman in 217 and the topiary lions, the hotel also personalizes horrors for Danny alone like the sentient fire hose, the ghostly figure in the cement ring, and the bloody visions on the walls. Danny's ritual preparation includes the dark trials with Jack's alcoholism, Danny's broken arm, the tensions in the family, and the hatreds, fears, and anxieties that are beyond Danny's ability to articulate. All of this is compounded by Danny's gift of the shining, the ability to inhabit the horrors in other people's minds. His shining also includes visions of Tony, a manifestation of his older self struggling to get out. Through these visions Tony guides Danny through a series of visionary experiences that serve as his archetypal journey into Hades. In fact, he receives a special password—REDRUM—that is supposed to guide him out of the shadows, but only serves to draw him further in. Among Danny's more horrific trials is his increasing distance from a father who challenges his innocence and integrity. Not only is he desperately trying to learn to read, to understand his parents, and to grow up, he also faces his own temptations to explore the evil of the hotel. These temptations get him into trouble and also help him identify with his father's own demons—perhaps the most dangerous test of his journey. Finally, after facing the woman in 217, the thing in the concrete ring, the dogman, and, in the end, his father, Danny realizes that he must face the hotel alone. As King puts it, he "had an adult thought, an adult feeling, the essence of his experience in this bad place—a sorrowful distillation: (*Mommy and Daddy can't help me and I'm alone*)" (429). Through his initiation Danny grows up early, and can face the unbelievable horror of his father (in essence, the hotel itself) turned into a homicidal thing and not flinch: "Go on and hit me. But you'll never get what you want from me" (428). In his initiation Danny only merges with the good that was in his father but was so hard for his father to access and sustain.

As we've seen throughout this study, reading the texts that were inspired by "The Fall of the House of Usher" causes us to look back and see the original in new ways. That is, King's "interpreta-tion" of it highlights overlooked aspects of Poe's text that enrich our view of Roderick, Madeline, the house, and the narrator.

As Leonard Mustazza writes, "King's echoes of Poe subtly invite us to do that which many might do anyway: to compare the work of the nineteenth-century master of the horror tale with that of his twentieth-century counterpart" (63). So, turning the tables on Poe, we find that like Jack Torrance, Roderick Usher is nervous, paranoid, and moody, and grows increasingly insane throughout the story. Both are aware that they live in a "sentient" house and are terrified—Jack tries to deny it as long as he can. Both of their psychic fears are symbolized by the explosive potential below these buildings—the creeping boiler in the Overlook's basement and the "deposit of powder, or some other highly combustible substance" in the Usher cellar (410). Like the sentient House of Usher, whose sentience was inexplicably characterized by its very structure, fungi, and reduplication in the tarn, the Overlook seemed to be powered by the collective mind of its former inhabitants, who channel invisible forces into inanimate fire hoses and topiary animals and create all manner of supernatural effects. Both Roderick and Jack are out of tune with their sentient abodes and are eventually destroyed by them. Jack and Roderick are both creative, writing plays and poetry, and each pours over texts that put them in dream states—Jack with the Overlook scrapbook and Roderick with his texts "over which Usher would sit dreaming for hours" (409). Finally, both try, but fail, to kill the women in their lives, for reasons that are vague and part of their growing deterioration. Madeline, a figure of death in life, brings to mind the dead/alive woman in room 217 of the Overlook Hotel. While they both seem to be dead, both can rise as retributive occasion demands. Madeline also relates to Wendy, who is left for dead but ultimately survives. All of these women are victims of the men in their lives, and, in the case of the dead ones, seem driven to revenge from beyond the grave. As Anne Williams notes, the "Male Gothic expresses femininity as subversion within—the madwoman locked in the attic who eventually escapes and burns the house down" (175). Much like Mother Norma Bates, these women are images of the undying feminine side of the unconscious mind, representing a power that cannot be permanently repressed. Roderick and Madeline, in fact, are twins, as are Norma and Norman psychologically, making them sides of the men's personalities that they desperately wish to repress, just as Jack perceives Wendy as a pesky conscience, stinging him like the wasps with her unfulfilled expectations and disappointment in him. In short, they are central forces in driving the plots of both stories.

Perhaps the most significant parallel between Poe's and King's narratives is the observers of the action—the narrator and Danny. Like the narrator, who is filled with sorrow, a sickening of the heart, and an iciness when confronted with the House of Usher, so Danny is guided by Tony into dark premonitions of the Overlook. While Jack is returning from his interview at the Overlook, Danny has a trance vision in which he sees the Overlook with "a green witchlight" that "glowed into being on the front of the building, flickered, and became a giant, grinning skull over two crossed bones" (31). He goes on to see destruction within the house, hearing loud noises and an unseen monster chasing him (31–32). Like Poe's narrator, whose feelings anticipate all that will happen (sadness, death, and destruction) and who sees the image of the cadaverous Roderick in the cracked and deteriorating house, Danny sees the whole future history of the Torrances at the Overlook, though he doesn't understand it all yet. Poe's narrator even has a kind of trance experience outside the House of Usher as he looks down at its reflection in the dark tarn. Feeling a "shudder even more thrilling than before," he comforts himself with the idea that it "*must* have been a dream" (398, 400). Thus, like Danny, the narrator is terrified even before he enters his strange new abode.

While, as Jeanne Campbell Reesman notes, King is influenced by the tradition of American Naturalism, he dips into much more than that, going back to Faulkner, nineteenth-century Gothicism through Poe, and by "a route obscure and lonely," all the way back to the "ultimate dim Thule" of ancient initiation rites and monomyths of the mystery cults of Egypt, Greece, and Rome (*Poems* lines 1, 6). With these materials King has concocted a classic modern Gothic tale, "subversive, delighting in the forbidden and trafficking in the unspeakable" (Williams 4). And what is unspeakable and forbidden here but that which he found within "The House of Usher"—the terrifying fall of the American family? In fact, Williams names "the *mythos* or structure" informing much of the Gothic as "the patriarchal family" (22). At the heart of such stories is the competition between masculine law and feminine revolt, both "Usher" and *The Shining* embodying the Gothic dread of fragile family relationships within an unstable setting that threatens to collapse—even explode—at any moment. Both stories feel like a kind of architectural and psychological Sword of Damocles, originating as they do in the deepest and most unstable reaches of the unconscious mind, symbolized by a haunted living space in which our closest relationships become intolerable—even horrifying—nightmares. In conversation with each other, these texts agree on what they are saying, to some extent, though not completely on how to say it. While Poe keeps motives and backgrounds at a dark distance, King brings the weight of complex personal and familial history to bear on every word spoken, bringing with this added narrative baggage a hotel large enough to store it all. What King loses in atmosphere, per-haps, with his realistic modern milieu, he attempts to make up for in audience identification and pathos, particularly by telling so much of his story through Danny's innocent eyes. By creating a hybrid text out of a postmodern-inspired eclecticism of sources and ideas, King, as well as anybody writing today, combines horror and authentic human drama in a way that captures the terrifying possibilities of family interaction.

NOTES

CHAPTER 1

1. For critical overviews of Poe's work, we examined J. Lasley Dameron and Irby B. Cauthen's *Bibliography of Criticism* and Eric Carlson's chapter on "Tales of Psychal Conflict" in his edited *Companion to Poe Studies*. A more recent effort to bring Poe Studies up to date may be found in Scott Peeples's *The Afterlife of Edgar Allan Poe*. We also relied on the annual updates compiled in *American Literary Scholarship*.
2. In this section on "The Fall of the House of Usher" and its sources, we rely heavily on Thomas O. Mabbott's discussion in his notes to the story found in *Tales and Sketches, Vol. 1*.
3. Burton Pollin suggests William Godwin's *Imogen, A Pastoral Romance* (1784) as another source text that may have influenced "Usher," though Thomas O. Mabbott doubts Poe ever saw this rare text.

CHAPTER 6

1. Although we draw on Jung broadly in this chapter, we are very well aware that there is an ongoing, and useful, critical revision of his theories (often called post-Jungian studies). We do not trace out the implications of these revisions in this chapter, largely because we want our claims to stay fairly close to the Jungian ideas Bloch drew on. Not only did Bloch refer to Jungian ideas in *Psycho*, he also collected Jungian texts. In the Robert Bloch papers at the American Heritage Center at the University of Wyoming, one can readily browse books by and about Jung that Bloch owned.

CHAPTER 7

1. It is probably fair to suggest that the critical evaluation of *Rosemary's Baby* is still in an early phase. Nevertheless, our chapter draws on several readings of the text that we found helpful. For representative

work that treats feminist themes, please consult the articles by Rhona Berenstein, Lucy Fischer, Sharon Marcus, and Karyn Valerius listed in the bibliography. For work that situates the novel within broader religious and textual concerns, see the work by Ronald Ambrosetti, Douglas Fowler, Robert Lima, and Maisie Pearson. For theological accounts of the "death of god" movement, please see the work of Thomas Alitzer and William Hamilton. Our approach to *Rosemary's Baby* differs from these latter works in that we draw on Poe's influence on Levin and on Levin's interest in popular culture.

2. Levin's description of the incarnate devil may well have been inspired by the demon depicted in *Curse of the Demon*, Jacques Tourneur's 1958 horror film about the investigation of devil worshippers in England. Tourneur's demon is a large, leathery creature with wings, large claws, horns, and big, evil eyes shown a couple of times in extreme close-up. Another dimension of the film that may have influenced Levin is the difficulty characters have in believing in the genuine power of these devil cults in light of modern scientific attitudes until it is too late.

BIBLIOGRAPHY

Abraham, Nicolas, and Maria Torok. *The Shell and the Kernel: Renewals of Psychoanalysis,* Vol. 1. Edited and translated by Nicholas T. Rand. Chicago: University of Chicago Press, 1994.

Alitzer, Thomas J. J., ed. *Toward a New Christianity: Readings in the Death of God Theology.* New York: Harcourt, Brace and World, 1967.

Alitzer, Thomas J. J., and William Hamilton. *Radical Theology and the Death of God.* New York: Bobbs-Merrill, 1966.

Ambrosetti, Ronald J. "*Rosemary's Baby* and Death of God Literature." *Keystone Folklore Quarterly* 14 (Winter 1969): 133–41.

Anderson, Quentin. *The American Henry James.* New Brunswick, NJ: Rutgers University Press, 1957.

Bailey, Dale. *American Nightmares: The Haunted House Formula in American Popular Fiction.* Bowling Green, OH: Bowling Green State University Popular Press, 1999.

Bakhtin, Mikhail. *Rabelais and His World.* Translated by Helene Iswolsky. Bloomington, IN: Indiana University Press, 1984.

Berenstein, Rhona. "Mommie Dearest: *Aliens, Rosemary's Baby,* and Mothering." *Journal of Popular Culture* 24.2 (1990): 55–73.

Bloch, Robert. *The Complete Stories of Robert Bloch: Final Reckonings,* Vol. 1. New York: Citadel Twilight, 1987.

———. *Once Around the Bloch: An Unauthorized Autobiography.* New York: Tor, 1993.

———. "Poe and Lovecraft." In *H. P. Lovecraft: Four Decades of Criticism,* edited by S. T. Joshi, 158–60. Athens: Ohio University Press, 1980.

———. *Psycho.* New York: Tor, 1989.

———. "The Shambles of Ed Gein." In *The Quality of Murder,* edited by Anthony Boucher, 216–24. New York: E. P. Dutton, 1962.

Bloom, Clive. "Introduction: Death's Own Backyard: The Nature of Modern Gothic and Horror." In *Gothic Horror: A Reader's Guide from Poe to King and Beyond,* edited by Clive Bloom, 1–22. London: Macmillan Press, 1998.

Briggs, Julia. "The Ghost Story." In *A Companion to the Gothic,* edited by David Punter, 122–31. Oxford: Blackwell, 2000.

Buranelli, Vincent. *Edgar Allan Poe.* New York: Twayne, 1961.

Burleson, Donald R. *H. P. Lovecraft: A Critical Study.* Westport, CT: Greenwood Press, 1983.

Cancalon, Elaine D., and Antoine Spacagna, eds. *Intertextuality in Literature and Film.* Gainesville: University Press of Florida, 1988.

Carlson, Eric W., ed. *A Companion to Poe Studies.* Westport, CT: Greenwood Press, 1996.

Carroll, Noël. *The Philosophy of Horror.* New York: Routledge, 1990.

Cavallaro, Dani. *The Gothic Vision: Three Centuries of Horror, Terror, and Fear.* New York: Continuum, 2002.

Chevalier, Jean, and Alain Gheerbrant. *The Penguin Dictionary of Symbols.* Translated by John Buchanan-Brown. London: Penguin, 1996.

Craven, Wayne. *Sculpture in America.* 1968. New York: Cornwall Books, 1984.

Dameron, J. Lasley, and Irby B. Cauthen, Jr. *Edgar Allan Poe: A Bibliography of Criticism, 1827–1967.* Charlottesville: University Press of Virginia, 1974.

Davison, Carol Margaret. "Haunted House/Haunted Heroine: Female Gothic Closets in 'The Yellow Wallpaper.'" *Women's Studies* 33 (2004): 47–75.

Dickinson, Emily. *The Letters of Emily Dickinson,* Vol. 2. Edited by Thomas H. Johnson. Cambridge, MA: Harvard University Press, 1958.

Dock, Julie Bates, Daphne Ryan Allen, Jennifer Palai, and Kristen Tracy. "'But One Expects That': Charlotte Perkins Gilman's 'The Yellow Wallpaper' and the Shifting Light of Scholarship." *PMLA* 111.1 (1996): 52–65.

Douglas, Mary. *Purity and Danger: An Analysis of Concepts of Pollution and Taboo.* 1966. New York: Routledge, 2002.

Edmundson, Mark. *Nightmare on Main Street: Angels, Sadomasochism, and the Culture of Gothic.* Cambridge, MA: Harvard University Press, 1997.

E. H. B. "Haunted Houses." *Occult Review* 3 (1906): 19–23.

Fetterley, Judith. "Reading about Reading: 'A Jury of Her Peers,' 'The Murders in the Rue Morgue,' and 'The Yellow Wallpaper.'" In *The Captive Imagination: A Case Book on "The Yellow Wallpaper,"* edited by Catherine Golden, 253–60. New York: Feminist Press, 1992.

Fiedler, Leslie. *Love and Death in the American Novel.* New York: Meridian Books, 1960.

Fischer, Lucy. "Birth Traumas: Parturition and Horror in *Rosemary's Baby.*" *Cinema Journal* 31.3 (1992): 3–18.

Foucault, Michel. *The History of Sexuality,* Vol. 1. Translated by Robert Hurley. New York: Random House, 1978.

Fowler, Douglas. *Ira Levin.* Mercer Island, WA: Starmont, 1988.

Frazer, Sir James. *The New Golden Bough*. Edited by Theodor H. Gaster. New York: Mentor, 1959.

Freud, Sigmund. "A Special Type of Choice of Object Made by Men." In *The Freud Reader,* edited by Peter Gay, 387–94. New York: W. W. Norton, 1989.

———. *The Uncanny*. New York: Penguin, 2003.

Gilman, Charlotte Perkins. *The Living of Charlotte Perkins Gilman: An Autobiography*. New York: D. Appleton-Century, 1935.

———. "Why I Wrote 'The Yellow Wallpaper'?" In *Charlotte Perkins Gilman: "The Yellow Wallpaper,"* edited by Dale M. Bauer, 348–49. New York: Bedford/St. Martin's, 1998.

———. "The Yellow Wallpaper." In *Charlotte Perkins Gilman: "The Yellow Wallpaper,"* edited by Dale M. Bauer, 41–59. New York: Bedford/St. Martin's, 1998.

Golden, Catherine J. *Charlotte Perkins Gilman's "The Yellow Wallpaper": A Sourcebook and Critical Edition*. New York: Routledge, 2004.

Grusser, John. "Madmen and Moonbeams: The Narrator in 'The Fall of the House of Usher.'" *Edgar Allan Poe Review* 5.1 (2003): 80–90.

Hall, Joan Wylie. *Shirley Jackson: A Study of the Short Fiction*. New York: Twayne, 1993.

Haney-Peritz, Janice. "Monumental Feminism and Literature's Ancestral House: Another Look at 'The Yellow Wallpaper.'" In *Charlotte Perkins Gilman: The Woman and Her Work,* edited by Sheryl Meyering, 95–107. Ann Arbor: UMI Research Press, 1989.

Hattenhauer, Darryl. *Shirley Jackson's American Gothic*. Albany: State University of New York Press, 2003.

Hedges, Elaine R. "Afterword to 'The Yellow Wallpaper,' Feminist Press Edition." In *The Captive Imagination: A Case Book on "The Yellow Wallpaper,"* edited by Catherine J. Golden, 123–36. New York: Feminist Press, 1992.

Heller, Terry. *The Delights of Terror: An Aesthetics of the Tale of Terror*. Urbana and Chicago: University of Illinois Press, 1987.

Henking, Susan E. *"Jung and Feminism: Liberating Archetypes,* by Demaris S. Wehr." Book review. *Journal for the Scientific Study of Religion*.

Hitchcock, Alfred. "Why I am Afraid of the Dark." In *Hitchcock on Hitchcock: Selected Writings and Interviews,* edited by Sidney Gottlieb, 142–45. Berkeley: University of California Press, 1995.

Hochman, Barbara. "The Reading Habit and 'The Yellow Wallpaper.'" *American Literature* 74.1 (2002): 89–110.

Hoeveler, Diane Long. "The Hidden God and the Abjected Woman in 'The Fall of the House of Usher.'" *Studies in Short Fiction* 29.3 (1992): 385–95.

Hoffmann, Daniel. *Poe Poe Poe Poe Poe Poe Poe*. New York: Avon Books, 1972.

Holland-Toll, Linda J. "Bakhtin's Carnival Reversed: King's *The Shining* as Dark Carnival." *Journal of Popular Culture* 33.2 (1999): 131–46.

Holy Bible. Oxford: Oxford University Press, 1998.

Howells, William Dean. *The Great Modern American Stories: An Anthology*. New York: Boni and Liveright, 1920.

Hume, Beverly. "Managing Madness in Gilman's 'The Yellow Wallpaper.'" *Studies in American Fiction* 30.1 (2002): 3–20.

Indick, Ben P. "King and the Literary Tradition of Horror and the Supernatural." In *Stephen King: Modern Critical Views*, edited by Harold Bloom, 15–26. Philadelphia: Chelsea House Publishers, 1998.

Ingebretsen, Edward J. *At Stake: Monsters and the Rhetoric of Fear in Public Culture*. Chicago: University of Chicago Press, 2001.

———. *Maps of Heaven, Maps of Hell: Religious Terror as Memory from the Puritans to Stephen King*. New York: M. E. Sharpe, 1996.

Irving, Washington. "Westminster Abbey." *History, Tales, and Sketches*. New York: Library of America, 1983.

Jackson's *The Haunting of Hill House*." In *Haunting the House of Fiction: Feminist Perspectives on Ghost Stories by American Women*, edited by Lynette Carpenter and Wendy K. Kolmar, 166–92. Knoxville: University of Tennessee Press, 1991.

Jackson, Shirley. "Experience and Fiction." In *Come Away with Me*, edited by Stanley Edgar Hyman, 195–204. New York: Viking, 1968.

———. *The Haunting of Hill House*. New York: Penguin Books, 1959.

———. *Just an Ordinary Day*. Edited by Laurence Jackson Hyman and Sarah Hyman Stewart. New York: Bantam, 1998.

———. *The Lottery and Other Stories*. New York: Farrar, Straus and Giroux, 1991.

James, Henry. "The Art of Fiction." In *The Portable Henry James*, edited by Morton Dauwen Zabel, 391–418. New York: Viking, 1959.

———. *Hawthorne*. 1879. New York: Collier Books, 1966.

———. "From the Preface to Henry James's 1908 Edition of *The Turn of the Screw*." In *The Turn of the Screw*, edited by Peter G. Beidler, 179–86. Boston: Bedford/St. Martin's, 2004.

———. *The Turn of the Screw*. Edited by Peter G. Beidler. Boston: Bedford/St. Martin's, 2004.

Jenkins, Philip. *Using Murder: The Social Construction of Serial Homicide*. New York: A. de Gruyter, 1994.

Jordan, Cynthia S. "Poe's Re-Vision: The Recovery of the Second Story." *American Literature* 59.1 (1987): 2–19.

Joshi, S. T. *H. P. Lovecraft: A Life.* West Warwick, RI: Necronomicon Press, 1996.

Joshi, S. T., and David E. Shultz. *An H. P. Lovecraft Encyclopedia.* New York: Hippocampus Press, 2001.

Jung, C. G. *The Archetypes and the Collective Unconscious.* Translated by R. F. C. Hull. Bollingen Series XX, Vol. 9, Pt. 1. Princeton, NJ: Princeton University Press, 1959.

———. *Symbols of Transformation.* Translated by R. F. C. Hull. Bollingen Series XX, Vol. 5. Princeton, NJ: Princeton University Press, 1956.

King, Stephen. *Danse Macabre.* New York: Everest House, 1981.

———. *The Shining.* New York: Doubleday, 1973.

Knight, Denise D. *Charlotte Perkins Gilman: A Study of the Short Fiction.* New York: Twayne, 1997.

———, ed. *The Diaries of Charlotte Perkins Gilman, 1879–87,* Vol. 1. Charlottesville: University Press of Virginia, 1994.

———. *The Diaries of Charlotte Perkins Gilman, 1890–1935,* Vol. 2. Charlottesville: University Press of Virginia, 1994.

Kolodny, Annette. "A Map for Rereading: Or, Gender and the Interpretation of Literary Texts." In *The Captive Imagination: A Casebook on "The Yellow Wallpaper,"* edited by Catherine Golden, 149–67. New York: Feminist Press, 1992.

Lawrence, D. H. *Studies in Classic American Literature.* 1923. New York: Penguin, 1977.

Levin, Ira. *Rosemary's Baby.* New York: Penguin, 2003.

Lima, Robert. "The Satanic Rape of Catholicism in *Rosemary's Baby.*" *Studies in American Fiction* 2.2 (1974): 211–22.

Livingstone, Marco. *Pop Art: A Continuing History.* New York: Harry N. Abrams, 1990.

Lloyd-Smith, Allan. "Nineteenth-Century American Gothic." In *A Companion to the Gothic,* edited by David Punter, 109–21. Oxford: Blackwell, 2000.

Lootens, Tricia. "'Whose Hand Was I Holding?' Familial and Sexual Politics in Shirley

Lovecraft, Howard Phillips. *The Annotated Supernatural Horror in Literature.* Edited by S. T. Joshi. New York: Hippocampus Press, 2000.

———. *The Call of Cthulhu and Other Weird Stories.* Edited by S. T. Joshi. New York: Penguin, 1999.

———. *The Dreams in the Witch House and Other Weird Stories.* Edited by S. T. Joshi. New York: Penguin, 2004.

———. *The Thing on the Doorstep and Other Weird Stories.* Edited by S. T. Joshi. New York: Penguin, 2001.

Magistrale, Tony. *Landscape of Fear: Stephen King's American Gothic.* Bowling Green, OH: Bowling Green State University Popular Press, 1988.

Magistrale, Tony, and Sidney Poger. *Poe's Children: Connections between Tales of Terror and Detection.* New York: Peter Lang, 1999.

Marcus, Sharon. "Placing *Rosemary's Baby.*" *Differences: A Journal of Feminist Cultural Studies* 5.3 (1993): 121–53.

Markow-Totevy, Georges. *Henry James.* Translated by John Cumming. London: Minerva Press, 1969.

Martindale, Colin. "Archetype and Reality in 'The Fall of the House of Usher.'" *Poe Studies* 1.1 (June 1972): 9–11.

Moore, Thomas. *Alciphron: A Poem.* 1877. Honolulu, HI: University Press of the Pacific, 2003.

Morgan, Jack. *The Biology of Horror: Gothic Literature and Film.* Carbondale: Southern Illinois University Press, 2002.

Murray, Margaret A. *The Witch-Cult in Western Europe.* London: Oxford University Press, 1921.

Mustazza, Leonard. "Poe's 'Masque of the Red Death' and King's *The Shining:* Echo, Influence, and Deviation." In *Discovering Stephen King's "The Shining,"* edited by Tony Magistrale, 62–73. San Bernardino, CA: Borgo Press, 1998.

Nardo, Anna K. *George Eliot's Dialogue with John Milton.* Columbia: University of Missouri Press, 2003.

Neumann, Erich. *The Origins and History of Consciousness.* Translated by R. F. C. Hull. Bollingen Series XLII. Princeton, NJ: Princeton University Press, 1954.

Newman, Judie. "Shirley Jackson and the Reproduction of Mothering: *The Haunting of Hill House.*" In *American Horror Fiction: From Brockden Brown to Stephen King,* edited by Brian Docherty, 120–34. New York: St. Martin's Press, 1990.

Oppenheimer, Judy. *Private Demons: The Life of Shirley Jackson.* New York: G. P. Putnam's, 1988.

Ouspensky, P. D. *A New Model of the Universe.* New York: Vintage Books, 1971.

Owens, E. Suzanne. "The Ghostly Double behind the Wallpaper in Charlotte Perkins Gilman's 'The Yellow Wallpaper.'" In *Haunting the House of Fiction: FeministPerspectives on Ghost Stories by American Women,* edited by Lynette Carpenter and Wendy K. Kolmar, 64–79. Knoxville, TN: University of Tennessee Press, 1991.

Pearson, Maisie K. "*Rosemary's Baby:* The Horns of a Dilemma." *Journal of Popular Culture* 2.3 (1968): 493–502.

Pecora, Vincent P. *Self and Form in Modern Narrative.* Baltimore: Johns Hopkins University Press, 1989.

Peeples, Scott. *The Afterlife of Edgar Allan Poe.* New York: Camden House, 2004.

Perry, Dennis R. *Hitchcock and Poe: The Legacy of Delight and Terror.* Lanham, MD: Scarecrow Press, 2003.

Poe, Edgar Allan. "The Philosophy of Composition." *Poe: Essays and Reviews*. New York: The Library of America, 1984.

———. *The Poems of Edgar Allan Poe*. Edited by Thomas Ollive Mabbott. Cambridge, MA: Belknap Press, 1980.

———. "Review." Nathaniel Hawthorne's *Twice-Told Tales* and *Mosses from an Old Manse*. *Edgar Allan Poe: Essays and Reviews*. New York: Library of America, 1984.

———. *Tales and Sketches*. 2 vols. Edited by Thomas Ollive Mabbott. Urbana and Chicago: University of Illinois Press, 2000.

Pohl, Frances. *Framing America: A Social History of American Art*. New York: Thames and Hudson, 2002.

Pollin, Burton R. *Poe's Seductive Influence on Great Writers*. New York: iUniverse, 2004.

Punter, David. "Robert Bloch's *Psycho*: Some Pathological Contexts." In *American Horror Fiction: From Brockden Brown to Stephen King*, edited by Brian Docherty, 92–106. New York: St. Martin's Press, 1990.

Reesman, Jeanne Campbell. "Stephen King and the Tradition of American Naturalism in *The Shining*." *The Shining Reader*. Mercer Island, WA: Starmont, 1991.

Riddel, Joseph N. "The 'Crypt' of Edgar Poe." In *The Selected Writings of Edgar Allan Poe*, edited by G. R. Thompson, 884–95. New York: W. W. Norton, 2004.

Savoy, Eric. "The Rise of American Gothic." In *The Cambridge Companion to Gothic Fiction*, edited by Jerrold E. Hogle, 167–88. New York: Cambridge University Press, 2002.

Scharnhorst, Gary. *Charlotte Perkins Gilman*. Boston: Twayne, 1985.

See, Fred G. "Henry James and the Art of Possession." In *American Realism: New Essays*, edited by Eric J. Sundquist, 119–37. Baltimore and London: Johns Hopkins University Press, 1982.

Silverman, Kenneth. *Edgar A. Poe: Mournful and Never-Ending Remembrance*. New York: Harper Perennial, 1991.

Spence, Lewis. *The Mysteries of Egypt: Secret Rites and Traditions*. Mineola, NY: Dover, 2005.

St. Armand, Barton Levi. "The 'Mysteries' of Edgar Poe: The Quest for a Monomyth in Gothic Literature." In *The Gothic Imagination: Essays in Dark Romanticism*, edited by G. R. Thompson, 65–93. Pullman: Washington State University Press, 1974.

Steiner, George. *Real Presences*. Chicago: University of Chicago Press, 1989.

Straub, Peter. "Introduction." *The Stepford Wives* by Ira Levin. 1972. New York: Harper Collins, 2002.

Thompson, G. R. *Poe's Fiction: Romantic Irony in the Gothic Tales*. Madison: University of Wisconsin Press, 1973.

Todorov, Tzvetan. *The Fantastic: A Structural Approach to a Literary Genre*. Translated by Richard Howard. Ithaca, NY: Cornell University Press, 1975.

Valerius, Karyn. "*Rosemary's Baby*, Gothic Pregnancy, and Fetal Subjects." *College Literature* 32.3 (2005): 116–35.

Wilbur, Richard. "The House of Poe." In *The Recognition of Edgar Allan Poe*, edited by Eric W. Carlson. Ann Arbor: University of Michigan Press, 1970.

———. *Poe*. New York: Dell Press, 1959.

Williams, Anne. *Art of Darkness: A Poetics of Gothic*. Chicago: University of Chicago Press, 1995.

Wolfreys, Julian. *Victorian Hauntings: Spectrality, Gothic, the Uncanny, and Literature*. New York: Palgrave Macmillan, 2002.

INDEX